MORE PRAISE FOR *IT HAPPENED ONE DOOMSDAY*

"If the apocalypse is going to be this much fun, sign me up!"
—M. C. Planck, author of
the World of Prime series

"Dru's apocalyptic adventures with demons, magical crystals, and crazy-making chaos are hellishly original and lots of fun."
—Helen Harper, author of
the Highland Magic series

"Add Laurence MacNaughton's Dru Jasper to the pantheon of Ree Reyes, Atticus O'Sullivan, and Harry Dresden. MacNaughton shatters his way through an apocalyptic good time, leaving a trail of broken crystals in his wake."
—Michael Haspil, author of *Graveyard Shift*

"Laurence MacNaughton sends readers on a fast-paced adventure into a fascinating world of sorcerers literally dealing with problems of apocalyptic proportions! *It Happened One Doomsday* will keep you turning page after page up until the end of the world!"
—Richard A. Knaak, author of *Black City Saint*

"From zero to apocalypse in sixty seconds! A fast-paced, action-packed supernatural road rally that had me on the edge of my seat . . . when I wasn't laughing out loud. Think Harry Dresden meets Stephen King's *Christine*."
—Mari Mancusi, award-winning author
of the Scorched series

"*It Happened One Doomsday* is an epic blend of magic, action, humor, and romance, delivered at breakneck speed on the road to Armageddon. Laurence MacNaughton knows how to unleash an apocalypse in style!"
—Angela Roquet, author of the Lana Harvey,
Reapers Inc. series

It Happened One Doomsday

LAURENCE MacNAUGHTON

IT HAPPENED
ONE DOOMSDAY

an imprint of Prometheus Books
Amherst, NY

Published 2016 by Pyr®, an imprint of Prometheus Books

Cover illustration and design by Nicole Sommer-Lecht
Cover design © Prometheus Books

This is a work of fiction. Characters, organizations, products, locales, and events portrayed in this novel either are products of the author's imagination or are used fictitiously.

Inquiries should be addressed to

Pyr
59 John Glenn Drive
Amherst, New York 14228
VOICE: 716-691-0133
FAX: 716-691-0137
WWW.PYRSF.COM

20 19 18 17 16   5 4 3 2 1

Library of Congress Cataloging-in-Publication Data

Names: MacNaughton, Laurence, 1975- author.
Title: It happened one doomsday / by Laurence MacNaughton.
Description: Amherst, N.Y. : Pyr, an imprint of Prometheus Books, 2016.
Identifiers: LCCN 2016007393 (print) | LCCN 2016020398 (ebook) |
    ISBN 9781633881877 (paperback) | ISBN 9781633881884 (ebook)
Subjects: LCSH: Magic—Fiction. | BISAC: FICTION / Fantasy / Urban Life. |
    GSAFD: Fantasy fiction.
Classification: LCC PS3613.A276 I84 2016 (print) | LCC PS3613.A276 (ebook) |
    DDC 813/.6—dc23
LC record available at https://lccn.loc.gov/2016007393

Printed in the United States of America

For Cyndi.

CONTENTS

1

THE PERFECT RING

Dru Jasper had no idea that the world was prophesied to come to a fiery end in six days. All she knew was that she had to ring up enough sales to pay the rent, or her shop, The Crystal Connection, would get evicted from its cramped storefront between the pawnshop and the 24-hour liquor store.

Worn out from a long day of cataloging rocks and hoping that one of her scarce customers would actually buy something, Dru pulled her brown hair back into a ponytail and carefully cleaned her thick-framed glasses.

The crystals, ancient artifacts, and leather-bound books lining the shelves of her shop all seemed to accumulate dust that had an obnoxious way of clinging to everything. Especially her glasses.

As she misted her lenses, a rumble of thunder rolled down the street. Which was odd because although the sunny Denver afternoon seemed unusually bleak, there was no sign of rain. A moment later, looking out her front windows, she realized it wasn't thunder at all.

With a snarl of exhaust, an old muscle car pulled up to the curb. Every inch of it glistened black and smooth as volcanic glass, from the sinister point of its long nose to the spoiler wing that rose up in back. The car rolled to a stop behind the old purple Lincoln Town Car belonging to Dru's sole employee, Opal.

At that moment, Opal got out of her car, a heavyset black woman in an orange-crush-colored knit top and a necklace of polished crystal tiger's-eye beads big enough to be actual tigers' eyes. When she stepped up onto the sidewalk in gumdrop-red platform sandals, one of them wobbled, and she accidentally dropped her paper cup of coffee, spilling it everywhere.

Opal paused in the process of picking up her now-empty cup to stare at her car's back tire. Which was slowly going flat, a nail sticking out of its sidewall.

Inside the shop, Dru winced in sympathy. She came out from behind the counter to help, quickening her pace when she saw the guy get out of his black car and approach Opal. With his thick dark hair, sunglasses, stubble, and black motorcycle jacket, he looked like nothing but trouble.

But much to her surprise, Mr. Motorcycle Jacket actually made Opal smile brightly. He walked back along the length of his long black car, opened up the trunk beneath the tall wing, and brought back a lug wrench and a jack. Without preamble, he got down and proceeded to change Opal's flat tire.

Through the shop's scratched front windows, Opal made eye contact with Dru. Her lifted eyebrows and pursed lips clearly expressed that she thought this guy was fabulous.

Then something around the corner, outside of Dru's line of sight, spooked Opal enough to make her hustle in through the front door of the shop. The bell jingled.

"Is that guy fixing your tire?" Dru asked in disbelief. She hurried to follow Opal toward the back room.

"Yeah, if I was single right now, we'd already be making plans, him and me. But whatever. You can be jealous later. You've got bigger problems." Opal turned and pointed outside. "Here comes your friend."

Dru's customers were mostly furtive sorcerers who shunned attention. But Rane was impossible to miss in a crowd. Six feet tall, built like a professional athlete, with a high blonde ponytail that bobbed with every stomp of her feet. Even when Rane was in a *good* mood she looked ready to smash something.

Rane marched straight toward the front door of the shop. And she was obviously not in a good mood.

"Oh, fudge buckets," Dru whispered. "Quick, hide anything fragile."

Opal rolled her eyes. "Everything in here is fragile. Including me."

In fact, nothing about Opal was fragile. Loud, sarcastic, and voluptuous, maybe. At least *voluptuous* was the current word she used to describe herself, formerly *full-figured*, *fluffy*, and (briefly) *goddess*. But certainly not fragile.

"She breaks anything?" Opal said. "I'm not the one cleaning it up this time. Thought you should know that."

Outside, Rane marched past Mr. Motorcycle Jacket, close enough that she nearly made him drop Opal's newly removed tire. She banged through the door the way she always did, the force threatening to tear off the bell that hung from the wall. It jangled in protest.

"Girl's got issues. Good luck with all that," Opal whispered. "And let me know when Mr. Hunky is done with my tire. I want to thank him properly." She ducked into the back.

Dru took a deep breath and slipped behind the counter again. "Hi, Rane," she sang out, trying to sound cheerful. And failing.

"Dude. You should totally tighten up that bell before it falls off. You don't want it beaning some jackwad on the head and getting you a lawsuit." Rane marched up to the counter and planted both palms on it. "Listen. I'm in big trouble."

Dru's smile froze. Rane had the singular ability to stir up trouble anywhere, even where there wasn't any. And she had a tendency to bring it into the shop with her. "What kind of trouble, exactly?"

"I need a new ring."

"Come on, Rane, give me a break—"

"Don't give me any crap, D. I had to try like fifty different rings last time before I found this granite one."

"It's flint, actually."

Rane propped one fist on her hip and shot Dru a dark look. "Seriously? This is *flint*? Like the sparky rock?"

"Well, yes. Although we, um, we don't usually call it that." Dru pointed to the mottled brown-and-gray stone ring. "Flint enhances strength and healing. And it's been used since prehistoric times to make tools and weapons. Considering how you spend your days, you know, hunting monsters and all, I figured it was apropos."

"Ugh." Rane rolled her eyes. "Well, that explains it."

"'It' what?"

Rane planted both palms on the counter again and leaned across it. Dru pulled back in wide-eyed wariness.

"Dude," Rane said somberly. "I've been fighting this infestation of little stinky gremlin types down by the river."

"Stinky?"

"Some kind of gas they put off. Nasty, slimy little beasties. But when they all jumped on me, and I punched one, super hard, it made sparks. And these guys lit up like the Hindenburg."

"That must've been . . . disturbing."

"Almost burned my face off. *Not* cool." Rane said it in a way that indicated she clearly blamed Dru. "So I need something a little less sparky and a lot more kick-ass."

"You're putting out a lot of magical energy when you transform. Probably too much for just one little ring. Out of all those rings we tried, this is the only one that really seemed attuned to you," Dru said.

"You mean the only one that didn't blow up in my face?"

And it was the only one that Rane had actually paid for. An important line item in Dru's bookkeeping universe. She folded her hands in front of her and forced a smile. "I'm thinking maybe rings just aren't your style. How about a nice amulet instead?"

Rane let out a long sigh. She stared deep into Dru's eyes, as if to let her know what a vast disappointment she was. In her flat monotone, Rane said, "It's like this. You know my transformation power *only* works if I'm actually touching something. If I want to turn into rock, I have to be touching rock. If I want to turn into metal, I have to be touching metal."

"Yes, I know, so—"

"*So* if I get grabbed up by some gi-*normous* creature and I'm hanging upside down by my ankle and this *amulet* is dangling over my head and it's not touching my skin? I'm totally hosed." She stared harder. "Get it?"

Dru nodded. "All right. I get it."

"Don't hose me, Dru."

Dru solemnly shook her head. "I would never hose you."

"Good." Rane clenched her right fist, the one wearing the flint ring. With a faint stone-grinding sound, patches of her skin took on the mottling of the polished stone ring, growing and merging until Rane's body had transformed into solid rock.

"You know, one of these days, someone is going to see you do that in public," Dru said. "You really want to end up on YouTube?"

"Already on there. No one cares. Help me out, Dru," Rane said, her voice coarse and hollow, as if it echoed up from a deep cave. "Seriously. I don't know who else to go to. You're my best friend."

Two incompatible thoughts competed for Dru's attention. One, that no one had called her a best friend since grade school. And two, if this was what it was like to be Rane's friend, what was it like to be her enemy?

Still, Dru couldn't help but feel just the tiniest bit warm and fuzzy inside. Even if Rane was more than a little scary as a living statue, and probably Dru's only paying customer today.

"Okay." Dru smiled. "Let's get you back into the storage room and see what we can find."

Rane turned human again with that stone-grinding sound and shot Dru a bright smile. "Thanks, D." She punched Dru in the shoulder and headed into the back room.

Dru was still rubbing her shoulder when the bell jingled up front. The solidly built guy in the motorcycle jacket pushed his way inside and took off his sunglasses. He had a swagger that some women might find cute. Or so she assumed.

But here in this shop, he looked completely out of place.

"Hi," she said when he got close enough. "Did you just change Opal's tire?"

He nodded dismissively, as if it were nothing. Puzzled, he frowned around him at the tall shelves crammed with minerals and crystals, charms, statues, candles, rare herbs, and everything else her supernatural-oriented customers wanted.

"Um, what kind of car is that?" Dru asked, not out of any particular interest, but just to avoid having to explain her shop to someone who was so clearly not a customer.

"A 1969 Dodge Daytona," he said. When she didn't reply right away, he seemed to mistake her silence for encouragement. "It's basically an aerodynamic, Hemi-powered Charger. When it was built, it was so fast NASCAR outlawed it. I restore old cars, especially Mopars. That's what I do."

"Hmm." She nodded, trying to look fascinated.

"Sign outside says 'The Crystal Connection.'" He looked around again. "What's with all the other stuff?"

Inwardly, Dru sighed. Anytime someone had to ask, the conversation never went well. "It's a shop for people who know magic."

"Card tricks, coins behind your ear, that sort of thing?"

"Not exactly, no." This was the part that always got awkward with people who wandered in off the street. "Mostly, this is a very specialized store. We help people who have unusual problems that can't be solved any other way."

Much to her surprise, he turned and looked directly into her eyes with a warm intensity. "Then maybe you can help me. I'm Greyson, by the way."

"Oh. Um, Dru." Trying to mentally reclassify him as a customer caught her off guard. "So, okay. Absolutely. What seems to be bothering you?" She pulled out her notepad and reached for a pen, but she accidentally knocked it across the counter.

Greyson caught it at the same time she reached for it, and when her fingers brushed his, a spark flashed between them, like static electricity, only brighter and shockingly cold.

The jolt of energy made the fluorescent lights above them sizzle and flare. Then a pop echoed from the breaker box in the back room, and all the lights went out, plunging them into deep shadow.

The only light came from Greyson's eyes, which glowed like red-hot coals as he gazed down at her. "I guess you could say I have an unusual problem."

2

THEN THERE WAS GREYSON

Dru had cured plenty of mystical ailments at The Crystal Connection, but she usually had at least some warning. A little time to prepare, research the right crystals, brew up a potion, braid a healing circle out of copper wire, that sort of thing. It wasn't often that a customer strutted in through the front door, shorted out the lights, and made the hair stand up on the back of her neck.

Never, in fact.

In the spirit of being prepared, Dru kept a flashlight under the cash register. But in the case of magical sparks and red glowing eyes, she needed something stronger. She reached for a crystal.

Her own magical power lay in the ability to enhance the inherent spiritual properties of crystals. Make them more potent than they were in nature. Powerful enough to fight the forces of darkness.

So her first instinct was to reach under the counter for a finger-length crystal of purple amethyst, which helped protect against any kind of psychic attack. But in the sudden electrical outage, she couldn't find the amethyst. Or her smooth, egg-sized whorl of iridescent tiger's-eye, which warded off curses.

Her fingers closed on a dagger-shaped wedge of spectrolite. In full daylight, it would have shimmered like oil on the surface of deep water, but in the gloom of the shop, she could only go by feel. At any rate, it was a good, basic, soul-protecting crystal, and it had saved her life before.

When she picked it up, a startling tingle ran through her fingers, as if the energy that had sparked from Greyson's touch now traveled into the crystal in her hand. The spectrolite glowed faintly from within, releasing a breathtaking rainbow of lights. The pool of multicolored light illuminated Greyson's rugged face and the entire front counter area.

She'd never seen a crystal do *that* before.

As she backed away from the counter, she held the glowing crystal out at arm's length, wondering if it would burn her. But as she got farther away from Greyson, the light faded and went out. And so did the red glow in his eyes.

Before Dru could make anything of that, a snap sounded from the breaker box in the back room, and the lights flickered to life overhead.

"I got it," Opal yelled from the back room. "Power's back on."

"Thank you," Dru called over her shoulder, and then she turned a wary eye on Greyson.

His eyes were now a piercing blue, with shadows under them that spoke of sleepless nights.

"So," Dru said. "This sort of thing happen to you a lot?"

"What, the power going out?" He shook his head. "Not really."

"No. I mean the glowy-eyes thing."

He seemed puzzled. "The what?"

Dru peered over the top of her glasses at him. "Maybe we should start at the beginning. What seems to be troubling you, sir?"

He dropped his gaze, and his broad shoulders hunched. It took him a long time to finally answer. "I keep having these . . . strange dreams."

Dru felt one of her eyebrows go up on its own. "What sort of dreams are we talking about, exactly?"

He let out a slow breath, then looked around to make sure they were alone. It took him a couple of tries to start talking. "It's always the same. In my dream, I'm turning into some kind of . . . monster. With horns. Claws. Fangs . . . You know what, never mind. This sounds crazy." Abruptly, he shook himself and started to back away, hands up. "Forget I said anything." He turned to go.

"Greyson. Wait." She started to come around the counter, but stopped when he did. "Give me five minutes. Tell me just a little more. Maybe I can make it stop."

He hesitated, then looked over his shoulder at her, eyes narrowed. She had the feeling he didn't often show weakness to anyone, much less a complete stranger.

But it sounded to her like he might have a real problem. If there was some kind of monster after him—or *in* him—she had to do everything she could to help. Now, before anything got worse.

"Just five minutes," she said again. "Then you can walk out of here, and it'll be like we never met."

Greyson seemed to weigh that carefully, then nodded once and came back to the counter. She waited for him to go on.

He glanced up at the lights, as if he expected them to go out again.

"Don't worry, it might be nothing," she said. "The electrical system in this place is a little iffy. Mostly because the copper wires run around through the walls and the ceiling in a way that makes a protective circle." She drew an imaginary circle in the air with her finger.

His gaze went across the ceiling, then returned to her. "Wouldn't that be a protective *rectangle*?"

She wasn't amused. "Forget about the lights for a minute. Tell me about the dream."

Absently, he scratched the stubble on his chin. "That's pretty much it. In my dream, I become a monster, and I'm standing side by side with three other monsters."

"Do they all look like you? Horns, claws, et cetera?"

"No. They all look different. We're just standing shoulder to shoulder, lightning crashing down around us. The sky is on fire. And I'm so *angry*." He looked down at his empty hands, and then his haunted gaze met hers. "In my dream, I'm so full of . . . *rage*. I just want to tear everything down. Everywhere I go, everything I touch is just destroyed."

"Destroyed, how?"

"Turned to dust. Everything. Everywhere. Laid to waste, by my hands. Until there's nothing left anywhere but scorched ashes. Doomsday. The end of the world." The anguish in his voice filled the air between them like a palpable thing. Though he looked cool and collected on the outside, she could see the vulnerability in his eyes. "And then I wake up."

A sinking feeling settled inside Dru. She wanted, so badly, to help him. But she'd have to convince him first.

She cleared her throat. "When did this first start happening?"

"A few months ago. Look, I know this must sound pretty weird."

She smiled a little. "Believe me when I tell you that around here, this isn't even in the ballpark of weird."

A slight nod on his part indicated that he accepted that.

From the back room, a distant pop echoed. Apparently, Rane had started trying on new rings.

Greyson seemed concerned, but Dru dismissed it with a wave. "You notice anything odd at home lately?"

"Odd?"

"Strange noises outside your window? Things misplaced? Night sweats?"

He shook his head. "No."

She leaned on the counter. "Hissing cats? Whispering voices? Crowds staring at you for no reason?"

"No . . ."

"A craving for raw meat? Aversion to crosses? Messages written in blood?"

"Would've noticed that. No."

"Hmm." Dru ran through a list of possibilities in her head. "Do you have any enemies? Is there anyone who wants you dead?"

"Not really."

"Not *really*?" She peered over the top of her glasses again. "Care to elaborate?"

He gave her an unreadable look. "No."

After drumming her fingers on the counter for a moment, she decided to let that go for now. "Cursed family history? Any ancestors who swore to get their revenge from beyond the grave?"

He cocked his head to the side. "I thought maybe you'd give me some kind of homeopathic incense or something."

"First, I have to figure out what's bothering you," she said. "Is there anything else you can think of, anything at all, that happened before all of this started? It could be something as subtle as a chalk mark on your door. Or somebody whispering Latin in your ear."

He gave her a long, silent look. "You're really serious about this supernatural thing."

While Dru struggled to respond with an inoffensive answer, Opal came up to the front counter, heels clacking. "Um, Dru?" She pointed meaningfully toward the storage room.

Another distant pop echoed through the store. And another. They kept coming, faster now.

Dru gave her best customer-service smile to Greyson. "Bear with me one moment."

She darted back to the storage room. Just as she opened the door, a flash lit the room, and the ring on Rane's finger exploded into skittering fragments.

Rane sat cross-legged on the floor, surrounded by open boxes. Charred bits of rings littered the floor. Her face was mottled red with frustration. "Dude, this is total crap. None of these are *working*."

"Can I help?" Dru stepped in through the doorway. Her shoes made gravel-crunching noises on the mess.

"Don't worry. I'll pay for those," Rane said, in a tone of voice that indicated she didn't think she should.

Dru tried not to think about the cost of the destroyed inventory or the amount of her almost-overdue rent. "Look, let's just slow down a minute. Maybe there's a way I can help you stop exploding things."

Rane held up a hand. "D. Seriously. Back off and let me do this." Her eyes glinted dangerously.

There was no way to win. After a moment, Dru forced a smile. "All righty. I'll be back." She shut the door behind her and leaned against it. Inside, another ring popped. Dru sighed in resignation.

Back up front, Dru sidled behind the counter again. "Okeydoke. One last thing. Have you tried any religious intervention? Church, priest, communion, anything like that?"

"Look, I've been to doctors. Tried a shrink, even. None of them helped. I was on my way to the liquor store next door. That's the best I've got."

"Well, I've got a better idea. Let's try something new." She went down the aisles in the front of the store. One by one, she pulled out cardboard drawers and sorted through various crystals and chunks of rock. She could feel the intensity of his gaze following her every step.

Blushing, though she didn't know why, she came back to the counter and spread out an assortment of crystals.

He picked up a softball-sized gray-and-tan lump of rock and turned it over.

"Careful. That's hollow." She snatched the geode out of his hand and set it down on the counter. After considering her options, she chose a shiny chunk of galena. Like most galena crystals, it looked like it had been formed from a half-dozen different little cubes all fused together, and it had a dark-mirrored sheen, like a highway patrolman's sunglasses.

She took a moment to weigh the crystal in her hand, until she could feel the faint whispers of its energy synchronizing with hers. "Here. Let's start easy, with a little lead-sulfide galena crystal. Let me have your hand."

He put his arm on the counter, and she pushed back the sleeve of his leather jacket. When she touched the galena to his wrist, the crystal popped with a cold blue flare of light, like an old-fashioned photo flash, accompanied by a sinister sizzling sound. Greyson yanked his arm off the counter and sucked his breath in through his teeth.

"Wow," Dru said, with a little thrill of triumph mixed with a tinge of surprised fear. She'd never seen galena react so spectacularly before. "Bingo. Looks like we have a demon."

"*Huh.*" Greyson shook his hand out. If he felt any pain, which Dru seriously suspected, he did a remarkable job of hiding it. "Demon, huh?" He shook his head and turned toward the door. "Time for me to go."

"Greyson, wait. I know it sounds bad. But chances are it's nothing. There are countless garden-variety demons out there trying to raise hell, so what you've caught is probably pretty minor."

After a couple of steps, he paused and faced her again. "Look, I don't believe in demons, or ghosts, or any of that." He glanced around at the cluttered shelves. "No offense."

Dru shrugged. "Doesn't matter if you believe in the demon or not. It still wants your soul."

A faint smile of disbelief, almost amusement, crooked up one corner of his mouth. He shook his head once, then turned to go.

But something held him back.

Dru waited. She'd seen people express this kind of disbelief in the supernatural plenty of times before. Even her boyfriend didn't believe, no matter how much he saw. She knew from experience that if she tried too hard to convince Greyson, she would push him away, and his problem would only get worse. As much as it pained her to stay silent, she bit her lip.

He let out a deep breath, then nodded his chin at the galena crystal she still held. "All right. I'll bite. First, tell me what makes the rock light up like that. Got an LED bulb in there, or . . . ?"

"Just an ordinary crystal. What lights it up is the thing inside you." She held up the galena for his inspection.

Greyson made no move to touch it again. The muscles in his neck tightened. "So according to your theory, I'm . . . what, possessed?"

"*Pfft*, no." She waved it off. "Well, maybe a little."

"A *little*?"

"Look. Let me try a few more crystals. If I'm wrong, you're no worse off. But if I'm right?" She let that thought hang between them for a moment, watching his face carefully. "If I'm right, you get a good night's sleep from now on. And your soul, even if you don't believe in it, stays safe and sound. Isn't that worth a shot?"

After another long, hard look around the shop, Greyson walked back up to the counter. Without another word, he tugged back his other sleeve and planted his arm on the counter. The expression on his face made it clear that he was only going to give her one more chance.

Inwardly, Dru sighed in relief. She knew she could do this.

Or at least, she hoped so.

"Okay, so, let's get you all fixed up. No more shocks, I promise." Dru tried a swirled green blade of agate against his skin. No reaction. She moved on to a heavily grained chunk of fossilized wood, then a wrinkly gleaming lump of natural copper. Nothing.

When she got to a finger-length wand of ice-clear petalite, she felt a subtle healing vibration flow through it. Much stronger than anything she'd ever felt before. Either she was a hundred percent on her game or Greyson's presence somehow made her crystals more powerful than usual.

Excited, she ran the petalite crystal up and down his arm and watched for any sign of discomfort. "Feel anything funny?"

"No." His tone explicitly indicated that he didn't expect to, either.

"That's fine. It's very rare for people to feel healing vibrations, but that's what I'm here for. It's what I do."

A loud bang echoed from the back room, and Dru cringed. She folded Greyson's hand shut over the crystal and noticed a gray metal ring on his index finger. Strange place for a wedding ring. "So, um, are you . . . married?"

"No." His gaze followed hers to the ring, then rose to meet her eyes with an irrepressible intensity. "Why?"

Despite her efforts to stay professional, she felt herself blushing. "No reason. I just had kind of a crazy idea, that's all. About your ring, not you. I mean, not about your *problem*. In particular."

"Just a ring. Bought it at a motorcycle shop."

"So, no sentimental value?"

He shrugged. "Not like it's a tattoo or something."

"Any chance you know what it's made of?"

He scratched his chin stubble. "Titanium. I think. You trying to tell me this ring is part of my problem?"

"Nah." Then she looked over her shoulder toward the back room. "I mean, *yes*. Definitely part of your problem. You should absolutely give up that ring. Immediately. Here, I'll take it."

He narrowed his eyes at her, but he pulled off the ring anyway.

"Sweet." She grabbed it from him. "Don't go anywhere!" She ran back to the storage room.

The floor around Rane was now littered with even more shattered rings. Her body had turned glossy reddish-brown, with light and dark stripes and swirls.

Dru pulled up short. "Whoa."

"Mahogany," Rane said, her voice rich and vibrant.

"Well, that seems . . . useful."

"Not. Unless I want to spend some quality time as a human matchstick." Rane pulled off the carved wooden ring and turned human again.

Her eyes had become red and puffy from unshed tears. She wiped them. "I think I'm in trouble here, D. None of this will work. I'm so totally hosed."

"No, no, honey." Dru knelt down next to her and held out Greyson's titanium ring. "Look."

Rane sniffed. "I've tried a bunch of different metallics. None of them took. I'm going to ruin everything you have. It's no good."

"Just try it. Really."

Rane sighed and slipped it on. She clenched one fist and waited. After a moment, a startled look passed over her face. With a sound like a gradually drawn blade, Rane's fist turned a lustrous earthy silver color. The effect spread up her arm and across her entire body.

She turned steely eyes toward Dru and smiled. *"Nice."* Her voice echoed with a metallic twang. "Druster, you've been holding out on me." She punched Dru in the arm.

"Ouch." Dru almost fell over. "Why do you always do that?"

"Oh, cowgirl up." Rane rose to her feet. She moved like liquid metal as she grasped Dru's hands in her own and hauled Dru up off the floor.

"Do not go outside looking like that," Dru said. "I *mean* it this time."

"Okay, fine." Reluctantly, Rane turned back to human, then pressed some cash into Dru's hand. "That's all I've got, D. You're a peach, you know? I could kiss you."

"Enough drama for one day. Out." She pointed to the door.

Rane carefully patted Dru's shoulder with just her fingertips, then marched out, grinning.

Dru looked down around her feet at the wreckage of Rane's shopping spree, mentally adding up how much it would cost to replace the broken rings. Right now, she just couldn't afford it. And she'd never get paid back, regardless of anything Rane promised. Plus, now someone had to sweep all of this up.

For a moment, Dru thought she might pull her own hair out. And then she made a deliberate choice, as she always did with Rane, to let all the stress go.

"Meh," she said, with considerable effort, and left it.

She got back to the counter just as the bell rang and Rane strutted outside in human form, admiring her shiny new ring.

Greyson watched her go. "She wearing my ring?"

"Different people have different problems," Dru said. "Let's focus on yours. Still have that petalite?"

He opened his hand to show her.

"Good. Hold it in your hand or keep it in your pocket at all times. Especially when you sleep."

"Why? What will it do?"

"It'll protect your soul and help you sleep. That's a start, anyway. But I want to see you back here in twenty-four hours, no excuses."

He nodded.

Just this small success, getting him to try the crystal overnight, gave her a greater feeling of triumph than she expected.

This was the whole reason she had her shop. To help people. To solve magical problems that no one else could solve. To push back against the forces of darkness and make the world a brighter place.

"And what about the dream?" he said, bringing her back down to earth. "The end of the world. Does it mean anything?"

It did. Dru was certain. It meant something terrible. She just had to figure out what.

3

HAVING RESERVATIONS

Greyson promised to return the next day. If there was a bright side to all of this, Greyson's payment for the crystal meant Dru had enough rent money for the month. That was something.

Meanwhile, Opal's eyes stayed glued to Greyson's every step out the door and back to his long black muscle car. "Mmm-*mmm*." Opal sighed. "For real, I'm about ready to lick peanut butter off that man's chest."

"Peanut butter?" Dru made a face. "That isn't even a thing."

Opal gave her a knowing look. "Is for me, honey."

"*Absolutely* didn't need to know that."

Outside, Dru's boyfriend, Nate, crossed the street toward them, lit by the warm Colorado sunshine. Well-dressed, brilliant smile, slightly geeky in a way that Dru always found disarming. But his well-mannered demeanor cracked as he shot Greyson a dirty look on the way past.

"Uh-oh," Opal said. "Apparently your boyfriend's all kinds of jealous of Hunky Davidson and his hot-mobile."

"Not a chance. Nate's not the jealous type."

Opal lowered her chin and shot Dru another meaningful look. "If you say so."

The door jangled, and Dru came around the counter with arms outstretched. "Honey! Hi! What are you doing here? I thought today was the big free day."

"Free day?" Opal echoed.

Nate gave Dru a quick kiss, then turned to Opal. "Free exams, fillings, extractions. For under-served populations."

"He means homeless people." Dru fussed with his tie and jacket lapels, trying to smooth them out. "So proud of you."

"But we don't call them homeless people." His smile practically lit up the room. "They're all just patients."

She beamed back at him. "How many? Patients, I mean."

"Lost count. Apparently, the line started last night, and it still stretched all the way around the corner when I ran out for lunch. But I wanted to see you before I head back to it. I'll be late. Planning to keep going until all of them are—" He broke off as the black muscle car's engine started outside with a sound like a rumble of thunder.

They both looked. The thud of the car's exhaust seemed to reverberate through the shop, powerful, menacing, dangerous. With a lurch, the long black car pulled away from the curb and rocketed down the street.

Nate's expression darkened as he watched Greyson drive off. "So who was that guy, anyway?"

"Just a customer. You know, I get all sorts in here sometimes."

"Indeed we do." Opal wiggled her eyebrows suggestively.

Behind Nate's back, Dru shot her a warning glare.

Nate sighed deeply. "Yes. I know. It's just that every day I worry about you being in this neighborhood."

"It's not like we're on East Colfax or something."

"Hmm. That reminds me." He reached into his jacket pocket and pulled out a small flashlight-sized device with six stubby metal prongs on one end. He clicked a button, and the metal prongs crackled with brilliant blue electricity. As the electrical arc crawled from one prong to the next, it left pulsing afterimages in Dru's vision.

"Jeez Louise." Dru backed away, blinking. "What is that?"

He let go of the button and showed her the bold black letters along the side of the device: SHOCK WAND. "It's a Shock Wand," he explained unnecessarily.

"So I see. Where'd you get that?"

"From Joe down the street."

"Joe, the crazy survivalist nut? The guy who's worried the CIA is reading his mind?" Dru pointed at her own head and made a swirly motion with her finger. "You know he just sits there dreaming this stuff up over foil pouches of freeze-dried space food, right?"

"That's high-protein fuel, by the way, and it's not that bad. Anyway, I picked up one of these for each of us. Capable of stunning a moose, apparently." He held it out to her, but she didn't take it.

"Pretty sure we don't have any rampaging moose around here." She glanced around at the shelves of crystals surrounding them. "Besides, we're standing in a shop stacked sky-high with magically charged crystals," she said. "The last thing I want to do is accidentally zap something and blow the place up."

Nate made the same face he always made when he was trying not to roll his eyes. He didn't entirely succeed. "Of course. I don't mean to interfere with the 'magic.'" He formed air quotes with his fingers. "I'm just worried about you, that's all."

"I know. And that's so sweet. But—"

His phone rang. With a sigh, he shoved the wand into her hands and pulled out his phone. "Dr. Corbin here."

Dru held the thing out at arm's length, as if it would bite her. She offered it to Opal, who backed away wide-eyed, shaking her head no.

"Correct," Nate said. "Tomorrow at seven. Perfect."

When Nate hung up, she tried to give the wand back to him, but he wouldn't take it.

"It's just a precaution," he said, "considering the neighborhood."

Opal picked up a box of crystals and huffed past him. "Excuse me, Mr. Nate. I happen to live just down the way, remember?"

"Present company excluded."

Dru decided to change the topic and set the wand down on the counter. "So what's tomorrow at seven?"

Nate's thumbs tapped on his phone. "Chez Monet."

Chez Monet was the hottest new restaurant in Denver. Nate had teased her that they'd eat dinner there when they were ready to get engaged.

Engaged. Her breath caught in her throat.

This was it. This was the moment. Tomorrow at seven, he would finally pop the question. She grabbed the counter for support, expecting the room to start swimming around her. It didn't, but she was still ready, just in case.

Nate was too busy tapping on his phone to notice. "Just a business dinner. Trying to get those new investors from Switzerland involved in expanding the dental practice. Chez Monet sounds like an ideal choice."

It took a few moments for his words to penetrate her daze. "Oh. Business meeting? So not . . ."

He paused and looked at her. "Not what?"

"Hmm?" Her brain frantically tried to change directions and failed. "Nothing. What?"

His phone chimed. He resumed tapping. "It's a pain trying to get everyone lined up. My dad, the investors, Tonya—"

"The *hygienist* will be there?" Dru asked, unable to keep the surprise out of her voice. Tonya was obnoxiously bubbly, busty, blonde, and had the insidious habit of "accidentally" brushing up against Nate at every possible opportunity.

"Like I said, big business meeting. Need all hands on deck."

Great. So not only was he *not* going to propose to her at Chez Monet, he'd be having dinner and drinks with a hot, flirty blonde with boundary issues. There was only one thing she could do.

"I want to go with you," she blurted.

Nate's thumbs paused, and he looked up from the phone screen. "Really? I thought you hated this sort of thing."

She did. "No. Not . . . Not at all. I, um, *want* to be more involved, anyway. With all the dental-ness." Which was more or less true.

Actually, she realized, it wasn't. At all. Inwardly, she cringed.

But the effect on Nate was immediate. A snow-white smile lit up his face. "Really? That's great. I'll set it up." He gave her a quick peck and headed out the door. "Have to run. Patients waiting."

"Bye," Dru said as the door jangled. She sighed and slumped against the counter.

Opal came back up front, carefully unwrapping a pack of bubble gum. "Dental-ness?"

Dru sighed again and held out the Shock Wand. "You want this?"

"Nuh-uh. Probably drop it down the sink drain and short out half the neighborhood."

Dru puzzled out how to pop the batteries out of the wand, then shoved it into the clutter packed under the cash register.

Chewing her gum, Opal tapped one long fingernail on the counter. "You know what you need to do?"

Dru didn't have the energy to answer.

"You need to make that man jealous," Opal said. "Maybe he didn't notice that buttercup hygienist yet, but sooner or later he will. Meantime? Make him worried about losing you. Underneath those librarian glasses and that girl-next-door hairdo, you are all kinds of hot, and he ought to know it. He doesn't even know what he's got."

"What he's *got* is a girl who's worried she's just too plain weird for him, that's what." Dru busied herself with straightening up around the cash register. "I can't expect Nate to understand magic. Hardly anyone believes in it, outside of actual sorcerers. But do I want him to, really? The fact that he's so *normal* is what keeps me sane in the middle of all this."

"Mmm-hmm."

Sometimes, Dru needed Opal's common-sense advice as much as her magical expertise. "Is it bad that I just want him to get down on one knee and propose? What's wrong with a white wedding? A stable home, so that if we have kids, they'll grow up someplace safe and normal and not have to worry about demons and monsters? *Real* monsters?"

"Oh, so you and Nate having kids, now?"

"I'm just saying. If we do." Dru grabbed the duster and swiped it across the counter with unnecessary force.

"Sweetie, I know what it's like to grow up around sorcery without being a part of it. My dad, my mom, my brother. But not me. Closest I got to magic is a sparkling sense of style."

"Not to be underrated," Dru pointed out.

"Thank you. Point is, I know what it's like, waking up every morning waiting for the curtain to go up, and it never does." Opal's penciled eyebrows wrinkled in concern. "But even if I'm just *around* magic, I'm okay with that. Having one foot in both worlds is just fine, if that's what you want."

"I just want to avoid making the same mistakes my mom made. Getting wrapped up in the danger and craziness of a sorcerer's life. Constantly being on the move. Always looking over your shoulder for the next creature or rival sorcerer who wants to ruin your life," Dru said. "I don't know if it's possible to have safety and stability, and also still have magic in your life. But that's what I want."

"You know, I think your mom tried to keep you safe from all that. That's why she never told you about your magical talent."

"No, she told me I didn't *have* any magical talent. Big difference."

Opal held up her hands. "Not saying it was right. Just saying maybe she was hoping you'd have a 'normal' life after all. Maybe she was trying to protect you from the craziness."

"Well, things ended up crazy anyway. And then I had to learn it all on my own."

"Well." Opal straightened up a shelf of tiny statues. "Least you got magic to learn."

"That's not what I meant."

"Mmm-hmm."

With an effort, Dru pushed herself away from the counter. "Where's the broom? I need to clean up after Rane. Again."

Opal popped another stick of gum in her mouth. "Well, somebody's got to. And you know, I'm busy."

4

NINETY-FIVE PERCENT RIGHT

Long before dawn, Dru woke up thinking about Greyson's dream.
Transforming into a monster and standing shoulder to shoulder
beside three others like him. Turning everything they touched into
scorched ashes.

"Doomsday," he had said. "The end of the world."

After that, Dru couldn't get back to sleep.

Something about his nightmare sounded uncannily familiar. She
knew she'd read about a similar dream somewhere before, probably in
one of the thousands of books she kept downstairs in her shop.

There were occasions that she hated having an apartment right over
her shop, which meant she could never get all that far from her work. But
right now it was truly convenient.

Except that it left her with several thousand books to sort through.

She pulled on a sweatshirt, went downstairs barefoot and sat in one
of the ugly armchairs in the back room, thumbing through stacks of
dusty books, trying to puzzle out anything she could about Greyson's
condition.

In the century-old padlocked journals of the demon-hunter Nicolai
Stanislaus, she found a passage about a captured demon claiming that the
"text of Doomsday"—whatever *that* was—was hidden among the causeways.

The causeways were a mythical maze of bridges and tunnels that
ancient sorcerers had supposedly built to ensure safe passage through the
netherworld, allowing them to walk from one point on earth to another,
sometimes thousands of miles away, just by stepping through a portal.
Somewhere in this labyrinth of portals, the demon had claimed, lay the
key to the end of the world.

The only problem was that no one had ever been able to locate a single such portal to the netherworld, and there was no proof that they'd ever existed. As far as Dru could tell, the causeways were just a wild myth.

Then again, demons weren't exactly known for their truthfulness.

Whatever the answer was for Greyson's problem, it stayed tantalizingly just out of reach. At some point, she fell asleep in her chair, the reassuring weight of the old books comforting her like a heavy blanket.

A pounding on the locked front door woke her again, but she ignored it. After some foggy contemplation, she realized that the warm glow surrounding her was actually the first rays of daylight.

About the time she decided that she really ought to get up and get dressed, the sound of splintering wood filled the air. A new shaft of sunlight poured in through the back corner of the shop.

"Yo, D," Rane called out. "If you're here, you should know your back door security could use an upgrade."

Wood groaned in protest, and the sunlight vanished with a slam. Rane's footsteps thumped closer through the dark maze of shelves and into the light streaming through the window. The moment Rane spotted Dru, she stopped short. "Oh, hey. I know it's early, but you don't mind if I borrow some of your books, right? Need to find some other way to pound out these stinky creatures besides lighting them up and practically burning my face off." She paused. "Are you in your jammies?"

Dru straightened up in the chair and moved the books off her lap. "Rough night. Got a lot on my mind."

"Let me guess. Problems with Nate, right? Best cure, go running with me, sweat it out." Rane crossed the shaft of sunlight from the room's only window, her muscled silhouette glowing for a moment in the light. She browsed Dru's bookshelves, pulling out occasional volumes and flipping through them.

A few brown-speckled pages fell out of one of the books and fluttered down to the floor. "Oops, my bad," Rane said.

Irritated, Dru snatched up the papers, took the book away from Rane, and sat down again. As she sorted the messily handwritten pages back into order, one particular passage caught her eye:

Now, there are seven of us. Seven angels or seven demons?
Neither.
Seven Harbingers. Seven creators of the new world, because today the world is too sick to survive. The day has come to wipe the slate clean. Do it over, and do it right.
Apokalipso voluta is the key. With it, we Harbingers will remake the world the way it was meant to be.

Dru rolled the strange phrase around in her head. *Apokalipso voluta.* Literally, it meant "the apocalypse scroll."

But with magic, nothing was ever straightforward. Hardly anything in a sorcerer's journal could be taken at face value. Sometimes, they even spread deliberate misinformation to protect themselves.

Although the sorcerers who came into Dru's shop were more or less dedicated to fighting evil in its various guises, that was where their common ground ended. Every sorcerer's agenda was as unique as his or her power.

Some used their abilities to settle old scores. Others hunted trophies among the creatures of darkness that stalked the night. And still others sought to quench a limitless thirst for esoteric, arcane knowledge.

Experienced sorcerers with delusions of grandeur and scant morals could take advantage of the lawless nature of the magical underworld. They could prey on weaker sorcerers, stripping them of their enchanted artifacts and research until others banded together to stop them.

Once the threat was eliminated, those alliances usually fell apart as the limited spoils of magic spread too thin. And so the cycle began again.

As a result, sorcerers tended to be elusive and paranoid by nature. They hid their research, writing journals by hand to guard their secrets. They couched their notes in vague metaphors and cryptic references, hoping to deceive and confuse their rivals.

But as Dru flipped through the handwritten journal, something about it left her feeling uneasy. Its brazen claims about remaking the entire world bordered on bragging, as if the anonymous author had absolutely no fear of discovery.

It was more like he or she actually wanted to be found. As if this journal was meant to serve as some kind of manifesto. A testament to why the world needed to be wiped clean and started over anew.

If that was true, then what was the apocalypse scroll, exactly?

She checked the book's spine. It was a plain, cloth-bound, hardcover journal. Midcentury, from the looks of it. No title or name written anywhere. The front cover was adorned only with the crude outline of a seven-fingered hand.

"Opal tells me you think Nate's going to propose," Rane said, interrupting her thoughts, which were going nowhere anyway.

Dru set the book down on a cluttered side table and wiped her glasses on her shirt. "Well, Opal also thinks I've got plain, girl-next-door hair, so you can't believe everything she says."

Still sorting through the shelves, Rane gave her an appraising look, but said nothing.

"What does that look mean?" Dru asked.

"Nothing, dude. Ever since you met Nate, you've been going all spastically *normal* about everything." Rane yanked another book off the shelf, causing a puff of dust to fly into the air. She flipped it open, then peered past the pages and pierced Dru with a long look. "You're sure you're not . . . I don't know. Bored?"

Dru sat up. "What?"

"Never mind. Not my business."

"Nate's not boring. Practical, maybe. Successful, definitely. But not *boring*. I like having an actual everyday conversation with someone. We talk about politics, instead of demons. Classical music, instead of ancient curses. The other night, we had an entire conversation about books we loved as kids, and I never mentioned *The Folio of the Forlorn*, not even once."

"Yeah, but I bet you wanted to."

"Maybe I like not having to worry about magic twenty-four hours a day."

"No way, dude. You know too much to ever be cool with that white-picket-fence routine. Face it."

Rane's words cut her to the core, though she tried not to show it.

Still, hot tears filled Dru's eyes. Quickly, she averted her gaze and tried to blink them away.

Rane froze, as if Dru had pointed a loaded gun at her. "Okay, um, sorry? Seriously. Don't freak out on me. Just . . . breathe."

Dru swallowed and wiped at her eyes. "Forget it. It's nothing."

Rane looked at the ugly chair across from Dru's, and then glanced toward the back door, as if she was planning an escape route. But instead, she stalked over to the other chair and lowered herself into it. "You, um . . . you want to talk?"

"No." Dru pretended to sort through the stack of books next to her.

"Okay." Rane resumed flipping through the pages of her book. "Sorry. I know you really like Nate and all, and it's *so* not my business."

"What is the big problem? For once, I'm finally dating a nice guy," Dru said. "Every time I've tried dating a sorcerer, it always ends in disaster. Just like it did for my mom."

"And everyone else. Join the club."

"Nate's different. He's stable, he's successful, he's crazy about me. I hope." She thought about Chez Monet and who was going to be there. "You know that blonde hygienist who works for Nate?"

Rane leaned closer, eyebrows knitted together. "What did she do now?"

"Nothing. Yet. It's just . . . I'm a little worried. Maybe Nate's not that into me."

Rane's face hardened. "Dude, I live by my instincts. And my instincts are right, like, ninety-five percent of the time. Even if Nate's not my type of guy, he's solid. He cares about you. He's always there for you. You remember that time you accidentally drank the sour fish potion and couldn't stop hurling?"

That particularly memorable experience was actually Rane's fault, but Dru didn't bother to point that out.

"Nate stepped up," Rane said. "He held your hair back all night while you were upchucking. And he cleaned you up. Took care of you. Right?"

"Thanks for reminding me," Dru said dryly.

"Look, I'd kill for someone like that. Vanilla or not, he's your man. I get it. If you're into him, you've got to fight for him, D. By any means necessary. Do not let some gold-digging bimbo get her claws into him." Rane stood, paced the cramped room for a minute, then flung herself down in the chair again and glared off into space. "Want me to beat her up? I'll do it, you know."

"I know. That's what scares me."

"Seriously." Rane brooded, apparently reliving a painful memory. "Just when you think you have everything under control. Right? Just when everything's all chocolate hearts and roses. That's when you let your guard down. And when you least expect it, *bam*." Rane punched the arm of her chair, shooting out a constellation of dust motes that glowed in the shaft of early-morning sunlight. "Whatever. You need a shower, and I need to get to work." She got to her feet, hefting the book. "Mind if I take this? I need to go hammer on those blue lime-pit critters."

"Today? In broad daylight?"

"Duh. Easier to find them in the daytime. Besides, the only people down there who will see anything are the homeless guys in their tents, and they'll be a lot safer when those stinky blue ankle-biters are history."

Dru stood and huddled deeper into her sweatshirt, feeling suddenly cold. "What kind of stinky are they, exactly?"

"What you mean? How many different kinds of stinky are there?"

"I mean, are they stinky like brimstone? Stinky like bad breath? What?"

"Bad breath. Definitely."

"Do they smell a little bit like garlic?"

Rane's face wrinkled in concentration. "Little bit, I guess, last time it rained. Kind of like tzatziki sauce gone way sideways."

"They're blue, they're from a lime pit, and they stink like garlic when they get wet. And they're extremely flammable. Right? I'd say calcium carbide."

Rane shook her head. "English please?"

"Calcium carbide. They used to make water lanterns out of it. It's blue, reacts with water, and it gives off an explosive gas. Your best bet is to lure these critters out into the open air and fight them there. Give the gas a chance to disperse. Then you can handle them."

Rane paused. "That's it? You sure? I don't need some kind of funky magic wand or something?"

"Maybe a fan would help."

"Awesome." Rane grinned. "Check you out, D. Smart and hot, all in one little package."

Dru blushed. "Whatever. Get out of here, and leave my books where you found them."

"There's no way Nate is going to give you up for that hygienist hussy. You're all that." Rane nodded solemnly.

Dru nodded back. "Thanks. You're sweet."

"Think so?" Rane grinned, showing teeth that looked like they could take a bite out of the hull of a boat. "Just remember, I got your back. You say the word, that chick is *toast.*"

5

RAT SIGNS

Dru slipped the honey-colored citrine crystal into a paper bag and rung up the sale. "Remember, from your front door, you put this in the *left* corner of the restaurant. Also, I put an extra little piece in the bag for you. That one goes in your cash register drawer." She hit the Sale button, and the drawer slid open with a chime, revealing the chunk of citrine she kept in her own change drawer. "See?"

Joe, the Chinese delivery guy, smiled. "Practice what you preach." He paid and took the paper bag.

"Prosperity and abundance," she said as he left. He waved and got into his car.

Opal caught the door before it closed behind him. Wrinkling her nose, she poked her head outside, then turned to look down the length of the shop at Dru. "You smell that? Some kind of chemical. Wind is blowing it right in."

Before Dru could answer, Opal's eyes widened in anger.

"That's spray paint! You little—" Opal launched herself out the door, hustling down the alley.

"Opal, wait!" Dru came around the counter and chased after her, haunted by visions of Opal getting jumped by spray-paint-wielding juvenile delinquents.

But in the alley between her shop and the 24-hour liquor store next door, she instead found one of her customers, Salem, spraying the finishing touches of a symbol on her broken back door.

As Opal shook her finger at him, working herself up into a tirade, Salem stepped back, black trench coat swirling around him. Ignoring

Opal, he tipped his silk top hat back on his head, pushed his long hair out of his face, and fixed his piercing gray eyes on Dru.

She stopped short, looking from his crazy, eyeliner-outlined eyes to the symbol he'd painted on her door, and back. "Salem? What's up?"

"Maybe you haven't noticed, but your door is broken," he said matter-of-factly, tilting his head toward the damage Rane had caused earlier.

Opal planted her fists on her wide hips. "I *know* that rat sign you painted on there is not gonna fix that door. All it's gonna do is bring trouble, and we don't need any more than we already have. Salem, I don't know *what* you're thinking."

"Sure you do." He pointed one finger to his temple and smirked at her. "Guess what I'm thinking right now."

Dru stepped between them. "Okay, enough. Opal, I'm sorry, I'll take care of this."

Opal dropped her chin and gave Dru a withering look. "Nothing but trouble, mark my words. Don't make me say 'I told you so' later on." With a dismissive sniff at Salem, she turned and headed back to the front door.

"She will anyway," Salem murmured. He locked gazes with Dru again, but she always had trouble maintaining eye contact with his half-crazed stare. Instead, she looked at the sign he had spray-painted on her rear door: an elongated hexagon beside a triangle, and beneath that, a smiley face without eyes.

It took a moment for the meanings to come to her. "'Crystals inside . . . um, somebody will help . . .'"

"*Kristalo sorcisto helpos,*" Salem said effortlessly in the sorcerer tongue. "'Someone here will use crystal magic to help you, when you need it most.'"

"Sure, but . . . Salem, in the entire world, there are, like, a few hundred true sorcerers, at most. What are the chances that one will happen to come through this exact alley and read this?"

His gray eyes widened with animal-like intensity. "We all move on the same paths, Dru. Magic attracts, like magnets. They'll come here, sooner or later. It'll seem like luck, that they saw this sign. But that's how magic works."

As much as she hated the ugly spray paint, she couldn't argue with him and his crazy eyes. "Speaking of signs, do you know a sign of a seven-fingered hand?"

He stared at her like a hungry wolf at wounded prey. "No."

It was plain he was lying. Alarm bells went off inside her head.

"Why?" he asked, edging closer. "Have you seen it?"

She backed up a step. "Uh, no. Just . . . always wondered about that one. Don't remember where I saw it. Long time ago. Anyway, what do you want, Salem?"

His black eyebrows drew together. "I need a way to focus. Three civilians have disappeared. We found their garages exploded outward, like something burst out and escaped. Traces of demon magic everywhere. And from the looks of it, there will be a fourth victim."

Dru suppressed a shiver. "Who?"

Salem shook his head in frustration. "I should be able to see the pattern. But I just can't put it together."

"Want me to have a look at the clues?"

He shrugged, as if the idea that she could see anything he'd missed was simply preposterous. "Just get me a crystal to help me focus."

She folded her arms. "Too bad you're not with Rane anymore. Why don't you get your new girlfriend to help you? What's her name again?"

Salem lowered his eyelids over his sharp eyes. "Just because you're BFFs with my ex doesn't mean you won't help me. As a *professional*."

She couldn't tell if he was complimenting her or insulting her. As if they were sharing some secret joke that she wasn't *really* a professional and he was just pretending to go along with her.

She sighed. All sorcerers were weirdos. It wasn't worth getting riled up about. "How about some red zincite? It can help you identify your gut feelings and trust your intuition. Want one?"

He took off his top hat, letting his long hair fall across his thin face. "You're too kind."

She led him back up the alley to the front door. But before he followed her, he waggled his fingers at the back door. The sound of mending wood and metal crackled through the alley as the broken lock knitted itself back together.

6
STRANGE BREW

The spiky red zincite reminded Dru of a pile of transparent plastic cocktail toothpicks. "Red zincite is good for clarifying your thinking. It also happens to remove hypnotic commands, just in case you start feeling very . . . sleepy . . ." She waved the crystal slowly back and forth over the counter.

Salem snatched it from her and peered closely at it. "Looks like a fine natural crystal."

"Nope. Dirty and artificial." Dru got a little spark of enjoyment from the glimmer of surprise on Salem's face. "Straight from the chimney of a smelting furnace in New Jersey. Natural ones are rare, and they're weaker. These smelter ones are industrial-strength, I promise."

Salem raised the crystal slightly, as if to salute her, and gave her a gaunt smile.

Opal looked up from the tray of crystals she was sorting. "Salem, I'm here to tell you, you're so skinny these days you don't look right. You been eating?"

"It's next on my to-do list." He tilted his head until his eyes glinted from beneath the rim of his top hat. "Dru, when you remember where you saw that seven-fingered sign, you tell me."

She forced a smile. "Oh, will do."

As Salem paid for the crystal, Greyson walked in through the front door. His attitude was so changed that Dru did a double take when she saw him. He walked taller, his eyes were brighter, and the brooding look that had plagued him before was nowhere to be seen. He strode up to the counter with a trio of coffee cups and a box of fresh-baked cinnamon Duffeyrolls.

"Just to say thanks." He cracked a slow smile.

Dru traded glances with Opal, whose wide eyes mirrored her own astonishment. Usually when they got surprises from customers, they were the unpleasant kind.

Salem turned to go but stopped and looked back at Greyson, studying him intently.

Greyson didn't notice. He was busy turning the coffee cups to read the markings on the side. "Went out on a limb here, but I think you're kind of a caramel latte girl." He pushed a cup toward her and another toward Opal.

"Damn," Opal said after the first sip. "That's exactly right. How'd you know that?"

Dru took a tentative sip and had to agree. It was her favorite. "Don't tell me you've been stalking my barista."

"Just a hunch, that's all," he said.

"Is this a new thing? Or do you always have hunches this accurate?"

He met her gaze evenly. "They've been getting better lately."

She had no way to tell whether Greyson had some kind of natural talent, whether this was a symptom of his problem, or whether he had, in fact, interrogated her barista.

"Anyway," Greyson said. "Just saying thanks for helping me."

"That's what I do," Dru said. "That's the whole reason for this shop. To help people."

"Mostly people who get their own selves into trouble," Opal muttered. She opened the box of cinnamon rolls with a sigh of satisfaction.

Without a word, Salem darted in and snatched a cinnamon roll, then made a beeline for the door. Greyson watched him go, looking slightly puzzled.

"Truth is," Opal said, "most people don't even know what kind of dark magic trouble they're getting themselves into until it's too late."

Greyson sipped his coffee and frowned. "Still not sure I buy this whole Ouija-board-and-voodoo-doll thing. But I did sleep better. That's enough for me."

Dru suppressed a smile. It was so obvious that Greyson didn't know the first thing about magic, but in a way that was kind of endearing.

It wasn't unusual, though. By and large, people without magical powers were oblivious to their existence. Those who witnessed magic and creatures of darkness firsthand usually tried to rationalize what they saw. And if they didn't, hardly anyone believed them anyway.

But that didn't stop occasional dabblers from treading where they didn't belong. "Mostly, people who don't know what they're doing get themselves into trouble trying to cast spells on other people," Dru said.

Opal picked up a roll with her fingertips and bit into it. "Mmm. Love spells, a lot of times."

Dru nodded. "We do get those a lot. Dark magic."

"Love spells are dark magic?" Greyson didn't look convinced.

Opal rolled her eyes. "Oh, Lordy. Yes. Anytime you try to cast a spell on another human being, that's dark magic. Comes back on you threefold. Trust me, nothing's so sad as a lonely person with three unrequited loves."

Greyson gave her a dubious look and sipped his coffee.

In her years of doing this, Dru had never seen anyone come into the shop who was so innocent about magic, and yet mired in so much trouble.

He hadn't so much as touched the dark arts, but here he was afflicted by the sort of soul-sucking problem that only the darkest sorcerers usually faced. She made up her mind that Greyson was worth saving, no matter what. "So the petalite crystal is working for you?"

"Apparently." He pulled the crystal out of his pocket and set it down on the counter.

But something was terribly wrong with it.

The petalite had been as clear as glass when she had given it to him. But just a day later, half of it had turned inky black. Sickly bluish-gray tendrils wormed through the remaining transparent part of the crystal, like smoke frozen in time.

"*Ooh*." Opal shuddered.

Greyson looked from her back to Dru. "What?"

Dru hesitated, afraid to touch the contaminated crystal with her bare hands. Instead, she rooted around under the counter until she found a pair of salad tongs and used them to gingerly pick up the crystal. "Did you let anyone else handle this at all?"

"Just me." He frowned. "Why?"

"Did you maybe bump into any weird strangers? Possibly you heard, I don't know, voices in the night?" She groped for some explanation other than the dark truth she suspected. "Maybe you've noticed something odd recently, like a window you didn't think you left open? Or inexplicable sounds in the moonlight?"

He folded his arms across his chest. "Inexplicable? No."

"Time for my break." Opal quickly placed several cinnamon rolls on a napkin and tottered away on her new stiletto heels. Behind her hand, in a stage whisper, she said, "Boy's got *problems*."

"I'm standing right here," Greyson said as she retreated.

"Thanks for the yum-yums!" Opal called.

Greyson turned sharply to Dru. "What does she mean?"

"She's a big fan of Duffeyrolls."

He gave her a look that was clearly not amused.

"Well." Dru cleared her throat. "There's no easy way to say this."

He leaned in, waiting.

Inwardly, she squirmed. She had spent hours this morning studying up on his monster dream, sifting through a stack of dusty, old books, most of them handwritten in Latin. Everything she had found indicated the worst. But she hadn't really believed it until she saw the decimated petalite crystal.

Greyson still waited, his patience clearly running low.

"You don't *have* a demon," Dru blurted out finally. "You're *turning into* one."

His expression didn't change. "Uh-huh. Okay."

"You still don't believe any of this, do you?"

His silence was answer enough. His disbelief was obvious.

She waved the salad tongs in frustration. "Just don't go away yet. Ordinary petalite is not going to cut it, apparently." Dru dropped the crystal into the lead-lined box she kept under the counter for magical contaminants. After considering it for a moment, she tossed in the salad tongs, too, then slammed the lid.

Later, she'd lock the box in her safe, hidden in the back room behind a framed picture of Ming the Merciless, where she kept anything that gave her the heebie-jeebies. But for now, she just had to get the crystal off her counter.

"Well, obviously the crystal works," Greyson said. "Just sell me another. Or a boxful."

"Wish it was that easy. But it doesn't work like that." Dru launched herself down the aisle, heading for the locked cabinet containing the most potent crystals she had. "Hope you don't have any other plans for today."

Greyson followed her, looking utterly unconvinced. "I'm telling you, I feel fine."

"Well, that's just dandy, but it won't last long. That petalite crystal?" She gestured toward the counter. "It should've lasted you *for life*. Instead, you burned through it in less than twenty-four hours."

"I take it that doesn't happen much."

"That just doesn't happen. Ever." She shook her head. "You know, I blame myself. I should've seen it yesterday. The way you reacted to that galena."

"You mean this?" He pushed back the sleeve of his leather jacket to reveal a swollen red burn mark on his wrist.

"Sorry." She grimaced, then unlocked the cabinet and started pulling out armloads of ingredients. "This time, let's try a more nuanced approach. This is going to require some meticulous experimentation."

"Is all this really necessary?"

"Do you want to avoid more nightmares?" She gave him a meaningful look. "Have a seat."

As the afternoon unfolded, she mostly relied on trial and error, using branching patterns of magic she'd learned through years of nose-in-the-book study, if not a whole lot of actual experience. That required methodically laying out different combinations of herbs and crystals. Some in their pure form, others reduced to their essences and blended together.

She ground up herbs into fine powders and applied them as poultices, looking for a reaction. She immersed crystals in purified water to transfer their properties into liquid form. From time to time, Opal offered advice from her perch at the register or dug up hard-to-find ingredients from the storage room.

Every so often, Dru checked her progress by pressing a rectangular ulexite crystal to her forehead, over her spiritual third eye, and gazing at Greyson. Ordinarily, the most she ever saw through the ulexite crystal was the change in someone's aura. But with Greyson, she could clearly see darkness surrounding him.

The tips of his fingers became shadowy claws. At the edge of his hairline, dark crescents seemed to jut upward, like horns. The sight gave her a chill.

The better she narrowed down the mix of ingredients, the more his shadow faded, leaving him looking more and more normal. It was an exhilarating feeling.

For the first time in a long time, Dru felt like a true expert. Charts and intersecting circles of magical properties laid themselves out in her mind's eye. She calculated proportions and combinations faster than she could explain them. All the while, Greyson patiently sat and tried every cure she handed him, one swallow at a time.

By the end of the day, Dru had finally concocted a potion that made Greyson's demon shadow vanish. Exhausted but triumphant, she decanted it into a skull-shaped glass bottle and slid it across the counter to him. "There. This will keep you safe for now. Take a shot every two hours. And stay as calm and focused as you can at all times. Meditation would help. This isn't a cure, but it's progress."

He gave her a tired smile. "You know, I just stopped by to bring you coffee."

An idea struck her, something she should have thought of before. "Oh, you know what else? I should probably get some sage and bells, and go clear out the energy in your apartment, too. In fact, if you have time, we should go over there together, so I can check you out and make sure you're all good." Dru caught the eyebrow Opal cocked at her and felt herself turning red for no reason. "Just a precaution."

Greyson glanced at his watch. "Maybe we could grab some dinner, too. Do you like Italian?"

Dinner. The word hit Dru like a splash of cold water. "Oh, fudge buckets. What time is it? We have reservations at Chez Monet." She surveyed the clutter of potions, powders, and empty boxes that covered the counter. "Like right now."

Opal stirred from her chair, where she had been experimenting on her nails. "Go, girl. I got this. Don't you worry."

"Really?" But she didn't dare risk giving Opal a chance to change her mind. As she hurriedly scribbled down a receipt for Greyson, she added her phone number. "Call me if anything changes. You'll be fine, Greyson."

He nodded. "I'll call you."

A little voice inside her insisted that she wasn't done here. That she needed to test the potion more thoroughly and make sure its effects would last. But she didn't have time if she wanted to make her dinner date.

She just had to trust that the potion would work, and nothing would go wrong.

7

HIGHWAY TO HELL

Dru stepped into the dining room of Chez Monet and took in the intoxicating scent of roses, peonies, and countless other flowers. "This place is magical," she whispered. But for once, she didn't mean it literally.

The crisp white linen tablecloths and softly glowing chandeliers were pretty much what she had expected. But she hadn't counted on the endless vases of flowers in every imaginable color.

Brilliant blues. Romantic reds. Delicate yellows. They stretched in all directions, framed by elegantly draped weeping willow branches. Like Monet's garden spectacularly brought to life.

Dru felt as if she'd stepped into a different world. As if she'd become someone more special, more fabulous. Someone with refinement and taste and wealth. And a dress with a neckline considerably lower than that of her usual T-shirts. She resisted the urge to tug it upward.

"You look stunning," Nate said softly. "Where did you get that dress?"

She'd had it in her closet for a year now. She'd even shown it to him when she bought it. Not that he'd noticed, apparently, but his appreciation now made up for it.

This dress was the only decent thing she owned: a burgundy satin number with spaghetti straps and a designer label. She'd been hoping to wear it if Nate ever got around to proposing.

When he got around to proposing, she told herself. *When.*

In the meantime, this might be the only chance she'd get to actually wear it. So she made an effort to enjoy it. And to project an aura of confidence that she desperately wished she felt.

Nate wore suits all the time. But she'd never seen him dressed quite this sharply before: a tailored charcoal-gray suit with a sky-blue Oxford shirt and matching blue tie. He looked like a movie star. Walking beside him gave her a warm glow.

As they crossed the dining room, she leaned closer to him. "After dinner," she whispered, "do you want to take a stroll through the gardens out back, just you and me?"

"Oh, there's Dad." Nate walked on ahead to greet him, leaving her behind. Dru felt a brief stab of disappointment. But they were here on business, after all. Meeting the filthy-rich investors from Switzerland, who apparently had an interest in expanding Nate's dental practice into a multimillion-dollar enterprise. No pressure or anything.

For the moment, their table was empty except for Nate's dad, Jack. When he stood up, he was easily the shortest man in the room, and his thick nose was accentuated by heavy glasses and a steel-gray beard. But he made up for his gnomelike stature with a tailored suit and an ever-present smile. He clapped an arm around Nate's back, then turned to kiss Dru on the cheek.

"Dru, my dear, you look younger and prettier every time I see you."

When she smiled, Jack gave her front teeth a critical frown. It was just a momentary glance, a mere instant of disapproval that vanished just as quickly. But the effect was enough to make Dru's hand fly to her mouth in embarrassment.

"Why does he always *do* that?" she whispered to Nate, as his dad spoke briefly to the maitre d'. "There's nothing wrong with my teeth!"

"Honey, we're a family of dentists," Nate whispered back. "He can't help it."

But that didn't mean she had to be happy about it.

Across the dining room, Tonya the hygienist appeared, smiling with dazzlingly perfect teeth, leading two bone-thin old men with paper-white hair and three-piece suits. She sauntered through the dining room toward their table, turning heads in her slinky red dress.

"That's them," Jack said over his shoulder to Nate. "They're brothers. Did I tell you that? Klaus and Wilhelm Zubriggen. Twins."

As they waited for Tonya and the investors, Dru leaned close to Nate. "If there was something wrong with my teeth, you would tell me, right?"

"Dad's a perfectionist," Nate muttered back. "He's never happy. Just focus on making nice with the Swiss twins."

Tonya, meanwhile, seemed to charm everyone around her the moment she opened her mouth. Absolutely no one frowned at her teeth, Dru noticed.

They all shook hands. When it came time to sit, Nate held Dru's chair, which he'd never done before. It was a nice touch. She tried to focus on that instead of how frazzled she already felt.

And then he held Tonya's chair for her.

Something about that simple act sent a stab of jealousy through her. No one else at the table seemed to notice. They were all smiles and nods, eagerly getting acquainted.

Dru appeared to be the only one who wasn't utterly charmed by Tonya's incandescent smile and eager attention. It occurred to Dru that there were plenty of other women like Tonya—women who didn't seem in the least bit as weird as Dru—who would be beside themselves with happiness to be sitting at this table with Nate.

Dru shook her head. She was driving herself crazy. She had to lighten up.

"So," one of the Swiss twins said to Dru in his thick accent, breaking her runaway train of thoughts. "You are ze wife of Jack?"

Eww. "Um, no. I am the girlfriend of Nate."

Klaus, or maybe it was Wilhelm, cocked his head. "Why do you say it like so?"

"Like so . . . what?"

"'Ze girlfriend of Nate.' So very strange. You are not from America?"

"Oh, I am totally from America." Dru smiled, then realized Nate and Jack both looked distressed, while Tonya looked slyly amused. "I was just . . . Never mind. I'm from around here. Where are you from?"

The twins traded glances before giving her a puzzled look. "We are from Switzerland. You do not know of Switzerland?"

"No, of course, I know—"

"No?" The man tsked his disapproval. "It is the finest country in Europe. You should know this fact."

"Yes. Thank you," she said, louder than necessary.

After a moment of awkward silence, Tonya said breathlessly, "I've never been to Switzerland. What's it like?" Which brought a new wave of enthusiastic chatter from the investors, sprinkled with occasional phrases in German.

Dru pretended to study her menu until they had ordered, then excused herself and headed for the ladies' room. As she passed by the hostess station, she heard her name.

"Dru! Over here!"

She turned. There, squared off against a broad-shouldered, sweating maitre d', was Greyson. The only person in the whole place wearing jeans and a motorcycle jacket. Here, he looked even more out of place than he had in her shop.

The look on his face told her something was terribly wrong.

She rushed over to him, peering around the bulk of the maitre d', who looked as if he was trying to body block Greyson from taking another step inside.

"Greyson, what are you *doing* here?"

"What was in that drink you gave me?" His pupils were obviously dilated. His unusually pale skin glistened with sweat. "Something feels really wrong with me."

The maitre d' shot Dru a surprised look. "You know this . . . gentleman?"

Greyson held his hands out, staring at them as if he'd never seen them before. "I feel so funky."

Dru pulled Greyson a safe distance away from the maitre d's deepening frown. That was when she noticed Greyson was wearing a black AC/DC cap that proudly proclaimed *Highway to Hell*.

She glanced pointedly at his cap. "What's with the hat?"

He looked over both shoulders to make sure no one was standing nearby, his motions exaggerated as if he'd been drinking heavily. Then he leaned close and growled under his breath, "Look, I don't know how to say this, but I'm getting horns."

"Horny?" Dru nearly choked.

"*Horns.*" He lifted up his cap and pointed at his forehead. Just above each temple, a peaked lump showed through his dark hair. "I thought they were bug bites, at first. But they just kept growing. I don't believe this is happening."

She reached up and, after a moment's hesitation, felt the inch-tall lumps jutting from his head. Smooth ridges, rounded points, and hot to the touch. "Yeah, hmm. Those definitely seem like little horns."

"I don't care how *little* they are," he whispered fiercely, tugging his cap back on. Another couple came in through the doors behind him. With wary glances, they circled around at a safe distance.

Dru tried to project confidence she didn't feel. "Don't worry. Everything is going to be okay."

He shot her a dark look. "There are *horns* growing from my *head*. Nothing about this is okay!"

That potion should have done away with any sort of demonic symptoms. Or at the least, things should have leveled off, not gotten worse. She'd never seen anything like this before. What vital clue was she missing?

"There's got to be something constantly re-afflicting you, accelerating your transformation. Your connection to it is only getting stronger. It's not the potion."

"You're sure about that?" he said.

"The potion might be helping, but not enough. Something else is getting to you. It could be a charm, an icon. A physical object that the potion can't touch. Maybe a cursed artifact of some kind."

His eyes narrowed. "What, like a voodoo mask?"

"I don't know! That's why I was going to check out your place, see what I could find."

"What was in that drink, anyway?" He belched suddenly, drawing another dark scowl from the maitre d'.

Dru winced and steered Greyson closer to the exit. "Well, to stabilize your spirit, I needed to *use* spirits. Like, actual spirits."

Greyson's eyes widened. "You mean I was drinking ghosts?"

"No, no, I mean alcohol. But special alcohol. The stuff I used was distilled from berries ritually harvested under a blue moon and filtered through Herkimer diamonds. Good stuff, and it should cleanse your spirit."

He belched again. "*Urrp.* So not ghosts?"

"Mostly vodka." A blast of stinky breath washed over her, and she tried in vain to wave it away. "Jeez. You didn't just slam down that entire potion, did you?"

The expression on his face warred between total denial and befuddled pride. "Maybe." He quickly added, "Tell me you wouldn't do the same thing, if you started sprouting horns."

"Are those getting longer?" She reached beneath his hat and squeezed his stumpy horns. "Does that hurt?"

"Who cares? No. They're *horns.* Get rid of them!"

"Dru!" Nate said behind her, making her jump. She spun around, suddenly guilt-ridden, although she had no idea why. She rubbed her fingertips together, still feeling the unsettling texture of Greyson's horns against her skin.

Nate approached them with a mystified look on his face. "Hey. Aren't you the guy with the old car?"

Greyson blinked unfocused eyes at him and turned to Dru. "Who the hell is this?"

"My boyfriend. Be nice."

"Him? Really?" Before Dru could reply, Greyson gave Nate a pained smile and held out a hand. "Hey, bud. Name's Greyson."

Nate looked him up and down, then reluctantly shook his hand. "Dr. Nate Corbin. How do you do?"

The handshake went on longer than it needed to. Dru watched the tendons flexing in both men's hands as each one tried to out-squeeze the other.

Her stomach did a flip-flop. She had no idea how she was going to explain this to Nate. "Honey." She took his arm and pulled him away from the testosterone-fueled squeeze contest. "Look, I hate to do this, but I need to get Greyson back to the shop. Right now. I'm so sorry."

Nate tilted his head in the direction of the table. "Maybe after dinner? Tonight is important."

"I know. I know. Big night for you, and I get that. So . . . how about you stay and talk shop with Hans and Franz? I'll go get Greyson cleaned up." She held up her hands. "I wouldn't do this unless it really was an emergency."

"Emergency? What's wrong?" Nate pulled out his phone. "Do we need an ambulance?"

"Probably not a good idea."

Nate hesitated, and his worried look turned into a frown. "Or maybe a cab, so he can sleep it off."

How could she explain? After a torturous moment of hand-wringing, Dru decided to come clean. A hundred percent clean. If Nate truly loved her, he would have to believe in *her*, even if he didn't believe in magic.

"Okay. So. This is going to sound a little weird, but here it is." She took a deep breath and explained as quickly as she could. "Right now, we have a magical emergency. Greyson here is about to undergo an awful transformation, a truly dangerous one, but I don't know why. This is a huge problem because the potion I gave him today should've worked, but it didn't. So I've got to get him back to the shop and find a cure for him, pronto. Right this second."

Nate stared at her for a few seconds, blinked, then chuckled. "I get it. You're kidding."

Dru clenched her hands at her sides. "Even if you don't believe in magic—"

Greyson stopped her with a touch on her arm. "You're right, man. She's kidding you. There's no emergency. I'm just a, *urrp*, rock collector. Looking for a gem."

"Oh." Nate looked relieved, if mildly disgusted. "Well. Mystery solved. I'm sure Dru can find one for you tomorrow, when the shop is open." Nate tried to steer Dru back toward the dining room, but she resisted.

"Think I've already found it." The urgency had left Greyson's voice, replaced by an easy drawl that only made Dru more worried. "And I've done my fair share of digging."

Nate hesitated. "Really? Where do you dig? Up in the mountains?"

Greyson gave Nate a lazy smile. "Wherever looks the most promising. Most digs don't pan out. But you want to know what the funny thing is?"

Nate's expression turned guarded.

Greyson leaned closer, looming over Nate just a bit. "Funny thing is, just when you think you'll never find what you're looking for . . . it turns up right in front of you. The perfect gem. When you least expect it. And no one else has claimed it yet."

"Is that a fact," Nate said evenly, standing his ground.

"It is."

Dru watched the exchange between the two men, seeing something going on just beneath the surface. Something unstated and primal, like two gorillas circling each other in the jungle. Neither of them was willing to back down.

She gripped Nate's arm and pulled him away. "Honey, I'm sure Greyson doesn't have time to chat." She shot Greyson a warning look.

"She's right," Greyson slurred, the pitch in his voice deepening dangerously. "She needs to come back to my place and check out my mojo. Ain't that right, Dru?"

Nate glared at Greyson, then turned aside and said to Dru, "What is he talking about?"

There's no time for this, she thought. *Greyson is transforming into a demon! Right now!*

Greyson stepped up close to them with a smile that seemed ever so slightly unhinged. "Well? Let's go, magic lady."

8
THE DEVIL INSIDE

"Why don't I buy you a drink, and we'll call it a night?" Nate said to Greyson with a forced lightness that wouldn't have fooled a kindergartner. When Greyson shook his head, Nate said, "I insist."

"Nate," Dru said, leaning in close. "I need to get him out of here. Fast."

"Going anywhere with him is a terrible idea," he replied in a low voice.

"Hey," Greyson barked. "The lady told you. We need to *go*."

Seeing Greyson's state deteriorating before her eyes, Dru realized there was no more time for this nonsense. She took Nate's arm and pulled him a few steps away. "Honey. This dinner is too important to mess up." He started to object, and she cut him off. "I'm taking Greyson back to the shop, right now, before he gets any sicker. I'll call Opal to help."

Nate put his hand over hers. "*After* dinner."

Greyson marched after Dru, but the bullish maitre d' put out an arm to block him, like a railroad gate coming down in his path. "I'm so sorry, *monsieur*. A jacket is required."

Greyson straightened the front of his leather motorcycle jacket. His eyes glowed bright red. "This *is* a jacket," he slurred, then swatted the maitre d's arm out of his way.

It barely seemed like Greyson put any effort into the motion at all. But the maitre d' staggered back as if he'd been thrown and collided with a waiter carrying a tray of glasses. The deafening crash of breaking glass turned heads throughout the restaurant.

"Okay, time to go." Dru left Nate behind and darted over to Greyson, took his arm, and turned him toward the door. He didn't resist. His face looked paler and more haggard by the second. "You're going straight back to the shop," she ordered. "Come on."

Greyson shook his head, not in denial, but as if he was trying to clear it. "Something's . . . not right. Dru?" Sweat tricked down the side of his forehead. "What am I doing here?"

His confused words sent a chill down her back. They might not even have time to make it to the shop. She tried to remember which crystals she had with her, in her purse.

Greyson swayed, and Dru hurried him out. She glanced back at Nate, who was eye to eye in an argument with the maitre d'.

Far beyond, across the restaurant, Dru saw Jack stand up and crane his head to look. Even from this distance, she could see the worry wrinkling his forehead. Beside him, the white-haired investors took their eyes off Tonya long enough to turn and peer severely toward the commotion.

She reached one arm up to Greyson's broad shoulder and gently pushed him out through the door. "Keep walking. Outside. Deep breaths. Sit down, if you can."

Nate caught Dru by the arm and yanked her back. "Where do you think you're going?"

"Nate, let go."

Greyson, heedless, stumbled outside.

Dru tried to pull away but couldn't. "Look at him. He needs my help."

"He needs to be arrested." Nate sounded worried. "Listen, he's drunk. Or on drugs. I'm not letting you go anywhere with him."

She stared Nate in the eye. "If you don't let go of my arm, this instant, Greyson could die. Do you want that on your conscience?"

"Die?" He blinked. "You can't be serious." Still, he released her arm.

Dru ran out the door and into the parking lot.

"Why don't we call an ambulance?" he called after her, but she kept running.

Ranks of shiny Mercedes, Lexus, and BMWs lined the pavement. Well-dressed couples came and went, some chatting, some holding hands.

She peered in every direction. No sign of Greyson.

A skinny valet with a bad complexion gestured toward the corner of the building. There, a path led around to the softly lit gardens tucked away behind the restaurant. Greyson leaned against the wall, his silhouette hunched in pain. As Dru watched, he lurched into the garden and disappeared from sight.

"Thanks!" Dru said breathlessly to the valet as she ran after Greyson. "Big tip later!"

Behind the restaurant, the garden felt hushed and close. Wide stone pathways meandered through the fragrant garden flowers, wet from a recent dousing with sprinklers. Empty wrought-iron chairs and tables sat scattered about. In the center, a hot-tub-sized lily pond glimmered under warm lights, crowned by an arched wooden footbridge.

Greyson, his back turned, leaned heavily against the wooden railing at the foot of the bridge, making it creak ominously. With a groan, he sank to his knees.

Dru ran over to him and took his stubbled chin in both hands, tilting his face toward the light. His irises glowed like hot coals. His skin was flushed red, deeper than a sunburn, the color of brick. He grunted in pain, revealing a row of sharp teeth.

It was happening. Happening right now, right in front of her. Greyson was transforming into a demon.

An ice-cold rush of fear shot through her. Her mind raced, searching for a solution.

He gazed up at her with pleading eyes. "What's happening to me?"

Dru dug frantically through her purse for crystals. "Greyson, listen to me carefully. I need you to look into my eyes and focus on your breathing. Keep it slow and steady for me. Can you do that?"

He did. Great, billowing breaths. Too powerful to be human.

She knew she had a quartz wand in her purse. A simple quartz wand, maybe three inches long. But she couldn't find it. Just makeup, receipts, several pens, spare key fob for Nate's new Prius, a Groupon she'd never used. In anguish, she dumped her purse out on the wet stone pathway and sorted through the mess with shaking hands.

Greyson heaved out a tortured breath and dropped to all fours. His hands clawed into the mulch and dirt, veins bulging. His skin darkened.

His AC/DC cap tumbled into the flowers and vanished, revealing the stubby horns on his head. They were twice the length they had been a minute before.

She found her quartz wand. About the size of her thumb, six-sided, and pointed at both ends. One of the most-powerful tools she had for smoothing out magical turmoil. She couldn't hope it would stop Greyson's transformation, but it might be enough to slow it down.

"Okay, let's sit up." She helped him into a kneeling position and held out the quartz crystal in the palm of her hand. "Put your hand over mine. Come on."

Greyson lifted his hand up from the ground, trailing dirt and fibers of mulch. It seemed like an enormous effort.

His hand wavered in midair. His fingers had become thick and knobby. His nails had grown into sharp black claws.

She was losing him to the demon.

"Greyson," she whispered. Tears stung the corners of her eyes. She had failed him. He was fading away before her. "Greyson, look at me. Please."

He tilted his head up. His eyes had become twin slits of glowing red menace. No pupil or white anymore, just one continuous glow, as if the inside of his skull were a blast furnace and his eyes were windows into the searing fire.

"Dru," he said, his voice hollow and raw. "I'm burning up . . . I can feel it . . . Scorching through me . . ."

"Just give me your hand," she repeated in a whisper. She edged the quartz crystal toward him.

With an effort, he placed his hand heavily on Dru's palm. His skin was hot to the touch.

The moment their hands met, a current of energy jolted through her, far more powerful than that first spark when they'd met. Waves of invisible force welled out of him, awash in rage, loss, and fear. Greyson's emotions overwhelmed hers until she couldn't tell where his feelings ended and hers began.

The onslaught of emotions threatened to overpower her. But she forced her voice to stay even and soft. "Greyson. Stay with me. Focus on me. Focus on my touch."

He gritted his teeth, fangs bared. "It *burns*."

"Stay with me," she said. "Don't give in to it. Don't slip away." In her palm, the quartz wand grew cooler, quickly turning cold as ice.

A crystal had never done anything like that before, not for her. Greyson seemed to have all the power of a sorcerer within him, but it was untapped. A vast depth of pent-up energy that flowed out of him and into her, amplifying her crystal magic.

She had read somewhere about the phenomenon of meeting someone, one singular person in the entire world, who could elevate your hidden talents to an incredible level. She couldn't remember where she'd read it, or why it was so dangerous, but she had no time to stop and consider all of the ramifications. She just had to go with it. Combining their powers was her only chance to save him.

"That's it," she said, trying to encourage him. "Let the healing energy in."

Greyson's eyes squeezed shut in pain.

"Open your eyes," she said. "Keep looking at me."

He did. She forced herself to stare into his fiery red gaze and hold it, not shrink back in fear. Any instant, he could tip over the edge and become a monster. If he did, she would be dead, and he would never be human again.

She wouldn't let that happen. She *couldn't*.

He'd come to her for help. Trusted her. Believed in her. She wouldn't let him down. She held his gaze until her eyes brimmed with stinging tears.

Like a block of ice pressed into her skin, the crystal spread a cold numbness across her palm. "Greyson. Stay with me." She repeated it over and over. A mantra. A meditation. A plea. "Stay with me."

She put her free hand on top of his, trying to cool the infernal heat radiating through his skin. Trying to calm him.

Just when she thought she couldn't take any more, the quartz wand cracked. She felt it as much as heard it, a sharp sound like an old-fashioned camera flashbulb popping between their fingers.

Greyson gasped. His head sagged.

"Greyson?"

He heaved great breaths. But with his head hanging down, she couldn't see his face.

Was he human? Had the crystal done its work?

"Greyson! Look at me."

Slowly, he raised his head and opened his eyes. Bright, deep, and incredibly compelling. Gazing back at her with a mixture of disbelief and gratitude.

She stared in amazement as his symptoms began to fade away. His skin lost its grayish tone, becoming tan and smooth. His fangs receded. His horns shrank down and disappeared into his thick black hair. In moments, he was normal again. Human.

"The quartz did it," Dru breathed, elated.

"No. *You* did it." An exhausted smile hitched up one corner of Greyson's mouth. "You and your sorceress ways."

"I don't know how. I've never done anything like that on my own before. There's something between you and me that . . . Never mind. Just take a breather." It was too much to process all at once. It was as if she had done actual, serious magic. Like a real sorceress. Her heart still pounded from the flood of sensations. "That was too close."

He kept hold of her hand. "Don't let me go yet. I'm not all the way back."

"I won't let go." She shook her head. "I'm right here."

Greyson put his other dirty hand—now completely normal—on top of Dru's. It felt strong and sure.

Footsteps slapped across the stone walkway toward them. Nate, at a dead run. "Dru! *Dru!* Are you all right?"

Greyson stood up unsteadily and pulled her to her feet. She turned toward Nate, arms out.

But instead of embracing her, he advanced on Greyson. "You!"

"Nate, hey!" Dru tried to catch his sleeve. "We're okay! Everything is okay."

"It will be when the police get here." Nate pulled out his phone.

Greyson lurched toward him. "Now, just hang on—"

"Back off!" Nate shoved Greyson back a step. Or tried to, at least, without much effect.

Greyson swatted Nate's hand away, making him stumble. Nate's shiny new phone hit the flagstone pathway with the unmistakable sound of breaking glass.

The broken phone tumbled and came to rest face up at Dru's feet, its dark screen fractured like thin ice. Distracted by the phone, Dru didn't notice Nate reach into his other jacket pocket until it was too late.

With one savage jab, Nate planted his stubby Shock Wand in the center of Greyson's chest. Writhing blue arcs of electricity erupted from the tip and scorched outward like fingers of lightning.

Greyson's body went stiff, arms jerking and trembling. His eyes rolled back into his head, and he fell to his knees. Nate kept the crackling wand planted against Greyson.

Dru's hands flew to her mouth. Shattered bits of quartz tumbled from her palms, twinkling like stars in the flashes of electric-blue light.

"Nate! *Stop!*" Dru watched in horror as Greyson's skin grew scaly and dark. Every muscle in his body rippled and flexed. Thick black horns sprouted from his head, longer than before, curling over like a ram's.

His leather jacket swelled and split at the seams. The body underneath wasn't human. It was a monster. Greyson—or the thing that had once been him—glared at Nate with baleful glowing eyes. He opened a mouth full of fangs and roared.

Greyson had become the demon.

9
BEHIND RED EYES

Dru wasn't a big believer in worst-case scenarios. There was always a solution. Always some way out.

Until someone turned into a demon.

In one swift motion, the dark creature sprang to his feet and whirled on Nate, seizing him by the throat in a meaty fist. With ease, he lifted Nate up, leaving his feet kicking in the air. The Shock Wand clattered to the ground and rolled away.

Nate, choking, beat his fists against the demon's thick arm. When that didn't work, he clamped both hands on the thick wrist and tried to draw in a breath. It came as a high-pitched whistle.

The demon just bared his fangs at Nate and growled.

Frantically, Dru scanned the scattered contents of her purse. There had to be something in there she could use.

She found a gray-silver cube. A galena crystal. It had burned Greyson before. It might work again. She grabbed the mirror-sided crystal in one fist and ran into the demon's line of sight, waving her arms. "Hey! Over here!"

The demon took one look at Dru and tossed Nate aside like a discarded bone. He landed with a resounding splash in the lily pond.

A freezing fear spread through Dru's body as the demon advanced on her with pounding footsteps. She backed up, crushing flowers beneath her heels, until her back pressed against the brick wall that surrounded the garden, its rough surface still warm from the vanished Colorado sun.

The demon loomed over her, silent but for his powerful breaths. He put two clawed fingers beneath her chin, lifting it. His eyes burned in a terrifying face.

Dru swallowed down her fear. As slowly as she dared, she reached up, as if to cup the demon's hand in her own. But hidden in her palm was the dense cube of the galena crystal.

She hesitated, then jammed it hard against the back of the demon's hand.

The effect was immediate. Searing white energy arced out from the space between their hands, swirling up the demon's arm and into his heart. He howled in pain and leaped back into a crouch.

For a moment, the glow in his eyes faded and she could see Greyson trapped somewhere inside. He looked around with growing alarm, as if trying to piece together what had just happened.

"Greyson, it's okay. It's me." She wanted to take a step toward him, but she couldn't will her feet to move. Her knees shook too badly. Only the brick wall behind her held her up.

He shrank back away from her. "*Stay away!*" The words were doubtless Greyson's, but the bellowing inhuman voice was rough and full of anguish.

With a grunt, he leaped up onto the brick wall that separated the garden from the parking lot. He was silhouetted against the night sky like some ancient gargoyle contemplating an eternity of damnation.

Despite her fear, she stepped forward. She had to reach him, help him. While she still had a ghost of a chance. "Greyson. Look at me."

At that moment, Nate erupted from the lily pond with a gasp and a geyser of water. "Help!" he croaked, coughing and splashing.

Without a sound, Greyson leaped off the wall, launching himself away into the night.

Instantly, he was gone, leaving Dru too overwhelmed to speak. The night air felt achingly hollow in the wake of his disappearance.

"Dru!" Coughing hard, Nate climbed out of the lily pond, water pouring out of his ruined suit. "What the hell just happened?" The look in his eyes was half disbelief, half haunted. As if he full well knew the truth but couldn't bring himself to accept it.

She didn't have time to wait for him to figure it out. She couldn't even give voice to her hurt, her anger, her panic. Because of him, Greyson was a demon now. Out there somewhere, fleeing into the night.

Alone. Tortured. Damned.

And it was up to her to save him. If she wasn't already too late.

10
MEANT TO BE BROKEN

Dru scooped her stuff back into her purse and left Nate in the garden, dripping wet and picking up pieces of his phone. She ran across the parking lot and got into the driver's seat of his new white Prius.

The horror on Greyson's face haunted her. The shock when he realized what he'd become. The real Greyson was still trapped inside that demon, his body twisted into something dark and evil. If there was any way to save him, if there was still any chance, she had to find it right now.

She started the car and pulled out onto the street. She headed north, the direction the demon had gone when he leaped out of the garden.

There were certain crystals she could use to try to track him down, but they were all miles away at The Crystal Connection.

Up ahead, a silver sedan sat parked at the curb, its lights flashing erratically, car alarm wailing. It was impossible to miss the deep depression in its roof where something had landed on it and leaped off again. Its shattered windows left a halo of broken glass sparkling on the pavement.

This was definitely the right direction.

Dru followed the street north for a few blocks, looking for anything else amiss.

Her skull throbbed with a pounding headache. An electric tingle coursed up and down her arm, strongest in the palm she'd pressed against Greyson's hand. She could still feel the ghost of his touch.

She'd never shattered a crystal like that before. In fact, she'd never cast a spell that was anything remotely of that magnitude. At most, her talents enabled her to charge up crystals, perform a few minor enchantments, and brew the occasional potion. But it was strictly low-key stuff.

Whatever her connection was to Greyson, it seemed to magnify her abilities in ways she couldn't predict. It elevated her powers into real, actual life-and-death sorcery. The thought terrified her and thrilled her at the same time.

But none of that mattered unless she could bring him back.

Ahead on the left, a geyser of water shot skyward. When she got closer, she spotted a broken fire hydrant lying on the sidewalk.

She cut left across traffic, drawing angry horn blasts and a split-second terror that she would total Nate's car. The next block looked quiet, until she found a streetlight bent at an angle.

She turned at that corner, pulse pounding. Up ahead waited another smashed car hood. Beyond that, shattered glass glittered in her headlights. She was close.

But still, no sign of the demon. Gradually, the trail of wreckage came to an end.

After a few more blocks, she circled around but found nothing. A few blocks after that, she realized she'd lost the trail.

She coasted to a stop on a residential street. Warm lights glowed in windows. Late-model cars sat safely in driveways. Swing sets and bicycles dotted smartly mowed lawns. It sent a pang of longing through her.

Part of her wanted to live here, on this street. Live a normal, safe life. No magic, no evil curses, no demons.

She could plant a garden. Trade muffin recipes with the neighbors. Have dinner parties.

But a little voice inside her insisted that she was surrounded by too much magic to fit in here. She knew firsthand that the world was full of foul creatures, ancient curses, and terrifying secrets that no human mind was meant to comprehend.

As much as she would love to put that all behind her and pretend that the world was safe and sensible, she just couldn't do it.

Like it or not, this was her calling, to fight back against the darkness.

North, she realized out of the blue. The demon kept heading north. He wasn't just fleeing randomly. He was headed toward something. But what?

Back to his source of power. Whatever cursed artifact it was that had afflicted Greyson. She kicked herself again for not checking out his place when he offered. How would she find it now?

She called Opal.

"Whatever happened, I didn't do it," Opal said by way of answer. "And did I mention I'm off the clock?"

"It's about Greyson," Dru said, rubbing her temples, trying to wish the headache away. "He's completely lost his marbles. Gone full-on demon."

With a click, the TV noises behind Opal went silent. "Oh, girl, I'm sorry. That's hard. He was a nice one, that Greyson," Opal said, sounding genuinely sad. "Anybody get hurt?"

Dru took a deep breath and let it out. "I'm a little shaken up, but I'm okay."

"Oh, I know *you're* fine. On account of the fact that Nate's not calling me from the hospital, screaming like a little girl. What I want to know is, did anybody *else* get hurt? Anybody dead?"

"Well . . . no."

"Anybody get their hearts ripped out? Literally, I'm talking? Dismembered, disemboweled, dis-anything?"

Dru made a face. "No! Yuck. Jeez."

"Well, things could be a whole lot worse, then. Am I right? This is just some everyday demon making trouble. So he goes a little crazy, trashes somebody's yard, maybe gnaws on a couple garden gnomes. A week later, he wakes up like it's a bad dream, and everything's back to normal. Meantime, all we can do is wait it out. And I can get back to watching my show."

"This isn't some garden-variety demon, Opal, trust me. This is serious trouble, the soul-devouring kind. Nobody's dead *yet*, but that could change." Dru sorted through her purse, its contents now damp and grimy from the garden. She found her notebook. "I need to track him down and do whatever it takes to bring him back."

"Back? Nuh-uh. I don't think so," Opal said, indignation raising her voice. "You remember Dru's rule number one?"

"Of course I do. It's my rule. But—"

"'Don't get involved in magic outside the shop.' First thing you told me on the very first day I came to work for you."

"Actually, the *first* thing I told you was, 'We opened forty-five minutes ago.'"

"Long as we're changing the subject," Opal said, "what's Nate say about all this? Hmm?"

It hurt just to think about. "Let's just leave Nate out of this for the moment."

"See what I mean? You know, if you want that man to put a ring on your finger and settle down, this is not gonna help make that happen."

"Don't you think I'm painfully aware of that?"

"I don't know if you're aware of it or not. You say you want one thing, but then you turn around and want to go chasing after this demon-boy like it's some kind of a mission you're on."

Dru held the phone out at arm's length and shook it, as if she could somehow throttle Opal. It made her screen go haywire, but it didn't do anything to calm her nerves. She brought the phone back to her ear.

". . . told me no magic outside the shop, is all I'm saying," Opal said. "Out on the street, you're not in control. Everything can go to pieces real fast. People can get hurt. People can get killed. Anything can happen."

"Well, *anything* just happened," Dru said. "Look, I know that there is practically zero chance I can fix this. But I have to try. This is my mess. It started in my shop. I have to fix it."

"Dru, you made that rule for a reason."

"Rules were made to be broken," Dru snapped.

Opal paused for an excruciatingly long time before she answered. "I'm gonna quote you on that. You know I will."

Dru flipped her notebook to a blank page. "The demon's heading north through town. Probably toward whatever's been re-afflicting Greyson. Something he's been exposed to on a daily basis." She stared at the blank page by the dashboard lights, trying to think. "Did he ever say anything to you about where he works, or where he lives?"

"Mmm . . ." Opal didn't sound too sure. "Said he had a workshop at his place. Where he fixes up old cars, that kind of thing. I wasn't really paying attention."

"Because you were busy picturing him naked."

"Damn straight I was. I'm not dead."

A workshop. That sounded like the right place to start. If Greyson had acquired some sort of cursed artifact and just set it on a shelf somewhere, it could've been re-afflicting him all along. Relentlessly breaking down his defenses. That would explain his quick transformation.

The question was, where was his workshop?

An idea struck Dru. "You didn't go to the bank today, did you?"

Opal sighed. "Let me tell you something, Dru, you don't even *know* how bad the traffic is on my way home. And don't forget you're not paying me mileage for this. It's a favor. So if you're on some kind of schedule—"

"Just *look* in the deposit bag, okay, please? If I remember right, Greyson paid with a check."

"A paper check?" A long rustling sound came through the phone. Opal muttered something under her breath. "Okay, yeah, I got it. Greyson Carter." Opal read off the address, and Dru wrote it down. "For real, Dru, even if he is there, what are you going to do about it?"

Dru looked over her shoulder and pulled away from the curb, speeding north. "If I can get there before he does, maybe I can find the source and break the connection."

"What if the demon gets there first?"

"I've got some amethyst with me. And a wicked galena crystal. I can probably slow him down."

"Slow him down?" Opal repeated, and the doubt in her voice made Dru realize she needed something much more drastic. "Slowing him down won't be enough. You know that?"

"You're right. I need something more direct. Some kind of brute force."

"If this demon is as bad as you say, what kind of brute force do you think could take him down?" Opal said. "A shotgun? A Mack truck? A tank?"

"Worse," Dru said, summoning up her courage. "I need Rane."

11

HOW TO CATCH A DEMON

It took three tries to get Rane on the phone. When she finally answered, a rush of wind noise blasted through the speaker, along with the rhythmic thump of sneakers on pavement.

"D!" Rane puffed. "What's shaking?"

"Remember that customer I had, Greyson? He's turned into a serious demon. I need to stop him. If he *can* be stopped." Dru took her eyes off the road long enough to read aloud the address from her notebook. When she looked up, she was hurtling toward the rear end of a parked UPS truck, its lights flashing. She swerved around it, heart thumping. "I need your help."

"Demon ass kicking? Count me in," Rane said. "You're like ten minutes from me. I'll be there in five."

"Okay. Hurry."

Dru could hear Rane breathing even harder. "In the meantime, stall him. But don't get, you know, *killed.*"

"How am I supposed to stall him?" Dru said.

"Cowgirl up."

"Right." Dru shook her head. "Wait, what does that even mean?" But Rane had already hung up.

Dru kept her sweating palms locked on the steering wheel as she careened through Greyson's neighborhood, worried some cop would pull her over and ruin everything.

But her fears were unfounded. It didn't look like a cop had set foot here in a decade. Sandwiched between the railroad tracks and a string of empty industrial buildings, the strip of brick single-family homes and one-level apartment buildings looked practically deserted.

Weeds grew along the edges of the broken sidewalks. Abandoned cars sat on dead dirt yards. Layers of graffiti covered up the boarded-up windows of empty houses.

She coasted to a stop in the middle of the road. There was no other traffic. At all.

The only sign of life was the occasional light in a window or the blue flicker of a TV.

She pulled up in front of Greyson's address, a former commercial building of some kind that looked as if it had been converted into an apartment with a small, attached warehouse or garage.

His workshop.

Afraid to get out of the car, Dru turned off the headlights and leaned across the seat to see what she could tell in the dark. It wasn't much.

Nondescript flat tan paint covered the old cinder block walls. The small windows revealed nothing, except for reflecting the caged light bulbs above the front double door and the garage-style door on the side. A simple black-and-white sign dourly advised, *No Trespassing*.

One thing missing from his place was the general sense of decay that pervaded the neighborhood. There was no graffiti on Greyson's building and no junk on the strip of grass out front, which actually looked green and healthy. The modest landscape was subtly well-groomed.

She wasn't sure what that said about Greyson, but she took it as a good sign.

At least the demon hadn't shown up yet. She'd have to work fast. Hopefully, she could find a way to get inside, track down the source of the demonic power, and break its connection to Greyson.

Pretty much impossible. But still, she had to try.

She took a deep breath and checked her crystals. With the quartz shattered and left behind in the garden, all she had left was the shiny cube of galena and a sparkling purple piece of amethyst.

Not much, but they would have to do. Mouth dry, palms sweating, Dru opened the car door and stepped out into the cool Colorado night. The breeze smelled vaguely like wet mud, as if a stream ran behind one of the streets, out of sight.

She looked both ways but saw no one. Down the street, an old car backed out of a driveway and chugged away in the opposite direction, red taillights like possessed eyes.

Dru decided to go the direct route first and walked up to try the worn brass handle on the front door. It was locked. Of course.

She felt along the ledge above the door for a spare key. She found only grit and something that she hoped was a dried leaf, not a spider.

Wiping her hands off on spare napkins from her purse, she circled the building, peering into the few windows, but she could see nothing. When she tried the one farthest from the street, it didn't budge. Actually, none of them budged. They were all locked tight.

She passed the garage door and peeked down the dark alley, seeing nothing but impenetrable blackness. She wasn't brave enough to head down that way. Maybe when Rane showed up.

She felt a sudden, guilty longing for the early days of The Crystal Connection. When she would start every morning by brewing a fresh pot of coffee, vacuuming the front entry, and turning over the plastic sign in the window that proudly announced, "Yes, We're Open!"

Back in those days, the world had seemed so full of potential. Everything was fresh and new. Anything felt possible. She'd been ready to help anyone who needed it. She'd been a little nervous, leaving a safe cubicle job and opening her own business, trying to run it all by herself. But the work was exhilarating.

Curing magic-hangover headaches and nausea. Finding the right ingredients for a good luck charm. Helping the occasional B-list sorceress track down a long-lost book, decode an ancient inscription, or identify an errant creature that had strayed too far into civilization.

Back then, working with a sorceress was like being invited backstage by a rock star. Every time, she had to resist the urge to squeal.

Back then, anything had felt possible.

Now she was keeping secrets from Nate, running around the wrong side of town, and close to ruining her only nice dress.

As she tried to psych herself up to step into the pitch blackness of the alley, the hairs on the back of her neck prickled up. Goose bumps prickled her arms.

The demon was here. She could feel it.

She turned to run back to the car, but she was too late. With a blur of motion, the demon leaped from the darkness above and landed with an earthshaking impact between her and the Prius. His hooves cracked the sidewalk underfoot.

The demon no longer looked even remotely like Greyson. Bare to the waist, his muscles rippled beneath skin that had turned scaly and midnight black. His curled horns had grown huge. His mouth was a nightmare of fangs.

Dru stepped back, gripping the amethyst crystal in her left hand, the galena in her right. "Greyson, it's me. It's Dru."

The demon's mouth stretched open, fangs glinting in the streetlight, and he let out a bone-shaking roar. The hot steam of his breath filled the air between them.

Cold fear urged her to run. But she kept her feet planted on the ground. Even if she could outrun him, if she fled now, Greyson would be lost forever.

The demon closed the distance between them in three long strides, his hooves clopping like gunshots on the pavement.

"Greyson." With every ounce of strength Dru could muster, she raised her gaze and stared the demon directly in his molten-iron eyes. "I know you can hear me. Fight it, Greyson. Fight it!"

Because if he didn't, she was doomed. Alone, she was no match for this thing, and she knew it.

The demon stopped, his breath blowing hot on her skin. With a deep grunt, he turned his head away and shook it side to side, his massive horns gleaming.

"Listen to me, Greyson. You're stronger than this. I know you. When we were in the garden, I felt that strength. I know you have it in you." She longed to reach out and comfort him, but the crystals in her hands felt like loaded weapons. She kept them close to her body. "Follow my voice, Greyson. Remember the way back. I'm here."

Slowly, the demon's head swiveled back around to face her. The lava-like glow was gone, replaced by glowing red irises.

Deep within them, she could see Greyson staring back at her. Barely, but he was there.

"Dru . . ." he whispered, his voice tortured and hoarse.

"That's it," she said. "Just breathe. You can do this."

"I . . . can't . . ." He staggered back, clutching his head with his huge hands. He let out a wordless groan that sounded more animal than human.

She moved to follow him. "You can. I can sense it in you. Don't slip away."

"Dru. I can't stop it." He panted. His voice dropped into a monstrous rumble. "Get back. I don't want to—" His words became an anguished growl.

Dru tightened her fists around the crystals. She could feel their energy humming in her fingers. Being this close to Greyson, even though he was corrupted by the demon, somehow magnified her power to an entirely new level. She knew there were forces unfolding here she hadn't even begun to understand.

"I'm not leaving you," she said. "We're connected. Can you feel it? Greyson, we can find a way. We *will*. Just stay with me."

He stumbled back, demon head thrashing side to side. Then he stopped.

When he next looked at her, his eyes faded behind the hellish glow. He ground out one last strangled word.

"*Run!*"

Somehow, through the fear that instantly flooded her veins, Dru realized with crystalline clarity that Greyson was trying to save her. It could have been his last conscious moment on earth, and he used it to try to spare her life.

Dru knew then that she'd die before she'd let the demon have him.

She brought up her fists, holding them a shoulder-width apart. A rush of energy sang through her, up and down both arms. She could feel an almost magnetic pull between the crystals. Together, they could protect her. She didn't know how she knew that.

But she *knew*. Felt it deep inside her core. The sheer magnitude of

Greyson's presence had unlocked a deep potential within her. It welled up inside her, ready to explode.

The demon straightened up and slowly flexed his arms, thick fingers working the air, primed to grab her. A sigil glowed red-hot on his hands: two triangles with rounded bases, connected by a bar across the top.

As they grew brighter and became white-hot, Dru realized what the sigil was. Scales. Like the scales of justice.

She had no idea what that meant, but she didn't have time to wonder. The demon lunged at her with blinding speed.

Dru drove the heels of her hands together, crystals clutched tight in her fingers. The magic flowed out of her at an indescribable rate, like a river bursting through the floodgates of a dam, many times more powerful than anything she'd ever known. It refracted through the crystals, changed, and emerged as a blinding blue-white glow that enveloped her fists.

The demon's hands struck the outside of her protective aura and halted midswing, as if striking an invisible wall. His touch sizzled.

She felt the impact reverberate through her defenses and into her, a searing pain that burned her soul even more than her skin. She staggered for a moment, then planted her feet and leaned in, desperate to stand her ground.

But the demon kept pushing her back. She fought to hold her place, high heels scraping across the driveway, but she was no match for him. He pushed her until she was pinned against the concrete wall by the alley.

There was nowhere else to go. He had trapped her.

Grinning, the demon pressed on, threatening to crush her behind her own enchantment. The pressure increased until her spell overloaded with a blistering flash and flared out of existence.

Leering, the demon lowered his smoking hands. The afterimage of the magical clash remained burned into Dru's retinas, superimposed on the demon's hulking body. In the sudden silence, her ears popped.

Dru tried to call her magic defenses back, but they were gone. She raised her shaking arms, so heavy she could barely lift them, and opened her sooty hands. The crystals in her palms were blackened, burned. They crumbled, and their remains slipped away through her numb fingers.

The demon opened his jaws wide, fangs wet and sharp, and let loose a terrifying growl.

From the darkness of the alley came a rhythmic clanging that grew louder and faster with every beat.

Rane streaked out of the alley, legs pumping. Her metal skin shimmered beneath the streetlight.

The red-hot glyphs on the demon's hands flared brighter. He raised his fists. But before he could strike, Rane drove her own fist into his face with a deafening clang that rang like a hammer striking an anvil.

The impact drove the demon back, lifting him up off his hoofed feet. He toppled to the pavement with an earthshaking thud, skidded flat on his back, and let out a heavy breath. Then he slumped and lay still.

Rane slowly bent over, hands clutched together under her chin. She sank to her knees on the sidewalk, hunched over until her metal forehead nearly touched the ground, then toppled over onto her side.

Dru, shocked, looked from Rane's still metal form to the demon and back. They both looked as if they could be dead. In the distance, a mournful police siren wailed.

The demon heaved a slow breath. Alive, but out cold.

With tentative steps, Dru crossed the short stretch of concrete and knelt down beside Rane, afraid to touch her, terrified some horrible magical affliction had overcome her.

With a sound like a sword being slid back into its scabbard, Rane became human again. Her skin lost its steely shine and turned tan and soft. Her straight blonde hair fell down over her face, partly obscuring her pained expression. She clutched her right fist and pressed it against her chest, breathing hard.

She opened one squinting eye and glared at Dru.

"Rane?" Dru whispered. "What's wrong?"

"Fuck," Rane intoned solemnly, as if it were a deep spiritual revelation, "that *hurt*."

12

THE MONSTERS WE KEEP

Dru pulled Rane to her feet. Even in human form, the woman was deceptively heavy, built like an Amazon in a bright pink tank top and jogging shorts that said *Bad* across the rear.

Unsteady on her feet, Rane held onto Dru for support, then pulled her into a crushing hug. "Dude, I thought you were a goner," Rane whispered in her ear. "When I saw that light . . ." Her voice caught. She drew in a breath that sounded like the beginning of a sob, then slowly blew it out. "Okay. Okay. We're all good, right?"

"Totally." Dru gave her a thankful squeeze. But Rane held on, tightening the hug into a back-popping embrace.

Dru tried to wriggle free, but it was like pushing against a brick wall.

"Did he hurt you, D?" Rane said into her hair.

"Ack. I can't breathe."

"Oh. Right." Rane finally let her go. She swiped at the corners of her eyes with the heel of her uninjured hand.

"Let me see your hand." Dru reached for her, but Rane pulled away.

"Whatever. I'm good to go." Rane circled the unconscious demon, who was stretched out mere inches from the front bumper of Nate's car.

"Thank you. For, you know." Dru pantomimed slugging the air. "If you'd hit him a little harder, I think I'd be buying Nate a new car."

Rane put her hands on her hips and glared at the demon. "So now what do we do?"

Distant police sirens grew closer. Down the street, blue and red lights began to reflect off the houses and trees.

Dru looked over her shoulder, down the dark alley. "Can we get him out of sight, at least?"

"Yeah. Bet he's heavy, though. Let me just get my game face on." Rane played with her rings. "I keep worrying I'm gonna use up this titanium ring. Better switch to the sparky rock." She closed her hand over the stone ring.

With a grinding sound, patches of Rane's skin turned the same speckled gray of her flint ring. The effect quickly spread until Rane's entire body transformed into solid flint. "Now let's do it."

Dru kicked off her heels. She struggled to lift Greyson's ankles, but Rane hoisted him up like a sack of groceries. Together, they carried him into the alley. There in the cool darkness, beneath a burned-out light bulb in a cage, was a steel door in the side of the garage. Rane kicked it open, denting the door and splintering the frame.

"Wait!" Dru whispered, realizing the futility of stealth at this point. "We don't even know what's in there!"

"So? Get the lights." Rane shifted her grip under his armpits and dragged him away into pitch blackness that smelled of gasoline and chemicals.

Dru fumbled blindly, fingers gliding around the jagged wood of the broken doorframe, until she found a light switch. Just as she was about to flip it, a spotlight lit up the alley, shining across graffiti-painted brick walls, wind-blown newspapers, clusters of dead leaves.

As quietly as she could, Dru eased the dented door closed and leaned all of her weight against it, hoping the damage couldn't be easily seen from the street.

Pulses of blue and red lights splashed across the front of the building, reflecting around her where they leaked in through unseen windows.

Across the dark garage, a cascade of metal crashed to the floor. "Sorry," Rane said. "My bad."

An idling car engine crept up, accompanied by the squawking of radio voices and the crunch of tires on loose gravel.

After an agonizing minute, Dru whispered, "Why aren't they leaving?"

"Probably running the plates on Nate's car," Rane answered from the darkness, not bothering to lower her voice. "Why, he got any outstanding warrants?"

"Funny." Dru waited, sweating, as the police cruiser idled out front.

She had the irresistible urge to swallow, but her throat was bone-dry. When had she become the kind of person who hid from the police?

She thought about walking out into the flashing lights, hands up, trying to explain. *You see, my customer turned into a demon. Then my friend punched him out. So it's all under control now, Officer, thank you.*

No.

She wondered if Nate would bail her out of jail.

Probably not.

After an eternity of pounding heartbeats, the lights and sounds faded away, leaving the three of them alone in the darkness. The demon's breathing echoed like a snoring horse.

Dru silently counted to ten, then flipped the switch. She blinked in the sudden glare.

The garage was easily big enough for three cars, but it held only one: the long, angular form of Greyson's black muscle car. It crouched behind Rane's back, its hood open just an inch, as if waiting to devour her.

Rane, still in stone form, had dropped the demon at her feet. Beside her, a tool tray was overturned, the source of the crash. A dozen shiny wrenches lay scattered across the concrete floor, and the corner of the metal tray was squashed flat under her stone heel.

The walls of the garage were lined with upright red tool cabinets. The swollen tanks of a welding rig sat in the corner, topped by a well-used tinted visor. Spare parts hung from the walls, surrounded by chrome hubcaps and old license plates in faded colors.

Rane glanced over her shoulder at the car. "Damn." She stalked around the car as if it would bite her. "This thing got a Hemi?"

"Something about that car gives me the creeps." Dru started to turn away, then gave it a puzzled look. Something didn't add up. "Wait, how did his car get back here?"

Rane cocked her head to the side, like a puppy.

"I mean, I assume he drove to the restaurant," Dru said. "So . . . wouldn't it still be there, in the parking lot?"

"Maybe he took a cab." Rane shrugged. "It's not like the car drove *itself* home."

"Strange." Dru shook her head. "Anyway, let's get Greyson restrained before he wakes up."

Rane gave her a stone grin that was half amusement, half disbelief. "Restrained?"

"If we can." Dru went through the tool cabinets, gingerly at first, then with more urgency, looking for rope, cable, duct tape, anything. "Unless you want to fight him again when he wakes up."

"Wasn't much of a fight," Rane muttered. But she started looking, too.

In a bottom drawer, Dru found a pile of thick metal chain. Long stretches of it were caked with oily grime and occasional patches of bright orange spray paint. But it felt solid enough to hold down an elephant. She grabbed a heavy handful and dragged it out across the floor. "What do you think? Chain him up?"

Rane found one end, then looked from Greyson to Dru and back. "Kinky," she said, waggling her eyebrows.

Dru sighed. "Whatever."

Near one of the walls of the garage, a pair of foot-wide metal I-beams supported the high roof. It didn't take long to prop Greyson up against the base of one of the beams and wrap chains around his arms and chest.

Rane jammed a long metal bolt through the ends of the chain and bent it into a pretzel shape. "That should hold him. For a while, anyway." With a grinding sound, she turned human again.

"Great." Dru looked down at her dress. It was completely ruined. Wrinkled, dirty, and torn at the hem. Now it had a black greasy smudge on the side, too. "Fantastic."

Rane wiped ineffectively at the smudge with a red shop rag. "*Way* better than the night I had planned. What's next?"

"I have to find a way to cure him. Without screwing it up again." Dru sighed with frustration. "Somewhere in here, there's a cursed artifact of some kind. We need to find it and break the connection."

"What does it look like, this artifact? Is it glowy or something?"

"That's the problem. It could be anything." Dru thought about the burning glyphs on the demon's hands. "My guess is it'll be marked with a symbol. Like the scales of justice."

"Okay. Find something with scales on it. *Sounds* simple. Don't you have a crystal that allows you to see enchantments? TV crystal or something?"

"TV rock. Ulexite. Yes, but it's back at the shop."

Rane folded her arms. "Hold up. If the evil hoodoo charm is in here with us, making this place ground zero for demon weirdness, doesn't that mean this is *exactly* the wrong place to chain him up?"

The two of them regarded the unconscious demon. His head hung down, thick curved horns hiding his face.

"You want to move him?" Dru said.

"Nope."

"Me either." Dru took a deep breath. "Look, I hate to split up, but I need you here to keep an eye on him."

"Where are you going?"

"Back to the shop to get more crystals. And check my books. I'll be back here in maybe an hour, tops."

For a brief instant, Rane looked deeply worried. Then it was gone, and Rane waved it off. "It's fine. You go. I'll keep an eye on him."

Dru thought about it. Maybe splitting up was a really bad idea after all. "I don't know what else to do. Is there anyone else we can call in on this? Salem, maybe?" She hated to bring up Rane's ex-boyfriend, but the situation was desperate.

Rane's face darkened. "No."

"Maybe I should call Opal, have her come over with some crystals and books."

Rane put her hands on Dru's shoulders. "You call in Opal, she'll get hurt, maybe worse. Regular people can't handle these kinds of problems."

"Opal's not exactly regular."

"But she doesn't have powers like we do. This thing is between you and me. So go back to the shop, get your own gear, and hurry back." As if sensing her reluctance to leave, Rane swept her into another bone-crushing hug. Then she took a deep sniff of Dru's hair and let her go.

"Um," Dru said. She wanted to say, *Did you just sniff my hair?* But she already had too much weirdness on her plate to deal with any more.

She backed away, grabbed her purse, and headed out. Just as she stepped outside, Rane called to her again.

"D."

That one syllable was loaded with emotion. Rane stood alone in the center of the garage, hugging herself. She set her lips in a thin line. "If he wakes up, gets violent? This could get freakishly ugly, fast."

"Uglier than now?"

"You haven't had to put down a demon before." Rane hesitated. "I have."

Put down a demon. The words echoed in Dru's mind, chilling her.

The haunted look in Rane's eyes made it absolutely clear what she meant. If Dru couldn't find a way to cure Greyson, he might never leave this garage alive.

13

SHADES OF GREYSON

Dru stood in the doorway, torn. She needed to leave, but she also needed to be here. In case Greyson broke loose and everything went to hell.

Leaving was too risky, she decided. Greyson's life was at stake. And possibly Rane's, if she couldn't handle him.

Feeling like she couldn't win, Dru came back inside and inspected Greyson's chains again. She figured they'd hold if the demon woke up. But she'd been wrong before. "Okay, change of plans. Whatever the cursed artifact is that's doing this, we need to find it. Fast. Let's tear this place apart."

Rane cracked her knuckles. "All *right*."

Dru put a cautioning hand on her arm. "I don't mean that literally."

"Hey, you want to save his soul? You work your way. I'll work mine." Rane pulled a box of rusty parts off a shelf and dumped it out on the floor with a deafening crash.

Dru scanned the garage. There was just so much stuff here, she wasn't sure where to begin. Then she remembered the glowing glyphs.

"Hey, you saw the scales symbol he had on his hands? I know I've seen that before. I need my books." Dru whipped out her phone and set down her purse. "I'm calling Opal. Executive decision."

Rane snorted. "Whatever. It's your party. You can invite your employee if you want."

"Opal's not just an employee," Dru said. "She's a good friend."

Rane waved her off and started rifling through toolboxes.

Opal answered on the third ring, speaking loud enough that Rane probably heard her. "You know I only work for you in the daytime, right?"

"Hi, Opal." Dru ignored Rane's sudden smirk. "Listen, we're in big trouble here."

"You find the demon?"

"That's the problem. If I'm going to save him, I need more crystals. Like right now. And you're my only hope."

Opal let out a long, frustrated sigh. "Only hope, huh? I was afraid you were gonna play that card. Now I've *got* to be there for you." With a hint of suspicion, she added, "Where is *there*, anyway?"

"Greyson's place."

"I was afraid of that, too."

Rane cupped her hands around her mouth. "Girls' night out at the demon house, Opal. When this is all over, we need beer. Lots. So bring it."

"Girls' night?" Opal repeated. "You think it's safe to give that girl alcohol?"

"Absolutely not," Dru said. "Look, we're trying to find whatever kind of cursed artifact has been afflicting Greyson. It'd be a lot easier if I had a ulexite crystal to see through. Or optical calcite."

"And you want me to go down to the shop and bring your stuff over." It wasn't a question.

Dru cringed, just a little. "And I need some books, too. There's a thick hardcover on demon idols by Lafayette on the back shelf. And I need the one by Tristram about banishing spirits. Plus the Stanislaus journals, the ones with the padlocks on them."

"Hold on, hold on," Opal muttered. "I gotta write this all down. Good thing I'm not *busy* or anything."

Dru was thinking too fast to fully catch the sarcasm. "And the blue parts bins in the corner beneath the giant amethyst? The ones with all the slide-out trays? Bring those, too."

"Which ones?"

"All of them. I need *everything*." Her phone beeped. She looked at the screen.

It was Nate. Calling from home.

Her heart leaped with hope, and simultaneously a jolt of anxiety shot through her. "Gotta go. Thank you so much. Hurry. But no beer." She switched over to Nate. "Honey, are you okay? Sorry I took your car. It was an emergency."

"I'm fine." There was a coldness in his voice that had never been there before. It sent a sudden icy spike of worry up her spine.

"Um, do you want your car back? I could come pick you up." She peered over at Greyson. Still unconscious. "In a little while."

"No," he said. "Just pick me up at the airport when I get back from New York."

"New York?"

"Yes, New York," he snapped. "It's the only chance I have to salvage things with the Zubriggen twins."

"What about the dinner?" But she already knew the answer. Dinner had been an utter fiasco. She tried to sound positive. "You prepared all of those reports, right? All the financial documents? Once they read those, they'll know your practice is a great investment."

Nate let out a deep, soul-searching sigh. "On paper, yes. But that doesn't matter. When you're investing in a business, Dru, you're investing in the people, too. You want to put your money behind people who are stable. Growth-oriented. People who have it together."

She hung her head. "Sorry about all of the drama tonight."

"*Drama?*" Nate made an inarticulate choking sound. "The whole reason I had you there at the restaurant was to show the investors that you and I are a happy, stable, professional couple."

Dru swallowed. "So, well . . . are we?"

"Are we what?"

"*Any* of those things?"

Nate paused. Then with an edge, he said, "What are you saying?"

Dru took a deep breath and watched Rane tear up the garage while Greyson, scaly-skinned and horned, slumped in his chains, unconscious. "I tried to warn you, Nate. I tried to explain exactly what was going on. Weird as it all sounds, I know, it *was* an emergency. I just needed you to *listen* to me."

She wasn't just talking about tonight, she knew. He'd never taken her work seriously, and it kept getting tougher to put a lid on her frustration.

She paced and bumped into a shelf full of junk. A can of black spray paint fell onto her head with a painful jab. She grabbed the can and slammed it back on the shelf.

Nate stayed silent, and she could picture him trying to sort everything out. As angry as she was, her heart ached for him. Nearly getting choked to death by a demon couldn't be easy for anyone to process, especially someone who steadfastly refused to believe in the supernatural.

"Look, I really am sorry," she said. "How's your throat?"

"Is this what you do?" He threw it out like an accusation. "Down in your little shop?"

"What you saw, what attacked you, that was real," she said as neutrally as she could. It was also entirely his fault, though now would be the wrong time to point that out, she decided.

"It's like I don't even know you," he said. "The real you."

"I'm not hiding anything," she said.

Just then, a resounding crash nearby made her jump. Her eyes instantly went to the demon, but he was still unconscious.

She looked around the garage, suddenly panicked to realize that Rane was nowhere to be seen. A door in the corner hung open, lights on inside, revealing the edge of a living room beyond, with a ratty couch and an aging lamp.

Rane poked her head through the doorway. "Sorry. Thought there was a secret door back here." Her head disappeared. "Guess not."

"Listen, we should talk," Dru said to Nate. "Maybe if I come over later?"

"No. Not after all this."

That cut deep. Tears stung the corners of her eyes. "How is any of this my fault? Why are you blaming me?"

"Look." He hesitated. "I don't want to talk. I've got to go."

"Wait, just wait one second. Okay?"

"I'm getting back the day after tomorrow. Pick me up at the airport, if you want to talk."

"Just let me deal with this situation here, and I'll call—"

"No. Don't call me." He let out a long, quavering breath. "I think you and I need to take a break."

She couldn't speak. The words died in her throat, leaving her choking, as if she couldn't get any air through.

"As a matter of fact, forget about the airport. I'll take a cab."

"Nate, I—"

But he'd already hung up.

Dru stared at the phone, and a gaping chasm of pain opened up inside her. She sagged against the cold concrete wall.

An intense pressure built up in her chest, making her feel like she would explode. But there was no way to release the pressure, and it just became a pounding pain that squeezed out all of her breath.

Rane stomped back into the garage, dusting off her hands. "Rest of the house looks clean. At least to me." She scanned the garage. "I don't see anything that screams 'insidious demon artifact.' Totally normal. Except, where are all the chickie posters?"

Still holding the phone because she didn't want to put it away and accept that the conversation was actually over, Dru gave Rane a blank look. "What?"

"Chickie posters. You know." Rane picked up a giant black crowbar and struck a pose, head tilted back, lips pursed, chest pushed out. Then she shrugged and tossed the crowbar aside. It clanged to the floor. "Seems like every serious garage has those posters all over. But nothing here."

"Maybe Greyson's just a classy guy," Dru answered absently. She almost dialed Nate back. She held her finger poised over the phone. But she couldn't touch the screen, as if it had suddenly gone toxic, coated with some kind of poison that would surely kill her. Her eyes filled with hot tears, and she squeezed them shut.

"Holy shit," Rane said and crossed the garage to Dru. "Did Nate just dump you?"

"N-no." Dru tried as hard as she could not to cry, but tears were already streaming down her face. "We're just . . . taking a break. I guess."

Rane blew out a breath but didn't say anything.

In the corner, chains clinked. A low, wet groan shuddered through the garage. The sound evoked some primal fear in Dru that she couldn't name. Her scalp tingled.

Slowly, the demon raised his horned head and gave them a red-hot glare. Dru quickly wiped away the tears.

The demon drew in a deep breath and roared, an almost physical sound that thudded through Dru's chest. Muscles rippling, he strained at the chains wrapped around him. They clinked and screeched as the metal links stretched taut to their limit.

Unfazed, Rane stalked around the demon and picked up the black steel crowbar like a club. With a metallic scrape, her hand and arm transformed into the dark shiny steel of the crowbar, quickly followed by the rest of her body.

She marched over to stand before the demon, stance wide, ready to strike. Rane was so much of a weapon herself that the crowbar seemed unnecessary. She turned her black steel face toward Dru. "That demon artifact? Better find it quick, before he gets loose."

The demon grunted, showing razor-sharp teeth, and his burning eyes opened wider.

Dru followed his gaze to the black car. The answer was so obvious she was shocked she hadn't seen it before.

"Oh, God," she breathed. "We didn't check the car. Could be in the trunk."

The demon threw back its head and howled, loud enough to pierce Dru's ears. As if it was conjuring something up from the pits of hell.

As the howl faded to a guttural moan, the black car coughed and rumbled to life. Twin lights flared on its nose, like the gleaming eyes of a poisonous insect.

Dru stared through the windshield at the driver's seat. There was no one behind the wheel.

The car's headlights flipped open, two on each side, burning like rising suns, blinding in their intensity. Dru threw up her hands to ward off the hellish glare.

Tires spun, spewing twin plumes of white smoke. An unholy screeching filled the garage, warbling through the air.

The evil artifact wasn't *in* the car, Dru realized too late.

It *was* the car.

With a lurch, the possessed car launched itself straight at Dru.

14
HEAT OF THE MOMENT

"Dru!" Rane shouted.

But Dru couldn't move. Sudden fear rendered her feet too heavy to lift. She stayed anchored to the spot.

The black car roared at her, brilliant headlights burning in her vision. She braced for the impact.

Just before the car reached her, Rane shoved Dru aside, sending her tumbling away across the concrete floor.

The car hit Rane in the legs with a sickening crunch of metal. She fell onto the hood, and it rammed her lower legs into the concrete wall.

The car pulled back, its front end mashed.

Rane, her metal face twisted in pain, slid off the hood onto the floor.

The car surged forward again. Rane sat up, struggling to escape, but the nose of the car pinned her torso against the concrete wall. Its crushed snout crumpled around her chest as if trying to devour her. The engine revved, spinning the tires into a frenzy, filling the garage with the acrid white smoke of burning rubber.

Across the garage, the demon threw back his head and howled, a gut-clenching sound.

Transfixed by horror, Dru stared at the reflection of the red glow seeping from beneath the car's slightly open hood.

She blinked. The red glow hadn't been there before the demon howled.

And it was the same fiery hue as the glyphs on the demon's hands.

With no time to formulate anything like a plan, Dru scrambled over to the car's fender, dug her fingers under the edge of the open hood, and lifted. The metal thrummed in her hands, vibrating with the relentless force of the engine.

In the ruddy glow, she saw all of the familiar but nameless parts of an engine she expected: spinning belts, twisting hoses, chrome gleaming with an unholy light. But it was the light itself that captured her attention.

On the underside of the hood glowed a pair of stylized scales. Just like the symbols on the demon's hands.

This was the connection, she realized with a surge of terrified triumph. This was the mark of evil, as rough as it was. It looked like someone had spray-painted it right onto the metal. If only she could find a way to break it.

Spray paint. The thought hit her with a jolt of adrenaline.

She launched herself across the garage and grabbed the can of black spray paint that had knocked her on the head earlier. She struggled to get the plastic cap off. It wouldn't budge.

Rane's terrified gaze caught Dru's and held it. Her mouth worked, trying to choke out words, but nothing came out.

"Hold on!" Dru yelled, running back to the car. With a grunt, she hammered the top of the spray can against the black car's fender. The plastic top flew off into the shadows.

Dru lifted the hood again and let loose a stream of black paint over the burning symbol.

The glow faded beneath the fresh paint, but surged back like a raging fire beneath a trickle of water.

She held down the spray top until her finger went cold and numb, filling the air with choking paint fumes. She kept spraying until the paint dripped and ran.

Die, she thought to it with every ounce of strength she could muster. *Die!*

The glow faded, but not completely. It remained, ruddy and faint. Still glowing.

Yet the tires slowed and stopped spinning. The engine dropped from a screaming race down to a thudding idle.

And then the paint ran out.

"No!" Dru whispered, shaking the rattling can. "No, no, no!" The paint came out in spurts and puffs, then died into silence. She tossed the can aside and shook out her numb finger.

"Neutral," Rane gasped. "Gear. Shift."

Dru stared at Rane. *Gear shift*. Of course.

The car door was locked, but the window was rolled down. Dru leaned in, practically crawling into the car, and grabbed the white knob of the gear shift where it sat on its long chrome shaft between the seats.

She wasn't sure how to shift it, so she pulled in every direction, without success. "Stupid thing. Let. Her. *Go!*" With a sudden jolt, the shifter moved.

The engine kicked up a notch, but the car began a slow roll backward. Dru scrambled back out of the window.

Rane, teeth gritted, pushed the car away from her. It inched back a little faster.

When the gap was wide enough, Dru took Rane's arm and, with strength she didn't know she had, dragged her out into the open. In metal form, the woman weighed as much as a refrigerator. Maybe more.

With a tortured screech of metal, the car's nose unwrinkled and smoothed itself out. The cracks disappeared from its headlights. They straightened and brightened.

As Dru watched, the front of the car became a flawless expanse of black metal. Then the headlights drooped closed, and the engine whined like an exhausted animal.

The glow from under the hood faded away. Without it, the engine guttered and died. For the moment, at least, it seemed the spray paint had worked.

In the far corner, the demon's chains sang like a chorus as he tried to break free, the metal links ringing out in unholy unison with each tug against the metal I-beam that held him prisoner.

Dru racked her brain for some way to knock the demon out again. But Rane was in no condition to fight. And without any crystals, there was nothing Dru could do.

The demon's muscles bulged as he twisted around, trying to change positions. The burning scales on his hands glowed red, then orange, and finally white-hot. The sizzling heat scorched the chains until they started to break apart.

He grinned, showing rows of shining knifelike teeth.

Dru's breath caught in her throat. In moments, the demon would be free. There was nothing she could do to prevent it.

"Rane, we've got to run." Dru shook Rane but got no response.

She was passed out on the floor, worn out from too much magic. Gradually, her body turned human again. Dru knew from experience that Rane would recover in a few minutes, but that was time they didn't have.

The last of the chains gave way with a ping. With a roar, the demon surged to his hoofed feet. His glowing magma gaze found Dru, and he bared his fangs.

Every instinct told Dru to run, but she stood guard over Rane.

Chest swelling, the demon tugged at the last chains still draped over his shoulders. They slithered to the floor with a metallic whisper.

The demon stepped over the chains. One step, then another, striding directly toward Dru. He stared down at her with inhuman intensity, his fiery gaze unblinking.

"Greyson," she said, trying to keep her voice from shaking. "I know you can hear me." She prayed she was right.

Something in the demon's face softened at the sound of her voice, and the tension went out of his fists.

"Greyson, it's me. Dru."

He cocked his head, as if struggling to remember her from the distant past.

She could barely make out a trace of Greyson in there, somewhere. Deep inside the demon.

She took a tentative step toward him. When he didn't react with anything more than a blink, she took another step.

A sound rumbled from deep inside the demon. Maybe a word. Maybe her name. But it couldn't survive the journey through the demon's thick throat and rows of teeth. It came out as nothing more than a growl.

But there was no menace in it. No threat. If anything, there was only pain.

Another step closer, and Dru stood within an arm's length of the demon. And she was terrifyingly aware of the fact that she didn't have a single crystal to protect herself with.

Nothing. She was utterly defenseless.

Carefully, Dru reached out one trembling hand. After a moment's hesitation, she placed it flat against the scaly skin of the demon's chest.

For some reason, she expected a jolt of pain when she touched him. But it was just a touch. Caring, close, and unexpectedly intimate.

His warmth quickly seeped into her fingers. And with it came the electric tingle of magic.

Except that the magic wasn't flowing into her. It was flowing *from* her. Into the demon.

Beneath her fingers, the ugly hue of the demon's skin began to fade away. Ever so slowly, the skin became human again. With freckles, fine hairs, a small scar.

The demon's breaths calmed to a human rhythm. The darkness faded from his face. The horns began to shrink, thinning and uncurling.

The energy kept flowing out of her, seemingly endless, in a way that she realized only happened when she was this close to Greyson. It resounded deep in her chest, like an echo of her heartbeat, and thrummed though her fingers into him. The effect was exhausting, but at the same time it made her want to sing with joy.

The demon's hoofed feet became human again, bare and pale. He shrank ever so slightly to Greyson's normal height.

But as quickly as the transformation began, it stalled out. The energy between them thinned to a trickle, and she had no idea how to make it continue.

Greyson's eyes flickered with a red glow, one moment human, the next demon. His angular face had become normal again, stubbled and tan, but stumpy horns still protruded from his dark hair.

"Dru." He choked out her name.

"I'm here," she said. "Don't worry. I'm here. Just hold onto me."

He placed one strong hand over hers, pressing her fingers harder against his chest. "It's not . . . working. He's . . . coming back."

"No, Greyson, no. You're almost back. I can sense it." But her energy was almost spent, and she could feel a new resistance building inside him. The demon, resurging once again.

Anguish welled up within her. She was so close. *So close.*

But it was too much. She couldn't make him fully human again. Her magic had run out.

His fingers turned black and gnarled. His nails lengthened into claws. "Can't . . ." he whispered. "Can't hang on."

Greyson seized her by the shoulders. A steely resolve washed over his face, tightening the muscles in his neck. He tilted his head down until they were eye to eye. "Dru. You have to run. Away from me, as far as you can."

Sudden tears threatened at the corner of her eyes. "Every time I touch you, you start to come back. There's a connection between us. You have to know that."

"Forget me." His breath warmed her cheek. "You can't save me."

"The hell I can't," she whispered. Then she raised her lips to Greyson's and kissed him with everything she had.

15

SOME GIRLS WANDER BY MISTAKE

Dru let herself become lost in the kiss. All sense of time or place disappeared.

When she finally forced herself to break it off, the air around her felt too thin for her to catch her breath.

Greyson's intense gaze gradually worked its way from her lips up the length of her face. He stared deep into her eyes, gold flecks in his blue irises reflecting the light.

He swallowed, the muscles in his neck working. "Guess I had a good reason to come back."

And he *was* back, Dru realized. She'd done it.

Greyson was one hundred percent human again. Rugged, handsome, smiling.

But definitely not Nate. That was when it all hit her.

Dru pulled away, hands flying to her chest as the full impact sank in.

She'd kissed Greyson. Not just an innocent peck on the cheek. Not just a ceremonial kiss to seal or break a spell. A full-on, hundred percent hot, passionate kiss.

And the part that she didn't want to admit was that she'd meant it. She couldn't deny that.

All of that added up to one undeniable fact: she'd crossed a line that could never be uncrossed. Greyson was a customer. Under her care. She wasn't sure if there was really a professional code of ethics out there for magic shop owners, but if there was, this definitely violated it.

"I can't believe you brought me back." The warmth was clear in his voice. "You're amazing."

"It worked," she said, trying to cover her lips without being too obvious about it.

Greyson gave her a puzzled look. He didn't seem to notice that he wasn't wearing a shirt. Or shoes. Or that his garage was entirely trashed. He looked like all he wanted was to sweep her back into his arms.

And the truth, as much as she tried to deny it, was that right now she desperately wanted him to.

Behind her, Rane coughed, a miserable, scratchy sound. Bringing reality back to shatter the enchanted moment.

Dru turned and rushed to her, helping her sit up. "Hey. Sweetie, are you okay?"

Rane, human now and worse for wear, pushed her blonde hair out of her face and looked up with half-lidded eyes. "Dy-no-*mite*." Her voice came out low and raw. "How 'bout you?"

"A little freaked out." The garage stank of exhaust and burned rubber. Dru waved her hand uselessly at the wisps of smoke. "Let's get you out into some fresh air."

"Ugh." Rane coughed. "Good thing I heal super fast. Gimme a minute."

Greyson stepped forward, hands outstretched. "Here, let me help."

"No!" Dru barked, drawing surprised looks from both of them. "I mean, um, you must be cold. Being half-naked and all. Why don't you . . . um . . . ?" The speech part of her brain felt as if it had shut down in his presence. "I have to take Rane outside. We're okay."

Greyson considered that, then nodded once, but didn't go anywhere. "All right." Dru got a grip around Rane's shoulders. "Up!"

With matching groans, the two of them got to their feet. Greyson looked like he could barely resist helping them up. He reached toward them, arms out, but stopped just short of touching them.

"We're fine!" Dru said with forced cheerfulness. She pulled Rane's arm up over her shoulders and walked her to the dented metal door.

"Is it still nighttime?" Rane studied the night sky above, lit a shady orange by the city lights. The moment the door was shut behind them, Rane said, "What's with the attitude? You're acting kind of funny. Even for you."

Dru leaned close as she half carried Rane toward the sidewalk. "I kissed him," she whispered.

A lopsided grin spread across Rane's face. "All *right*. Right here, sister." She held up her hand.

"No! This is not a high-five moment." Dru took a deep breath of the clean night air and found her way out of the alley to the front driveway. Seeing Nate's white Prius parked at the curb gave her a twinge of regret.

Rane sagged painfully against the corner of the building. "Damn. I hurt all over. I'm not ashamed to admit it." She brightened. "Wait, is Opal bringing beer?"

Dru shook her head. As much as she tried to stay calm, she felt torn up inside. "That was a terrible thing I just did in there. I cheated on Nate. I kissed a customer. I'm a horrible person."

Rane stared at her for a moment, then burst out laughing.

Dru folded her arms as Rane guffawed. "It's not funny!"

"Oh, check you out with all your guilt. Gimme a break." Rane cocked her head at Dru. "You grew up Catholic, didn't you?"

"Hey, I—" Dru scowled at her. "That's not the point."

Rane cocked an eyebrow. "Dude, you just saved a man's life in there. Don't you get that? You're a hero."

"*You're* the hero. You jumped in front of that car for me."

"Good point." Rane sighed and gazed off into the distance. "Look, if Nate's even half the man he needs to be, he'll understand. It's not like you ran off to the tropics with some cabana boy."

"Still. Greyson's a customer. And nothing's settled between me and Nate."

"Whatever. You and Nate are taking a break. He'll just have to deal." Rane pushed off the wall and put her hands on Dru's shoulders. "Dude, I was all set to crack Greyson on the head with a crowbar. And you stepped right in and saved his *soul*. From a demon. That makes you a hundred percent awesome."

Dru wasn't sure she believed that, but it felt good to hear it. She toyed with her glasses. "I guess. Maybe."

Rane clapped her on the back. "Congratulations. You're now officially a sorceress."

Dru stared at her in disbelief.

Rane mistook her doubt for confusion. "Look, it's not like you have to take a test or get a license or anything. Tonight, you were twice as badass as most of the ones I know." With her fingers, she tried to fix Dru's hair. "Plus, you've got that whole, I don't know—" She made a swirly motion around her face. "That whole naughty librarian thing going on. Kind of hot."

"What?"

"Kidding." Rane put her hands up. "But Greyson digs it, obviously. Now quit feeling sorry for yourself and repeat after me: I'm a sorceress."

"I'm not doing this." Dru turned and walked to the curb and back, shaking her arms out as if she could somehow fling the tension and insanity away from her.

Rane was still there at the corner, waiting for her. "Come on, say it. Say 'I'm a sorceress.'"

"This is ridiculous. I'm going back inside."

"He's still alive, right now, because you're a *sorceress*." Rane gave her a meaningful look. "I don't know why this is so hard for you."

Dru looked down at her ruined dress and tried in vain to straighten it. "I don't know. It's just . . . all my life, sorcery was this whole rock-star thing. You know? When I was growing up, my mom was always hooking up with these crazy sorcerers. Some of them were terrible. Some of them could do some *amazing* things. But I could never do any of it myself."

"I know. Your mom told you that you didn't have any talent. I've heard this story like a million times."

"Well, she wasn't entirely wrong. I have just a smidge of talent. That's it. I never developed any real powers, no matter how hard I tried. And I've tried *super* hard."

"I know. I was there." Rane made a face, apparently reliving some awkward memory.

Dru sighed. "All I've ever been able to do is a few crystal tricks. That's it. Maybe brew up some potions that never *ever* seem to work right. So eventually I just, you know, opened up The Crystal Connection. I figured if I can't fight the bad guys on my own, then the least I can do is help the real sorcerers any way I can."

"But tonight was different. Right?"

Dru shrugged. "I don't know how to explain it. It came from inside me. I didn't even know it was there."

"That's totally what I'm talking about," Rane gushed. As much as Rane ever gushed, in her solid monotone. "When the power comes from inside you, that's how you know. You are *so* a sorceress."

"But I've never done anything like that before. I've always needed crystals."

"Because that's your thing. You have crystal powers. I have transformation powers. I need to be touching a solid substance in order to turn into it. But then you came up with the whole ring idea, so I always have something touching my skin. So I can always transform. Those rings help a lot."

"Like the crystals help me."

"Correct. Point is, somebody else picks up a crystal, they can't do what you do." Rane held up her hand with the titanium ring, now scorched and pitted by magic. "Greyson wore this ring, but he couldn't go metall-o. *I* can. That's what makes me a sorceress. You, with the crystals, same deal."

Dru shook herself. She still couldn't believe it. The idea of actually being a sorceress was just too big an idea to handle.

Rane punched her in the shoulder. "Welcome backstage, rock star."

"Ow. Thanks."

"So what do we do next?"

Dru collected her thoughts. "Now, we try to break the spell on the evil death car from hell. That should keep Greyson from hulking out again."

"I thought you spray-painted that hunk of junk."

"It's just spray paint. Not real magic. Would you bet Greyson's soul on a can of Rust-Oleum?"

Down the street, tires squealed, and they both turned to look.

"This party just keeps getting better," Rane said as headlights hurtled toward them.

16

PARTY LIKE IT'S 1969

Opal's massive purple Lincoln Town Car rocketed toward them. She almost blew right past Greyson's place, but at the last second, she slammed on the brakes. The front tire hopped up onto the curb and banged down again onto the street.

Nate's Prius was the only car parked on that side. The Lincoln plowed up behind it with a shriek of brakes. Dru was terrified Opal wouldn't be able to stop the heavy car in time, and her mind was filled with visions of broken glass and tow trucks with flashing yellow lights.

But the long purple Lincoln squealed to a halt with less than a foot to spare between its massive chrome grille and Nate's defenseless bumper.

Opal got out and came around to the sidewalk, arms loaded down with bulging canvas tote bags in designer patterns.

"I brought it all, Dru. There's more on the seat," Opal said, huffing as she tottered toward them on clicking heels.

She set the bags down on the driveway and let out a relieved sigh as she straightened up. Her gaze went from Dru to Rane and back again. "What, did I miss something?"

"Hell yeah." Rane grinned. "Dru got all smoochy hot with Greyson."

"That's not funny," Dru snapped.

"Really? 'Cause I find it hi-*larious*."

Opal lowered her chin and gave Dru a disbelieving look. "Nothing should shock me anymore."

"Can we just focus on the demon problem, please?" Dru picked up one of the tote bags. As always, when loaded with crystals, they were insanely heavy. "It's complicated."

"Oh, girl, it's *always* complicated." Opal shook her head with obvious disapproval. "I'm not saying a word. Not for me to judge." But her head kept going, side to side, like a bobble doll. "Nuh-uh."

Dru sighed and lugged the bag inside.

Greyson stood beside his black car, arms crossed, frowning at it. At least he was wearing a shirt now. A plain white T-shirt that did nothing to hide the hard outlines of his shoulders and chest. She felt guilty just looking at him, but it wasn't easy to look away.

He nodded as they came in. "Evening, ladies." Then he went back to scowling at the car.

Dru set down the bag and went over to stand next to him.

He leaned down closer to her. "I don't remember much. How bad was I?"

"Pretty bad, actually."

As Rane and Opal brought in the rest of the stuff from the car, Dru told Greyson everything, including the way he'd somehow animated the car to attack them. She finished up by showing him the glyph under the hood, now buried under a blotchy black smear of spray paint, so thick it had dripped down the underside of the metal.

She deliberately avoided any mention of the kiss. It was like trying to steer around an iceberg, knowing that ninety percent of the danger was lurking beneath the surface. But Greyson didn't bring it up, either. He just pinched his cleft chin and nodded as she explained everything.

"There's one big thing I don't understand," she said at last. "Why did the car fix itself *after* I sprayed out the glyph? It's almost like the car is receiving its cursed energy from somewhere else, and I interrupted the flow." She took off her glasses and tapped her teeth with an earpiece. "I wonder if the flow could restart later. Or maybe it already has, and it needs to build up to a certain threshold. There's just so much we don't know."

"But either way, you're telling me Hellbringer could attack you again," Greyson said.

"I'm sorry, who?"

"Hellbringer." He nodded his chin at the car. "That's what I call it."

"You named your car *Hellbringer*?" Dru put her glasses back on. "Doesn't that sound a little, I don't know, fate-tempting-ish?"

"I had a good reason. I planned to document the whole rebuild online. I needed a catchy name. Didn't realize the full ramifications, obviously."

She peered over the top of her glasses. "You *named* your car Hellbringer."

He shrugged. "Thought about changing it when I realized I couldn't get a decent license plate. The closest I could get was H-E-L-L-B-G-R."

"Sounds like Hell Burger."

"Hell Booger," Rane called.

Greyson ignored her. "You get my point."

"I don't care if you named it Cupcake," Rane said, marching past them. "It's still evil. Let's take care of this thing the old-fashioned way." She tightened her fist around her ring and transformed into titanium.

Greyson's eyes went wide in surprise. He'd never seen her do that before, Dru realized. But there was no time to explain. She chased after Rane. "Wait, don't!"

Rane hesitated just long enough to shoot Dru an uncompromising glare. "Back off. This piece of junk tried to run me over."

"Well, pounding on it might just wake it up again. You really want to risk that? Besides, even if we melted this thing down into a pile of slag, it could still channel that demonic energy straight to Greyson. It has claimed him, and only a spell can break that connection."

Rane reluctantly lowered her fist. "Fine. Then let's push it off a cliff somewhere. Or ship it to California and drop it in the ocean."

"Distance doesn't matter." Dru shook her head. "Hellbringer could be at the bottom of the Mariana Trench, and it would still reach out to him. We're just lucky that it's right here, where we can do something about it."

"Oh, yeah." Rane turned human again with a whisper like sliding metal. "I feel *oodles* of lucky right now."

"So what do we do?" Opal said. All eyes turned to Dru.

She took a deep breath. This wasn't going to be easy.

Greyson pointed at Rane. "Did she just turn into metal?"

"It's okay. She does that all the time. Opal, you remember that time we had to break that curse of the lake deity?"

Opal put her hands on her hips. "I remember for a week after that my hair smelled like leftover sushi. I am *not* holding the ceremony bowl this time."

"Where were those circle diagrams?"

"The last two Stanislaus journals." Opal held up a finger as Dru dug through the bag of books. "But I am not planning on smelling like fish again. My cat just about licked me bald."

"Well, luckily for us," Dru said, pulling out the two padlocked journals, "it's not a lake deity this time."

"Oh. Well. Should be a piece of cake, then. Why would I possibly worry?"

Dru fished in her purse until she found a Starbucks napkin and a pen. She scribbled down a list of crystals: galena, sulfur, black tourmaline, amethyst, and a few others that might be helpful. "Do me a favor and find these, please. The clearest ones we have, not necessarily the biggest. The closer in size they are to each other, the better."

Opal sighed and leaned close. "Figures. I *should've* brought beer." But she took the list.

Dru spotted a spool of thick red wire hanging on the wall of Greyson's garage. She pointed it out to Rane. "Find a sharp knife, slit the insulation off the wire, and pull it off. All we need is the copper core."

"How much?"

"I'll tell you in a minute. But probably the whole roll."

As Rane nodded and headed for the spool, Greyson stepped up to Dru. "I feel like I should be part of this team effort."

"Good. For starters, don't turn into a demon again." She gave him a tired smile. "Best thing you can do? Draw out a chalk circle on the floor. Make sure it completely encloses the car. And it has to be as close to perfect as possible. We can't be too far off."

He turned to look at the car, frowning.

She drew out a circle in the air with her finger. "Get some string, tie it to something heavy to anchor it beneath the middle of the car, and use that as a compass to draw the circle." She squinted at the car. "But I don't know how you're going to work around the tires."

He scratched his chin, obviously trying to visualize a circle surrounding the car. He jerked a thumb toward his tools. "Floor jack. Don't worry, I'll take care of it."

"Thanks."

As he walked away, Dru felt a flush of satisfaction. For the first time, things might finally be under control. She watched Rane stripping wire and Opal sorting through rocks. Then she took the padlocked journals to an empty corner and sat down on the floor to study them.

It wasn't long before she realized things were about to get much worse.

17

MATHEMATICS OF A MADMAN

It took over an hour to sift through the cramped, sometimes psychotic handwriting of Nicolai Stanislaus. An eastern European pioneer of demonology, he had laid the theoretical groundwork for fighting the forces of darkness in the modern era. If anyone's expertise could be trusted, it was his.

But hidden in the faded, ink-stained journals was nothing but bad news.

Stanislaus likened demonic influence to radio waves, which were still a pretty revolutionary concept in his time.

Think not of the cursed artifact as evil in and of itself, but as an antenna which must receive its wireless signal from another source of unimaginable darkness, then channel it to its chosen victim.

That didn't sound good. From what Dru could make out, the car, Hellbringer, wasn't the actual source of Greyson's problem. It was just part of a larger system of evil. A receiver, of sorts.

A properly executed circle may break the connection and insulate the artifact from further evil influence, but only for a time.

"A little more vague, please?" she muttered. She could construct a magic circle like nobody's business, but how much time could she buy Greyson? A month? A day? An hour?

The journal didn't answer that. And it didn't say anything about kissing, either. She still didn't know why that worked, or whether it would ever work again. But sooner or later, she might get another chance to find out.

All Dru knew for sure was that trapping the car in a circle was a temporary solution at best. It was more like changing the channel, so the car couldn't receive any more transmissions from hell. But the source of darkness would look for another way to reach Greyson. Unless she could find the key to breaking the curse.

But how? Even if she managed to scramble Hellbringer so it was off the grid, what then? How could she find the source?

The tedious process of refining his calculations had driven Stanislaus completely insane. It was easy to see why.

Dru twisted her hair in knots trying to figure out the proper diagrams for the circle she needed. Finally she narrowed it down to a seven-point star, which wouldn't be the easiest thing in the world to recreate on a concrete floor. Especially using copper wire.

She dredged up some geometry from the depths of her memory and used her phone's calculator to figure out the angles, sketching out the circle on the back of a napkin.

Greyson leaned over her shoulder. "Shouldn't there be an app for that?"

Without looking up, Dru sighed. "That would be nice."

She wanted Greyson's help. But she couldn't shake her feelings of guilt.

She tried to think of Nate and all the good times they'd had. Not the angry Nate, the one who blamed her for everything, who refused to listen when she told him the plain truth. The one who wanted to take a break.

Take a break. What did that even mean?

She'd call him, she decided, when he got back from New York. He'd be much more likely to answer the phone after he talked the investors into signing on the dotted line. Then everything would be fine. They could work it all out over a romantic candlelight dinner at Chez Monet.

She frowned. Maybe a different restaurant next time.

He just needed a chance to calm down and pull himself together, that was all. And in the meantime, she had to do her best to keep Greyson safe.

Aching and stiff, Dru got to her feet. "Want to help me lay down the wire?"

"Wire?" Greyson said, following her across the garage.

"The chalk is just a guideline for the wire. I'll show you."

Together, they laid down a circle of copper wire around the car, using Greyson's chalk marks as a guide. Then they used seven straight lengths of copper wire to create the star inside the circle, twisting the ends where they met. They had to shove two of the wires beneath the edges of the tires to make them fit.

Dru sat cross-legged on the cold concrete floor, attaching each crystal to one point of the star with a loop of copper wire. She crawled completely around the circle, wiring up each crystal in turn, finishing with a handsome cluster of dusky purple amethyst.

Greyson came over to stand behind her. "What's that one for?"

"Amethyst is for protection. Just in case there's any psychic backlash when we scramble the car's reception. Could get a little zappy." She pointed at a shimmering black spike of tourmaline on her right. "That one will take most of the heat."

He nodded to her left, at a noxious yellow lump of sulfur. "And that one?"

"Sulfur acts like a filter. Soaks up negativity. When we activate the circle, the energy that the car's receiving right now has to get routed somewhere," she said. "Every crystal has a specific function. But where you put them in relation to each other is crucial, too. All the parts have to fit just right. They have to work together."

He considered that. "Like building an engine. Only, instead of a camshaft or lifters, you've got little rocks."

She cocked her head up and studied him, feeling a smile perk up the corners of her lips. "Yeah. Kind of like building an engine." She held her fingers an inch apart. "Maybe just a teensy bit different."

"I bet." He held out a hand. "Getting up?"

"Nope. I'm good right here. Ready to go."

"Speak for yourself," Opal said, tottering over in her new sparkling lemon-sherbet-yellow heels. "I said it before. I think this is a bad idea."

Rane crossed her arms. "You didn't say that before."

"Well, I *would* have, if anyone had asked my opinion."

Dru sat back with an exhausted sigh and admired the circle. "Good teamwork, everybody."

"Yay," Rane deadpanned. "You really think this is going to work?"

Dru gave her a sour look. "You might want to stand back a little."

Opal backed up halfway across the garage and said, "Okay, everybody. Here we go. Duck and cover. Hardhats if you got 'em."

"Everyone's a comedian." Dru cupped the amethyst beneath her hands, leaned over it, and focused as hard as she could.

Nothing happened.

She let out a tense breath, aware of everyone staring at her. "Just getting warmed up. Give it a second."

She closed her eyes. Focused again. Rane had called her a sorceress. Could she be right?

Dru tried to feel the magic rising inside her. Flowing through her. She willed the amethyst to charge up in her palm.

Nothing.

She strained, trying to summon up the power she'd felt earlier. But either she was too tired or she was doing something wrong.

She let out an explosive breath and sat back, shrugging her shoulders to let out some of the tension.

Opal checked her watch. "Well, if that doesn't work, I don't know what's gonna. You sure you followed those instructions right?"

"Of course I'm not sure. Stanislaus was an insane demonologist, not Martha Stewart." Dru tried to collect her thoughts. Something was blocking her.

Either the curse was an order of magnitude stronger than she thought, or Greyson's presence was interfering with the spell.

It had to be the strength of the curse. If her theory was right so far, then Greyson's proximity should make her spell *more* powerful, not less.

But why? What power lay within him that could amplify her magic so much? Could he possibly be a sorcerer without even knowing it?

She tried not to dwell on mysteries she couldn't answer. She didn't have to know how his presence helped her, exactly. She just had to accept that it did.

Closing her eyes again, she cupped the amethyst in one hand and held up the other. "Greyson?" she said softly.

Without hesitation, his strong fingers wrapped around hers. He gave her a reassuring squeeze.

Across the room, Opal sighed. "We're gonna be at this all night, mark my words. How late is Starbucks open around here?"

Dru opened her eyes. "You know, maybe that's not such a bad—" She didn't get a chance to finish.

An electrifying jolt shot through Dru's body, peaking in a sizzling flash that made her hair stand on end. The points of the copper star flared bright enough to light up the room.

Foul smoke from scorched wiring and melting metal prickled the back of her throat, and her mouth filled with a coppery aftertaste.

She sensed Hellbringer's infernal presence through the smoke. As it climbed across her skin, she felt the demon bound into the car, its very essence enshrined within the black-painted steel.

Hellbringer wasn't just a cursed artifact. The car itself was a demon in its own right.

As if it whispered into her ear, she could hear its raging desire to run wild across the land. To roam free in the wind.

And with that craving for freedom came a complete absence of fear. It wasn't afraid of death, destruction, or even being cast back into the pits of hell. The only thing Hellbringer feared was imprisonment.

Its solitude echoed through the smoke. The car had been locked away during most of its time on earth. Trapped. Unable to taste the freedom and relentless speed that defined the core of its being.

Hellbringer roused itself from exhaustion and reached toward her. Her consciousness briefly touched the swirling edge of Hellbringer's energy, a chaotic, primordial force that threatened to draw her in whole.

For a terrifying instant, she feared Hellbringer would pull her soul in through the crystal circle. Before the car could reconnect to whatever source of evil had cursed Greyson, Dru closed the magic circle, trapping Hellbringer inside.

Magic feedback jolted through her, again and again. Wave after wave of magical energy crashed against the bounds of the circle, pummeling Dru where she sat. But the circle did its work.

As Dru held on with all of her willpower, the intensity of each wave started to diminish. Strangely, she felt a pang of guilt, as if she had just kicked an animal.

A dangerous, aggressive animal who wanted to be free of its cage. An animal ruled by instincts and hungers that threatened innocent lives. But still, for the briefest moment, she could almost understand Hellbringer.

One after another, the crystals fractured, as if they'd been dropped from a great height. The individual lights of the dying rocks flared through her tightly closed eyelids. The afterimage of the copper circle, and the star within it, became a flash of orange zigzags on a red background.

Then it was over.

Dru dropped the burning hot amethyst and scrambled to her feet. When she stumbled, Greyson caught her. She sagged against him, her head spinning. A pounding headache shot up the back of her neck and throbbed across the top of her skull, making her nauseous.

The amethyst crystal crackled with vanishing motes of bright blue light, like a just-popped flashbulb. It gradually went dark, leaving behind nothing but a grayed-out cinder.

"Damn." Opal blinked. "Never seen a circle light up like that before. Did it work?"

"Think so," Dru murmured into Greyson's strong shoulder. And then she straightened up and saw his face.

The horns were back. Shorter than they'd been at the restaurant but still there nonetheless, where they hadn't been a minute ago. Worse, his eyes once again glowed red.

With a terrible sinking feeling, she backed away.

"Dru, what's wrong?" His voice trailed off as he saw his hands. The tips of his fingers ended in sharp black claws. He slowly turned them over, as if waiting for everything to go back to normal. It didn't.

Without another word, he rushed over to the oil-stained shop sink in the corner of the garage and bent to inspect his face in the streaked mirror.

Dru hurried after him. "It should have worked." Mind racing, she backtracked through all of her calculations, the combination of crystals, the configuration of the circle, trying to determine where she could have gone wrong. But there was no way to know.

Greyson's clawed fists tightened on the edge of the sink. "Then it's only a matter of time. Sooner or later, I'll become the demon again."

"Not as long as I'm here." She waited until she had his attention once more. "If we're going to cure you, Greyson, we need more information."

"About what?"

"That symbol under Hellbringer's hood," Dru said. "Did you put it there?"

Greyson shook his head no. "It was there when I got the car."

"And where did you get the car from?"

He hesitated. "An estate auction. Why, is that important?"

"It depends." An ominous feeling settled in the pit of her stomach. "Whose estate was it?"

18
LOT SIX HUNDRED
AND SIXTY-SIX

A s it turned out, the auction had been handled online, so Greyson didn't know whose estate it was.

Refusing to give up, Dru promised him that she would figure out their next move, no matter how long it took. She didn't imagine that it would take all night.

Opal brought them all coffee before the only nearby Starbucks closed. But she kept yawning so much, Dru couldn't stand the guilt and sent her home around midnight. Determined to stay and work this through to the end, Dru flipped back and forth through the pages of her old books, scribbling notes on napkins.

Eventually, Rane led her from the cold concrete floor to Greyson's cramped combination of living room and kitchenette. Even though Greyson insisted that he felt fine, Dru didn't feel comfortable leaving him unsupervised, and Rane refused to leave her side.

As the hours dragged on through the dead of night, Dru caught herself nodding off while trying to redo her Stanislaus calculations. She sucked down every last drop of coffee, but it wasn't enough. She was utterly exhausted. Her eyelids grew too heavy to stay open.

She took off her glasses and decided to rest her eyes. Just for a minute, she promised herself.

It seemed like only a moment later that Dru awoke with a start. Dawn sunlight streamed in around the edges of the window shades in Greyson's apartment. It fell in golden swaths across the cluttered living room, illuminating a pocked dartboard, a well-used weight bench, and a half-rebuilt engine stuffed with red rags.

Her phone told her it was six in the morning. "Son of a guano," she muttered under her breath, then scrambled to find her glasses. A blue plaid blanket dropped from her shoulders.

Glasses on, she looked around from where she lay on the couch, disoriented and foggy-headed in the morning light.

Greyson's furniture was old and worn, and that was being kind. A black-and-white checkered flag was draped in one corner. Car parts clustered on every available surface.

The wall behind her was covered with snapshots of old muscle cars in various states of disassembly and repair, punctuated by finished projects gleaming with fresh paint. The whole wall was an unfamiliar mishmash of bright paint, stripes, and shining wheels.

In the center of it all hung a framed snapshot of a scraggly-haired teenage boy, obviously Greyson in his high school years, shoulder to shoulder with a grinning freckled girl and a thin-faced middle-aged man in a leather jacket, the three of them leaning against what looked like a bright orange Corvette.

That was the only picture with people in it. The rest were nothing but cars.

The welcoming aroma of coffee filled the air. Greyson sat on a stool in his kitchenette, pecking at the keys of an old laptop. A black leather cowboy hat crowned his head as if it belonged there, hiding his horns. But his glowing red eyes were impossible to ignore.

They cut across the room to her, unreadable. "Morning," he said.

Looking at him now, in the clear morning light, there was only one thing she could think about.

The kiss.

The thought of it brought a rush of blood to her head, making her giddy. And confused.

She had no idea how to sort out what she was feeling. About him. About Nate. About the insane concept that she, herself, could actually be a sorceress. Everything was happening too fast.

From the armchair beside her, a chainsaw-like rumble made her jump. Until she realized it was Rane, snoring openmouthed. Most of

Rane's body was hidden under a blanket, but the arms and legs that stuck out didn't look like they were attached at the right angle, as if she'd simply splatted onto the couch from a high altitude.

Dru got to her feet carefully, afraid to wake Rane. But then again, Rane could probably sleep through an aboveground nuclear test.

As Dru crept toward the kitchenette, Greyson stirred and got out a mug emblazoned with a five-pointed Mopar logo.

"Thing only makes one cup at a time." Greyson opened a kitchen cabinet, revealing shelves of ramen noodles and Spam. He got out a single serving of coffee and started it brewing. "I don't get visitors all that much."

Dru gave him a sad smile. "Ever?"

His red eyes met hers briefly, then glanced behind her. She followed his gaze to a half-empty bag of cat food sitting on the floor by the back door.

"There's a stray cat, hangs out in the alley sometimes. A red tabby. Likes tuna."

"Really? What's his name?"

Greyson shrugged as if he didn't care, but a slight hesitation beforehand told her that he did. "Doesn't seem to need one. Mostly he responds to 'Want some food?'"

She watched Greyson as he fixed her a cup of coffee from his single-serve machine. Everything in his life seemed to be built around cars, not people. As if he had given up on any personal connections and devoted himself to things that couldn't talk back.

She cleared her throat. "So, who are the people in your photo? They seem nice."

He didn't answer at first. When he did, it was without meeting her gaze. "My family."

"Do they live around here?" In the silence that followed, she added nervously, "Do they work on cars too?"

He slid a steaming mug of coffee in front of her. "Cars can be tough to fix. But at least they *can* be fixed. Some things can't." Buried under his gruff tone, she could hear the hurt in his voice.

She decided it would be better to leave that topic alone. Whatever had happened with his family, Greyson seemed to have honed his mechanical skills to wall himself off from the human world.

No wonder he had forged such a strong connection to Hellbringer. The car attracted him, played to his biggest defenses, and his loneliness provided an opening for the demon's power. He was the perfect target.

"You said you needed info about the estate," Greyson said, interrupting her thoughts.

"That the car came from? Yes, absolutely. Did you find anything?"

By way of answer, he turned his laptop screen to face her. It was a list of auction items. A very long list.

She scrolled through it, not sure what she was looking for. She found the usual items she'd expect to see in a big estate sale: furniture, jewelry, miscellaneous antiques. But then things got a little strange.

A collection of rare insects. A medical autoclave. A sixteenth-century German tapestry depicting a scroll with seven wax seals.

"Well, that's something you don't see every day. Book of Revelation," she explained at his quizzical look. "Biblical prophecy about the end of the world. Who would want to hang that in their home?"

The deeper she got into the list, the weirder things became.

A stuffed Alpine ibex. A test tube incubator. An alphabetized collection of bat wings.

She pointed at the screen with a growing sense of dread. "This was no ordinary estate. Who was the owner?"

Greyson shook his head. "They don't give any names. But I did find an address in New Mexico. The weird thing is, when you look it up on a map, you can see the road, but no house. The road just ends."

"In the middle of the neighborhood?"

"No. Middle of the desert."

"So not exactly the sociable type." Slowly, Dru nodded. "That makes sense. I'll bet they had some obfuscation spells in place." Before he asked, she added, "Camouflage."

"So you think this person was a sorcerer?"

"Had to be. Monstrously powerful one, too. Or someone who made an infernal bargain."

Greyson didn't look convinced. "Or maybe just someone who liked to collect weird antiques."

She jabbed a finger at the screen. "Who else has a laboratory-grade fume hood and a vacuum pump in their house? And jars full of dead animal parts?"

Greyson's red eyes narrowed. "Maybe a veterinarian."

"Sure. A veterinarian who operates on *demons*." Dru kept scrolling through the list, more worried by the moment. "If this is all from one house, it must've been huge. There are over a thousand items here. Are there any books?"

"Think so." He took the laptop, typed for a moment, then turned it back to her.

Dru's jaw dropped open.

The Prophecies of Paloma.

Severina's Spirit Guide.

The Scripture of Ephraim.

Dru pointed at the last one. "That's part of the Wicked Scriptures. I thought they'd all been burned."

Greyson looked uneasy. "The Wicked Scriptures?"

"About everyone dying horribly in a fiery doomsday at the end of the world." She kept going down the list, and the books kept getting darker. "Some of these are seriously bad mojo from the Middle Ages. *Formulaes Apocrypha.* That's all about questionable studies into the nature of primordial destruction. And the *Treatise Maleficarum.* A who's who for the pits of hell." A horrifying thought seized her. "I can't believe they auctioned this stuff off to the public. You know what kind of creeps are going to buy these books?" She stood up and paced the tiny kitchenette, a hard knot forming in her stomach.

"Anything in here tell you how to undo what they did?"

"There's too much stuff here for one lone sorcerer. It had to be a group of sorcerers, all acting together. If even one of them was still around today, they wouldn't have let this stuff get auctioned. No way. Which means they're all dead," Dru said. "Whatever they were up to, it probably got them all killed. This is seriously worse than I thought. *Tons* worse."

A crash from the living room signaled that Rane was awake. She rolled to her feet and blinked in the morning light, looking stunned. "Hey. I miss anything?"

Dru just stirred her coffee and glanced at Greyson.

He lifted his leather cowboy hat, revealing his horns. "Morning."

"Ooh, still demon-y. Least you're not trying to kill anyone. And plus you're bitchin' stylish, so, win-win." Rane lurched across the living room, long arms stretching wide, mouth yawning open wider. "*Ahh* . . . Coffee. Black."

"Out of mugs," Greyson said. "She got the last one."

"Whatever. We'll share." Rane straddled a chair and picked up Dru's mug, downing it in three gulps before she set it down and tapped the rim for a refill.

"There's more." Dru pointed at the laptop. "Apparently, Hellbringer hails from some evil sorcerer group's mansion in New Mexico. Possibly haunted."

Rane draped a heavy arm over Dru's shoulders and hugged her close. Her skin radiated a sleepy warmth. "Cool. Road trip."

19
DON'T TRY THIS AT HOME

Nate's white Prius trundled southbound on the empty highway at exactly one mile per hour under the speed limit. Denver was hundreds of miles behind them. Ahead, endless hills of sunbaked New Mexico earth rolled out of the distance, evenly dotted with tufts of dry green scrub and spiky yucca. Beyond, dark clouds rose over the deep blue silhouettes of mountains, threatening to overtake the clear, bold sky.

Before they'd left, Rane had pointed out how much she liked seeing Dru in a "prom dress," which immediately made Dru insist on running home to get cleaned up and put on skinny jeans and some road-trip-worthy shoes.

Now, Dru slurped down the last syrupy drops of her Frappuccino through its overly long green straw and regretfully nestled the empty cup back into the holder.

As the desolate highway droned along beneath the tires, she wished Greyson would say something. Anything. He'd barely spoken a word in the last couple of hours. Even Rane was quiet in the back seat, possibly napping.

Dru kept wanting to ask Greyson how he was doing, but she held back. It was fairly obvious he didn't want to talk. Besides, who would be happy about being stuck in half-demon form, with horns, claws, and glowing eyes?

She felt terrible about his condition, though she hadn't caused it. At least she had broken Hellbringer's connection to whatever dark force was behind all of this. She presumed that kept Greyson from getting any worse. But she still didn't know how to break the curse for good.

"Just to keep you in the loop," Greyson said abruptly, breaking into her thoughts, "it's getting late, and we're getting closer to sunset. We need to pick up the pace."

Dru flexed her aching fingers on the steering wheel. "Well, I can't change the speed limit."

"Too late to point this out, but I do have a *much* faster car parked in my garage."

Dru shook her head resolutely. "No one is going anywhere in Hellbringer. That thing stays parked."

"Even after your spell? I was under the impression that you short-circuited the instrument of ultimate evil. Now it's just an ordinary car, right?"

"Still."

"Still, now you're wondering if you should've let me drive." He sounded sure of it. "You enjoy danger. You just don't want to admit it. That's why you're in this line of work." He turned his dark sunglasses toward her and gave her an unusually frank smile.

Part of that smile might have been from the potion he'd been sipping on all afternoon. She'd formulated a new potion before they left, a simpler one with more quartz infusions to strengthen his willpower and steel his resolve.

So far his demon symptoms hadn't gotten any better. But they hadn't gotten any worse, either. That was something.

"Believe me," she said, "I'm not a big fan of danger. The less, the better."

"You say that, but you're still driving us across the desert in search of some crazy haunted mansion that's not on any map. That's what I like about you. You're full of contradictions."

"Maybe," she admitted after a long moment, and a slow smile spread across her face.

It felt so great to be out of the city, on the open road, heading toward the unknown. Completely unlike her usual self, but unexpectedly invigorating. Like a cool drink of water when she didn't even know she was thirsty.

Plus, she was completely at ease with Greyson. Sitting next to him felt so effortless, so right. As if they'd known each other for years. Even the way he looked at her had a puppy-dog quality to it. The thought made her smile even wider.

He smiled back, teeth shining in the sun, red eyes still hidden behind his dark sunglasses. "Come on, you've got to be tired. Pull over and let me drive."

"Why on earth would I let you drive? Especially after you've been drinking out of that skull-shaped bottle all afternoon?"

He scrutinized the bottle. "I thought you made this potion lower-octane."

From the back seat, Rane barked out a laugh.

Greyson turned toward her, sunglasses flashing. "I'm sorry. Question from our studio audience?"

Rane leaned forward between the seats, wearing Greyson's leather cowboy hat. Dru did a double take, but decided not to ask.

"Dude," Rane said, "she's not going to let you drive her boyfriend's car. Period."

Greyson just grunted and faced front again.

An awkward silence descended. The desert slid by, endless.

"Speaking of your boyfriend," Greyson said finally. "Isn't he going to wonder where his car is?"

"No, Nate's in New York. As long as I get back to town in time to pick him up at the airport, everything's going to be fine."

Greyson glanced at his watch. "So what's Nate's deal, anyway? What kind of sorcerer is he?"

"Oh, no, he's a dentist."

Greyson raised an eyebrow. "A *dentist*?"

"What?" she said. "Why does everyone always say it like that? There's nothing wrong with a dentist."

"I just never pictured you . . . Never mind."

"Pictured me what?"

Greyson just shook his head.

"Pictured me *what*?" Dru slapped her palm on the steering wheel.

"Naked?" Rane said from the back seat.

"Hey." Dru pointed back over her shoulder. "Pipe down back there."

"Greyson, do not question the dentist thing." In the rearview mirror, Rane's half-lidded eyes scowled at Dru from beneath the hat brim.

"Please, please tell me you're not going to launch into your whole flower manifesto again. Are you?"

"No . . ." Dru sighed. "Anyway, I wouldn't exactly call it a manifesto."

Greyson cocked his head at Dru, waiting.

She sighed. "Rane doesn't want to hear it."

He folded his arms. "Then it must be good."

A warm glow spread through her. She couldn't help herself. "Okay. So, the thing about flowers—"

Rane took off the cowboy hat and bopped her with it. "Jeez-*us*. Not again."

"*So* . . ." Dru said. "You remember in that restaurant, Chez Monet? They had all the flowers?"

"My recollection's a little fuzzy."

"Right. Sorry. Well, everywhere you look, they have these gorgeous vases of miniature red peonies. Beautiful. And they happen to be my favorite flower."

"That's why Nate picked the restaurant for you?"

"No." *That would've been nice*, she thought. "No, that's just their thing. But that's not the point. I've always loved peonies because they're pretty unusual. But typically they don't get a lot of respect. Right?"

Greyson shrugged.

"Okay, well, what kind of flowers get all of the attention? Roses. Red roses. Because they're all dramatic and bold and romantic. Right? Well, sorcerers . . . I've known a bunch. A *bunch*. And they tend to be long on drama and short on commitment. They're like thorny roses." She looked up in the rearview mirror at Rane. "Present company excluded."

"No, go ahead," Rane said, tossing the hat over her shoulder. "I am *so* thorny."

Dru turned her attention back to the road. "And what I really want is a red peony. Less dramatic, sure, but completely dependable." She let out a breath. "You see what I'm saying?"

"No." His sunglasses made his expression unreadable. "But obviously you need to get more flowers."

"I mean I just want a normal life."

"Except," Rane said, "there's one big, fat problem with your theory. In reality, Nate's an a-hole."

Greyson tried to hide his smile.

Dru waved it off. "Oh, don't worry. It's just, you know . . . a little thing we're going through."

Rane leaned forward between the seats. "Okay, dude. Let me ask you. When a guy says, 'We should take a break,' what does that mean? Isn't that kind of like saying, 'I'm a selfish jackwad who only cares about myself'?"

Dru tried to shrug it off. "I'm sure he didn't mean it," she said quietly, but that sounded hollow even to her.

"Told her this on the *phone*," Rane said.

Greyson visibly winced. To Dru, he said, "Are you okay?"

She nodded, feeling a hard lump form in her throat.

"He's seeing someone else?" Greyson said.

"No!" Dru said at the exact moment that Rane said, "Probably."

Greyson made a dismissive wave. "Sorry, not my business. Just have to seriously question any guy who'd give you up."

Dru just glared at Rane. *Probably?* How could she even think that?

Rane caught the look and shot it right back. "Sorry, have I entered an alternate universe where Nate can do no wrong?"

"Good thing is you've seen your dentist's true colors," Greyson said. "Maybe there's someone out there who *will* treat you right."

Dru kept her gaze locked on the empty highway ahead. This conversation was spinning out of control, and suddenly all she wanted to do was stop the car and get out. But they were stuck together in the middle of the desert.

No one else could understand how badly she wanted to just live a stable life, for once. Because deep down inside, she didn't feel like she belonged in the weird world of magic. She'd never been a sorceress.

Until now.

The real question, the scary question, the one lurking at the edge of her mind like a dozing bear that could maul her at the slightest provocation: could she handle this? All this magic?

Or would it burn her out, crush her, leave her broken and unfulfilled and alone, like so many sorcerers she had known over the years?

She glanced at the clock on the dashboard. Greyson was right. They had to hurry if they wanted to make it before nightfall.

With a twinge of reluctance, she forced herself to press down the gas pedal and edge up past the speed limit.

It didn't solve anything, really, because the desert was still just as vast and endless. But it felt good. It felt like the tiniest taste of freedom.

From behind, Rane placed her strong hands on Dru's shoulders, giving them a quick squeeze. "You'll be okay."

"I know," Dru said with a sigh, tilting her head until she could see Rane's eyes. "We'll work it out."

"One way or another," Rane said.

Dru risked a glance over at Greyson and watched the stubbly outlines of his face as he stared out at the dry rolling hills. Wondering what he was thinking, what he was seeing out there in the unfocused distance. What he was keeping locked away inside.

He sat up suddenly, squinting into the distance.

She tensed. "What?"

He pointed. Branching off the main road, a cracked narrow blacktop driveway stretched away into the distance, as if some giant had used a black magic marker to draw a single dark line across the desert.

"We're here," Greyson said. "That has to be the address from the auction. The mansion where the sorcerers lived."

And likely where they died, Dru thought.

20
EVIL IN MIDCENTURY MODERN

Despite the illusion of nothingness that showed on the map, their destination stood out clearly against the desert. It gleamed in the distance long before they reached it, a shining white heat ripple against the drab earth tones of the dry hills. As they approached, and the building's outlines became clearer, Dru stared in disbelief.

It was a mansion, all right. But this was definitely not the haunted mansion she had expected.

The structure was all curves, without a single angle to be seen. Some nameless architect had sculpted it from an organic expanse of domes, curved walls, and flying buttresses that soared up and around with all the majesty of Saturn's rings.

It looked like the entire contents of a NASA warehouse had been melted together, painted space-capsule white, and dotted with portholes and wide oval windows.

Overall, the effect was hauntingly beautiful, but at the same time downright weird.

The blacktop ended, and the road became dirt. A faint track forked off to the right of the bumpy unpaved road, perhaps headed around behind the mansion. But from the looks of it, no one had used it in decades. Dru kept heading straight.

As she rolled the car to a stop on the long driveway, she craned her head up for a better look. The dark round windows that dotted the house seemed to stare down at them, unblinking, like the eye sockets of a sun-bleached skull. Dru stared back, searching for any sign of what lay inside, but the windows revealed nothing of the mansion's secrets.

A gust of wind buffeted the car, plinking grains of sand across the windshield. Nothing else moved in the still desert.

After trading glances with Greyson and Rane, Dru unbuckled her seatbelt and stepped out of the air-conditioned car into the prickling heat. Somehow, the New Mexico air failed to warm the chilly presence of the sorcerers' mansion.

The sound of the car doors shutting was oddly loud in the desert.

"Serious trouble, D," Rane said behind her. Dru turned to look, pulse quickening.

But Rane merely waved at the front of the Prius, now a disgusting carpet of splattered bugs and reddish road dust. "Nate'll blow a gasket when he sees this."

With a wry smile, Dru hitched her purse up onto her shoulder. "I'm sure Nate will survive."

"And hopefully," Greyson said, surveying the sorcerer's mansion through his dark sunglasses, "so will we."

Together, they made their way up the curved walkway. The front door proved to be a huge arch split by double doors made of tinted glass.

"No one lives here anymore, right?" Dru asked, looking at Rane, then Greyson. His forehead wrinkled in concern. Rane just shrugged.

After a moment of hesitation, Dru swallowed and tried the doors. Locked.

"All right, give me some room," Rane said, edging past Dru. "Glass doors always make a mess when they break."

"Wait, hold up," Greyson said. With a metallic jangle, he pulled a key ring out of his jacket pocket. "When I was cleaning Hellbringer the first time, I found these in the glove box."

"Seriously?" Rane said, sounding disappointed as Greyson unlocked the door with a soft click. "That was my only chance to have fun on this trip."

The doors swung inward with a thin screech, as if the steel hinges contained tiny demons rudely awakened from a deep sleep.

The domed foyer inside led away into darkness, punctuated by thick beams of sunlight streaming in from the round windows. The cool air wafting out through the open door, refreshing as it felt, also carried an unwelcome tinge: the tang of recently disturbed dust, along with years of sun-baked loneliness, and the moldering odor of forgotten things.

Before heading inside, Dru took a last look back over her shoulder at the parched desert hills, searching for any sign of life. But the dirt road was empty all the way to the horizon. Nothing moved except the clouds creeping in from the distance and the blistering disk of the slowly setting sun.

As Greyson moved to enter the foyer, Dru spotted a faint line of symbols etched into the floor just beyond the threshold. She stopped him with an outstretched hand. "Wait. See those?"

Rane bent down to get a closer look at the symbols, frowning. "Rat signs? Here?"

Greyson folded his arms. "Rat signs?"

"The correct term is *sorcisto*, the language of magic," Dru explained, digging in her purse for a ulexite crystal. "At some point, sorcisto got shortened to *sorcio*, which is Italian for 'mouse' or 'rat.' And since these signs are popular with the more, um, *alternative* sorcerers, they're called rat signs." She pulled out her round-cornered crystal of ulexite.

"Oh, sure," Rane said. "*Now* you have your TV rock on you."

The ice-clear ulexite was banded with countless milky lines, all perfectly straight. Pressed against the skin of her forehead, it felt like the grain of unfinished wood. In ordinary hands, ulexite formed a natural lens, transmitting light with fiber-optic clarity. Hence the nickname, TV rock.

But Dru had a more esoteric use for it—sensing enchantments hidden from normal sight.

As she suspected, the crystal revealed a faint magical barrier twining across the floor just inside the entrance. Untold years ago, the pale, brassy glow had probably burned hellishly bright. But whoever had cast the spell hadn't tended to it in years, and the magic had frayed from disuse until it couldn't stand even the slightest disturbance.

Dru carefully stepped across the threshold onto the polished concrete floor. The broken seal flickered slightly at her passage, then faded back into its slumber. "Keep a lookout for more signs like that. If they put a ward on the front door, there are probably more."

Their footsteps echoed hollowly as they explored the house. Every oddly shaped room sat empty and forlorn.

No furnishings, no decorations. Just subtle shifts of color on the walls and floors where things had sat for decades before being carted away. The few rooms that sported any carpet were worn from innumerable footfalls and littered with furniture indentations, but whatever had made them had vanished in the auction.

She could still sense traces of powerful magic from spells cast in and around the house in the past. But that was all they were. Traces. Brief, sour tingles in the back of her throat. A ghostly whisper along the back of her neck.

There had been powerful magic here once. But it was long gone now. Everything was gone.

Stumped, Dru wandered through one bare room after another until she stood in the center of the house, an echoing open space with a vaulted ceiling where all of the mansion's wings met at a starfishlike crest. The long blades of a ceiling fan spread out like the rotors of a military helicopter, motionless and silent.

With clanging footsteps, Rane mounted a nearby spiral staircase and headed upstairs.

"Wait," Dru called after her. "Let's not split up."

"Dude, this place is dead empty." Rane stomped her way up to the next level and hung over the railing, her long hair framing her face. "Total wild goose chase. Unless you know something I don't?"

"All I know is that we need to find some kind of clue about who created Hellbringer and why." Dru blew out a frustrated breath as Rane shrugged and wandered away through an upstairs archway. "Guess this was a waste of time," Dru muttered.

"Could be worse," Greyson said, crossing the vast room to stand beside her, his thumbs hooked into the belt loops of his jeans. "Look, if there's anything in here, we'll find it."

"Really? Because in places like this, I usually get a heebie-jeebie vibe. Not here."

"Something's here," Greyson said with a subtle nod. "I know it."

The utter certainty in his tone caught Dru's attention. "How exactly?"

He turned to look directly into her eyes. Though his eyes still glowed red, there was no false bravado there, no bluffing, just cool confidence. "Gut feeling."

"And you get gut feelings like this often?"

"Only when trouble's on the way." He shook his head. "Can't explain it, really. But when something bad is close by, I get a bad feeling."

"Except when it comes to Hellbringer."

He scuffed his boot on the old carpet. "That's a special case."

"Hmm." With anyone else, a mysterious "gut feeling" could be dismissed as everyday intuition, Dru thought. But what if this was something more?

What if Greyson's hunches had a magical explanation?

She folded her arms. "When did this start, this feeling? When you first got the car?"

"No. Been happening ever since I was little." His expression softened. "My dad used to call it my sixth sense. But that was his thing, not mine."

"What do you mean?"

"My old man used to do magic tricks. Read your mind. Make things disappear, pull a quarter out of your ear, all that. But he took it to a whole new level. You could bring him a broken toy, and he'd just snap his fingers, and it would be fixed." Greyson raised his fingers and snapped them. "Just like that. I don't know how he did it. He said it was magic. He seemed to believe it. So did my sister."

Dru studied him for a long moment, the chiseled features of his face, the openness in his gaze. "And what about you? Do you think it was real magic?"

"No." He looked away, at nothing in particular, and the muscles in his jaw worked. "Maybe. Tell you the truth, these days I just don't know anymore."

"But he fixed things. Just like you fix cars. Like Hellbringer." Dru nodded to herself. The pieces of Greyson's puzzle started to connect in her mind. There were still big gaps, but the overall picture emerged. "Greyson, listen, if your dad was a sorcerer . . ."

Greyson's red gaze became guarded, wary.

"If he had magic in his blood, then chances are, you do, too. But you've never had any training."

"Hey, I didn't even know real magic *existed* until I met you."

"Well, there's a term for people with untapped magical potential. *Arcana rasa*. It's rare. Happens to be dangerous, too. It makes you a magnet for the forces of darkness." She started to pace. It all clicked. "That explains why my crystals get more powerful when you're around. We have a sort of magical synergy."

He chewed that over for a moment. "You trying to tell me that I'm somehow, what, turbocharging your crystal powers?"

"Basically, yes. With your untapped magical energy." She wasn't completely certain, but the theory fit the facts. "Greyson, if you really are *arcana rasa*, that makes you a target. Demons crave power. That's why they try to feed on those with potential. But having that energy inside you also gives you a chance to fight the demon off. If you know how."

He gave her a long, lingering look. "What if I don't want this power?"

"If I'm right about this, and I could be wrong, then it doesn't matter if you want it or not. Whether or not you use your potential, it's still inside you, trying to come out."

"Because I'm close to you."

"We're sort of on the same frequency. Our magic is intermingling."

He stepped closer, and his nearness made it suddenly hard to think. "What does that mean, exactly? For us?"

She wanted him to back away, and at the same time she desperately wanted him to come closer. The two conflicting desires felt as if they would tear her apart. "Ever since we met, your magical potential has been spilling over into mine. Making my crystals more powerful. But in the long run, this could turn out badly. It's dangerous for both of us."

"I don't know about that." His voice dropped low and urgent. "If you kiss me again, it won't turn me back into a demon, will it?"

Her cheeks flushed hot, and somehow that only made everything worse. She dropped her gaze. "No. That only worked once, when we made that, um, connection."

"Well, I don't know much about magic," he said. "But whatever kind of connection we've got, I don't want to break it. Not if it makes us stronger."

She started to tremble. She wanted to reach out to him. Wanted to kiss him again. But she couldn't. She didn't know if it was wrong, exactly, but it didn't feel right.

"Things could spiral out of control," she said softly. "Someone could get hurt. Literally."

"Maybe," he said, stepping so close that she could feel the heat radiating from his body as he reached for her. "Or maybe being a little out of control is just what you need right now."

21
BORN UNDER A BAD SIGN

The spiral staircase creaked and popped as Rane swung one leg over the upstairs railing, straddling it. "I *so* want to live in this place. You guys find anything? *Oh*."

Dru had already stepped back away from Greyson by the time Rane's loaded "Oh" echoed through the vast central room. But it was too late.

Rane slid down the length of the banister, corkscrewing down until she hopped off onto the mansion floor, fixing Dru with a knowing look all the way.

Dru cleared her throat. "So, um, we should keep searching. Look for more rat signs. On the floor, the walls, anywhere. They could mark another warding spell. Or maybe a secret door." She turned her back on Greyson, then immediately felt as if she'd lost something precious. She could feel his presence behind her. The intensity of his gaze on her back.

"Okay, secret doors," Greyson said finally. His footsteps exited the room. "We still haven't checked the garage yet."

Dru nodded, trying to avoid Rane's penetrating eyes.

"So." Rane feigned wide-eyed innocence as she sauntered over. "Whatcha doin', D?"

"Nothing. Let's just keep going."

"Uh-huh."

"Quit looking at me like that."

"Over here," Greyson called from the doorway. "Hellbringer must have been kept down this way."

Thankful for the distraction, Dru followed after Greyson, who led them past rows of porthole windows that looked out on the empty miles of desert that surrounded them. The heat from the afternoon sunlight warmed Dru's skin as she passed through each thick beam of light. The darkness in between was chilly by comparison.

The garage turned out to be a vast dome, perfectly round and easily big enough to fit a trio of Greyhound buses. Hangar-style doors curved around one quarter of the perimeter, opposite an expansive window that dominated the other side.

Like the rest of the mansion, the echoing garage seemed spotless at first glance, but a closer look revealed drifts of dust and unidentifiable scraps of trash littered about. The smells of age and blown-in desert sand thickened the air and made it difficult to breathe.

Another scent lurked in the still air. An underground scent, the smell of dirt and long-buried rocks. The skin on the back of Dru's neck prickled as she realized what it reminded her of.

A freshly dug grave.

The echoes of Greyson's boots ricocheted around the garage. He studied the floor as he went. When he reached the exact center, he knelt down and ran his fingers across a streak of tire marks.

Dru crossed the cavernous garage to the massive window, a curved grid of glass nearly as wide as a city street. It looked out over the desert hills behind the mansion, toward the blue smudge of the mountains on the horizon. Ominous clouds roiled in the distance, reaching out forbidding fingers toward the mansion even as she watched, casting a chilling shadow across the landscape.

In the middle distance, the monotony of the desert ended at a brown rocky ridge. The clouds above seemed to change course around it, leaving it in an oasis of sunlight. Something seemed odd about the way the afternoon sunlight slanted through the rocks near the ridge. But it was too far away to tell why.

Dru took off her glasses, breathed on the lenses and wiped them off on her shirt, then tried again.

Squinting hard, she could barely make out a strange rock formation rising up over the ridge. A stone archway.

But not a natural, lumpy, wind-scoured arch.

This archway had machinelike precision. A perfectly smooth, sculpted shape. Something made by human hands.

She couldn't be sure at this distance, but it looked easily big enough to drive a truck through. And it happened to be in the middle of the desert, on private land, far from anyone's eyes.

Hidden from everyone . . . except the sorcerers who lived in this mansion.

"*That's* not a coincidence," she muttered. As soon as they were done here, she decided, they needed to check that out.

"Found more of those rat signs," Greyson called, crossing the garage. When he reached the far wall, a door-sized section swung open with a raucous metal screech, trailing loose cobwebs. Beyond, a rough-hewn rock staircase descended into darkness.

Rane strode toward the opening, transforming into metal with a faint scraping noise. "Behind me," she ordered.

Greyson stood his ground, body tensing, ready to fight. "I didn't even touch it."

"You're tainted by the demon," Dru said, hurrying over. "Just your presence may have triggered something. Let me have a look, make sure there aren't any warding spells." She dug her rounded rectangle of ulexite out of her purse. It confirmed her fear.

With the crystal pressed to the skin between her eyebrows, it was easy to see the magical warding spell beyond the secret door. Unlike the ward at the front door, this one hadn't been triggered until the door was opened, so it was still very much intact. And dangerous.

A curtain of frozen energy hummed just inside, giving off an electric mosquitolike whine. Flickers of sinister blue magic crackled and branched across its surface. As each strike faded, a jagged new one flashed out closer to her. She had the uncanny feeling it was tracking her movements as she inspected the doorway.

She was extremely careful not to touch anything. "This one's at full strength, and it's nasty. But it's only on the inside of the doorway, not the outside. Looks like it might let us in, but never let us back out."

"Like a Roach Motel. For people," Rane said, sounding grudgingly impressed. She transformed back to human form with a faint metal hiss. "If there's anything truly freaky evil in this whole place, it's got to be down there. So we go in, right?"

Dru studied the pulses of energy crawling around the inside of the doorway. Without knowing the original spell, it could take days to figure out how to disarm it.

"That was a rhetorical question, by the way," Rane said. "Of *course* we're going in."

"Just hang on," Dru murmured, looking hard. As she slowly paced back and forth in front of the doorway, the magical lightning tracked her movements, lashing out from every edge.

Except the bottom right corner.

Dru kept pacing back and forth to be sure, but it seemed as if that corner was a dead spot in the spell. Possibly the sorcerer who set this up had left it there deliberately, as a means of escape if necessary. Or possibly it had just been a casual mistake while weaving the spell, a slip of the wrist that left a tiny opening she could exploit.

"I have an idea." Dru lowered the ulexite crystal and braced herself for a wave of vertigo as her eyes adjusted back to ordinary sight. Thankfully, it passed quickly. Without the crystal, the ward was invisible, but just as deadly. "Greyson, what happens if you put the wrong fuse in a car's fuse box?"

He shrugged. "Depends. If the fuse is too low, it could blow right away. If it's too high, you might burn out something important before the fuse finally goes. Why?"

"Because I have a fuse on me." She knelt down and dug through her purse until she found a cotton-candy-colored crystal two inches across. "Pink halite shorts out patterns of negative energy. If we're lucky, this could short-circuit the warding spell, take it off-line, at least for a little while."

"Halite," Greyson said. "Isn't that rock salt?"

"Yes, indeedy. It'll dissolve harmful spells *and* de-ice your sidewalk." She hesitated, then held out her hand. "I could probably use your help with this."

"I thought you said it was dangerous, combining our magic."

"It is." She jutted her chin at the dark doorway and its now-invisible spell. "But that ward is even more dangerous."

With a slow nod, Greyson gently took her hand. At that instant, as if a switch had been flipped on, a newfound strength surged through her. As much as she feared the intensity of their magical connection, she thrilled at the way the halite crystal began to glow in her other hand with a soft, rosy light.

Carefully, she slid the crystal along the floor, into the weak corner of the spell. She felt a tiny jolt up her arm, and an insectlike whine buzzed through her ears for a moment before it faded away.

"Huh," Dru said, letting go of Greyson. "I think it's—"

A shattering noise blasted out of the doorway on a gust of hot wind. Flaming embers twined and curled in the empty doorway, like burning moths, leaving red-hot trails in their wake. A stench of hot soot filled the air.

Dru checked with the ulexite crystal again. The shimmering curtain of energy was gone. But the original spell remained inscribed across the width of the threshold, like neon graffiti. It pulsed erratic bursts of energy into the pink halite.

"The ward is down for now. It'll come back, but as long as we leave that halite in place, we'll be safe." Dru lowered the ulexite and blinked. A cobweb-choked torch hung from a rusted bracket at the top of the stairs. She stepped carefully through the doorway and pulled down the torch. "Anybody got a light?"

They traded glances.

Abruptly, Rane grabbed the metal basket at the tip of the torch and struck her flint ring against it. Sparks brightened in the darkness, and the torch lit with a satisfying flicker of flame, casting a warm glow on the hewn rock steps.

She grinned, holding up her ring finger. "Sparky rock."

"Oh. Handy." Brandishing the torch, Dru moved toward the dark stairwell.

"Wait." Greyson put a firm hand on her arm. "Let me."

"Both of you, hold up." Rane tightened her fist around her titanium ring and transformed. "If anything's going to hit us," she said, "I want it to hit me first."

Before Dru could argue, Rane headed down, surprisingly quiet on her metal feet.

They descended the steep, narrow steps into stale air thick with the cold scents of foul chemicals and long-dead fires.

The transition from bright, open rooms and desert sun to the darkness of tight, cobweb-shrouded stone raised a deep animal fear in Dru, a desire to turn around and flee this sinister place, with its cold, shoulder-cramping walls and dangling webs.

A voice inside her told her to get away while she still could, before whatever waited in the blackness below rushed up out of the shadows.

With every step deeper, the torch flame reflected off Rane's silvery skin, multiplying a hundred times off the moving curves of her muscled arms, her flowing hair. She took each step with intent, like a soldier marching to war. She never looked back.

The certainty in Rane's lead gave Dru confidence. Rane had done things like this before. She lived to fight the forces of evil.

But now that she thought about it, Dru realized she had always heard Rane's experiences related from the safety of the shop's front counter, and her stories always ended in triumph.

The sorcerers who never returned didn't live to tell their stories.

She repressed a shiver.

After a seemingly endless descent, the passage opened onto a ledge. Above them, the rock soared away in a rough-hewn ceiling.

Dru raised the torch high. They'd entered a dome-shaped chamber, itself easily the size of the mansion above. From the ledge where they stood, near the top, narrow stone steps curved down to the floor, perhaps three stories below.

The torchlight fell softly on the floor far beneath them. It was crowded with benches, scientific apparatus, storage tanks, and a hundred unidentifiable things, all long abandoned. A sorcerer's workshop like none she had ever imagined. Whatever research had taken place here in the deep darkness, it had been executed on a massive level. A veritable factory of magic.

Greyson grunted. "Guess the estate auctioneers missed something."

It was too difficult to see much from this height, with only one torch to light the way. She handed it to Greyson and brought out the ulexite crystal again.

Through its watery effect, she saw the subtle background glow of a thousand arcane objects. Mostly books and spell components, it looked like, stacked on shelves that clustered into islands between workbenches and wide, shallow pits whose purpose eluded her.

The distant center of the chamber was completely clear and empty, except for four trenches arranged like the points of a compass. They still glowed with the remains of a long-ago spell. A spell powerful enough to leave its mark years, perhaps decades, later.

Rane peered out into the darkness past the ledge. "This place looks dead to me. You see anything, D?"

"It's not dead," Greyson said, his voice low and urgent. "We're being watched. I can feel it."

Dru lowered the ulexite and shot a questioning look at Greyson.

The torchlight flickered on the chiseled planes of his forehead and jaw, leaving his eyes in shadow. A faint, ruddy glow circled his irises, like the dying rays of sunset reflecting off red clouds. "That trouble I told you about? I can feel it. It's down there."

22

EVE OF DESTRUCTION

Together, they descended the stone staircase that ringed the outside edge of the underground chamber. Earlier, Dru had felt claustrophobic and trapped. But in this wide-open cave, she felt exposed and vulnerable.

As if a thousand eyes watched her, but she could see no one.

As they reached the bottom of the steps, Dru took the torch back. Its light fell on dusty, bare light bulbs suspended from thick black wires over every workbench. The power lines rose up into the shadows, strung from dangling ropes or wires, and vanished into the darkness. Here and there, brown copper pipes snaked along the ground, making right angles, their seams green with corrosion.

"This place has power and water," Dru said. "We need to find the controls. If they still work."

"I'll take care of the mechanicals," Greyson said. "You handle the magic."

He turned to go, but Dru caught his arm. "Wait. We can't split up. We only have one torch."

"Keep it," Greyson said, his red eyes glowing. "These demon eyes aren't all bad. I can see just fine." With that, he vanished into the darkness.

"Okay, creepy." Rane watched after him for a moment, then turned her attention to the workbenches around them. "So. Serious laboratory these guys built down here. Or maybe a bomb shelter."

Dru held the torch up high, casting a warm flickering light on a workbench full of glass beakers and flasks, then a shelf full of old books and stacks of rolled-up parchment. "Whatever this place is, I hope something down here tells us how to break Greyson's curse."

She had no idea where to even begin looking. She tried to remember which direction she'd seen the four long trenches that still glowed with the remnants of a vanished spell.

Behind Dru, a metal drawer shrieked open, making her jump. She turned.

Rane, still in metal form, bent over an open drawer, examining the contents. "Rocks," she said flatly. "Your specialty, not mine. You want to look?" She slammed the drawer and yanked open another. The metal squealed.

"Rane!" Dru barked, hurrying over to her.

"What? I'm not touching anything."

"There might be someone else down here. They'll hear you!"

"Well, we've also got the only flaming torch in the whole freakin' place. So we're not exactly stealthy." Rane slammed that drawer and moved on to a workbench stacked with glass jars holding some kind of biological specimens. "Do you want any of those crystals in there?"

"Crystals?" Dru opened up the drawer Rane had just closed, but with considerably more care.

Rich purple amethyst. Iridescent tiger's-eye. Splintered black tourmaline. She gasped. Unwrapping a bundle of black oilcloth, now stiff with age, she found a gorgeous wand of radiant green vivianite like none she'd never seen.

There were easily a dozen major crystals in here, each one more fabulous than the last. Ten times—maybe a hundred times—better than the stuff she could afford to stock in the shop. She crammed a few of the smaller ones into her purse until it threatened to burst its seams.

In the last drawer, she found an ugly mud-colored lump labeled "Coprolite."

"Yuck." She turned up her nose.

Rane must have seen the look on her face, because she instantly appeared at Dru's shoulder, shining silver in the torchlight. She jutted her chin at the drawer. "What's that one?"

"We don't want it, trust me." Dru shut the drawer.

Rane immediately yanked it open again, making the brown lump roll over on its bed of green felt. "Why, what's up with it? Demon stone? Ultimate evil? What?"

"No. Just coprolite," Dru said, making a face. "It's fossilized dinosaur . . . um . . . poo."

After a surprised moment of silence, Rane seized the brown lump and held it up in her metal fingers. "Fossilized dinosaur shit? Seriously? That's a thing?"

"We don't have time for this. Forget the rocks. Look for anything that speaks 'demon spell' to you."

Rane pulled her head back. "You mean, like, *literally* speaks to me?"

Dru sighed, but it came out as a nervous stutter, as the agitation kept building up inside her. "I saw some kind of magic pits in the floor. I think they were this way. Come on."

They wandered past lines of half-burnt candles, battered cauldrons, a desk stacked high with books and loose papers.

Dru had already walked by a pinned-up drawing of the stone archway before she realized what it was. She hurried back and looked it over. A St. Louis–style archway with a stone ramp leading up to it and magical notes scribbled all around it. "That's the archway out back!"

"Guess so," Rane said, sounding unimpressed.

Dru studied the symbols scrawled around the edge of the paper. The first looked like football uprights turned upside down. The second symbol was a circle with a diagonal line drawn across it. "*Sekura koridoro*," she translated. "'Secure passageway.' The symbol below that says that this is a safe road to follow."

"Road?" Rane said.

"Not literally a road. Could mean some kind of escape route." She pointed to a flattened hexagon symbol, just like the one Salem had spray-painted on her door, and the column of symbols below it. "*Kristalo.* 'Crystal magic unlocks the road.' Whatever that means."

"Hey!" Rane excitedly punched her shoulder. "Maybe these nutjobs managed to build a portal to the causeways."

Dru shook her head. "Don't you think if the causeways ever existed, somebody would have found a portal by now?"

"Maybe there *aren't* any portals anymore," Rane retorted. "That's why they built one."

Dru fought the urge to roll her eyes.

"Their generator is dead," Greyson said, emerging from the darkness into the torchlight. "We're stuck with the torch. Did you find anything?"

"Just this, whatever it is." Dru waved a hand at the diagram of the archway. Turning to Rane, she said, "I highly doubt it's a portal to the causeways."

"The what?" Greyson said.

Dru sighed. "According to the stories, way long ago, ancient sorcerers built portals and tunnels through the netherworld. Shortcuts from one place to another. You enter in Rome and come out in Cairo, that sort of thing. And, if you believe everything you read, some pretty scary sorcerers supposedly used the netherworld as their personal domain. Building fortresses there. Safeguarding their greatest treasures. Carrying out unspeakable experiments. Creating an empire of magic in the netherworld. And all of their bridges and roads, those are the causeways." Dru shook her head. "But they're a myth. No one's ever found the causeways."

"Whatever." Rane yanked down the drawing and folded it up. "We're taking this with us."

A photo slipped off the table and fluttered to the floor. Dru picked it up, and a jolt of recognition went through her when she saw the black-and-white snapshot.

Four women and three men alternately stood or sat somewhere in the desert. The men all had long sideburns and shaggy hair, two of them with mustaches, one with a cowboy hat. The women wore bell-bottoms, crazy-patterned dresses, and hairstyles that Dru hadn't seen outside of old family photos from the sixties.

No one smiled. They all made the same cryptic sign: one hand held palm-out, joined by two fingers from the other hand.

A seven-fingered hand. Just like the one drawn on the front of that journal.

Seven Harbingers, they'd called themselves.

"Oh, God," she realized out loud. "I bought that journal from an online auction." Doubtless the same auction where Greyson had bought Hellbringer.

In the photo, now brittle and tan with age, the Harbingers' wide eyes all had the same crazed look. It made goose bumps rise on the back of her neck. Maybe the whole thing was staged, a bit of post-hippie drama captured for the ages. Or maybe it was a gleam of true madness. She had no way to know.

She flipped the picture over. Sprawling handwriting in faded ballpoint ink read, "Severin, Alistair, Marlo . . ." She couldn't make out the rest of the names. But those three were legendary sorcerers from the twentieth century.

Severin, Alistair, Marlo. She'd heard terrible things about them. Dark incantations, horrifying age-old secrets unleashed, rumors of murder and worse.

"Dude," Rane said to Greyson. "Gimme your hand."

When Greyson held out his hand, looking puzzled, Rane smacked the fist-sized lump of brown coprolite into his palm.

"No joke," she said slowly. "That shit is a hundred million years old."

Greyson wasn't paying attention. He turned and stared into the darkness, his face going blank. "Do you hear . . . ?" He didn't finish.

Rane rolled her eyes. "Hear what?"

He dropped the rock. With a lurch, he set off into the gloom, as if called away.

Dru traded worried glances with Rane, then followed him. "Greyson? Where are you going?" She caught up to him and tugged on his arm, but he pulled free without even breaking stride.

As she chased after him, he led her past the last of the workbenches into the open center of the chamber, a dirt-and-gravel clearing that extended beyond the torchlight into endless gloom. He marched onward without any hesitation, each stride purposeful and yet somehow vacant, as if sleepwalking.

"Greyson?" Dru's voice shook. She stopped at the border of the clearing.

Rane touched her shoulder. "Something's wrong. I'll go first. Stay tight."

Dru stayed close behind her, following Greyson, until he stopped in front of one of the four long trenches she'd seen from the top of the stairs. They were laid out like a plus sign. In the center lay the charred remnants of a long-dead bonfire, filled with the blackened remains of bones.

At the outside end of each pit lay a bleached-white horse skull, facing out. The one at Greyson's feet had something painted on the wide arch of bone between its hollow eye sockets.

Dru crept closer until she could get a clear look.

A pair of scales. Just like the one painted under Hellbringer's hood. Just like the one that had glowed on Greyson's hands, after he had become the demon.

He stood motionless and vacant, as if mesmerized. Dru backed away from him.

Rane's metal feet rang softly on the gravel as she circled the ceremony site, looking at the other horse skulls. "This one has a symbol of a bow and arrow on it," she said, pointing, then went to the next one. "A sword." When she reached the last one, she cocked her head. "Looks like . . . fangs? I dunno. Mean anything to you?"

Scales. Bow. Sword. Fangs. Dru shook her head.

Rane pointed to the gravel pit in front of the horse skull with the sword symbol. "The gravel there looks darker. Like maybe it's been dug up recently."

"Don't touch it," Dru warned her. "Not yet. Give me a sec."

"We don't *have* a sec." Rane shot a worried look at Greyson. "Something seriously bad is about to happen."

"Just let me think." *Scales. Bow. Sword. Fangs.* The symbols whirled around in her head. She couldn't put it together. What were they? She burned with frustration.

Scales. Bow. Sword. Fangs. Dru pressed her fingertips into her forehead, thinking.

Four horse skulls.

Four horses.

"Dru?"

"Still thinking!"

Rane bent down, one hand hovering over the disturbed gravel pit. "What if I dig this up? Will it break Greyson's curse?"

It hit Dru then, like being dropped into icy water. The cold realization washed over her, as impossible as it was, stealing her breath away.

"Oh, Greyson." She studied his blank face, suddenly wishing she didn't know. When she reached up and laid a hand on the scratchy stubble of his jaw, he blinked, startled.

"What?" He looked all around, at the pits, at Rane, and finally at Dru. An impenetrable worry haunted his eyes. "What's wrong?"

In a flash, the words came back to Dru from her childhood.

"'When he opened the third seal, I looked, and there was a black horse,'" Dru whispered. Her head felt suddenly, nauseatingly light. The vast cave seemed to spin around her.

Greyson caught her arm and steadied her. "Dru? What's going on?"

Gently, she took Greyson's hand and turned it over. The skin was rough and thick from too many hours in the garage, but there was no trace of the demon's burning glyph. "The rider had a pair of scales in his hand," she whispered.

Greyson frowned. "What are you talking about?"

"The book of Revelation." Tears blurred her vision. "It's not just any curse afflicting you, Greyson. That's why this has been so hard to beat. I'm not sure we *can* beat it."

His eyebrows drew together, an unspoken question.

"Greyson, I don't know how to save you. You're . . ." She swallowed down the hard lump in her throat and looked straight into his red eyes. "You're becoming one of the Four Horsemen of the Apocalypse."

He stared at her, the disbelief in his face gradually transforming to confusion, then horror. Despite his tough exterior, she could tell her words had shaken him to the core. "What happens next?"

"Doomsday. The end of the world."

The muscles in his jaw rippled, and then he quickly shook his head. "Tell me you know how to stop it."

"If I'm right, that means there are *four* Horsemen. Maybe if we find the others, maybe we can cure all of them at once. That could conceivably break the curse."

"*Other* Horsemen?" Rane straightened up, her steely gaze boring into Greyson. "How are we supposed to find the rest of them?"

With a blood-chilling roar, the gravel pit at Rane's feet erupted in a spray of dirt. Red scaly claws shot up from below and latched onto her ankles. Rane let out a startled cry as the claws dragged her feetfirst down into the gravel, like quicksand.

23

DEVIL IN THE DARK

As the scaly claws dragged Rane into the pit, her metal fingers clawed into the dirt, digging long, parallel troughs. But they did nothing to slow her down.

Dru stood transfixed with horror. She wanted to run and help, but a cold rush of fear froze her to the spot. She couldn't move. She could only stare in stunned terror as the pit of gravel swallowed Rane's feet, then her calves, and then her thighs.

Greyson didn't hesitate. He charged directly across the ceremonial site toward Rane. A fiery glow lit him up from below. His footsteps left burning imprints on the ground, ruddy glowing footprints crawling with yellow points of light. Waves of magic raced up his body, clinging to him. But he didn't seem to notice.

Greyson's presence released some kind of infernal energy from the unholy ground. But what would it do to him?

He grabbed both of Rane's arms. His face contorted with effort as he dug his heels deep into the dirt. The unholy energy slithered over his body, wrapping around him.

With a breathy grunt, Greyson heaved. Rane's metal body went taut, like a rope in a tug-of-war, suspended for a moment between the pit and Greyson's bulging arms.

Rane, wide-eyed, looked up at Greyson wreathed in flames, then glanced over her shoulder to Dru for help. "Dru!" she yelled. "Problem!"

"Hang on!" Dru jammed the torch upright into the dirt, set down her massively heavy purse, and dumped out the crystals she had just gathered from the cabinet. Green vivianite. Violet amethyst. Black tourmaline. Where was her galena?

Greyson let out a tortured groan, baring his teeth. With a final pull, he wrenched Rane free of the gravel. The two of them tumbled across the ground.

A spray of rocks erupted from the pit. With a screeching roar, a red scaly creature clawed its way out of the pit. Hunched, reptilian, bow-legged, it looked nothing like the human being that it had probably once been. A long, wickedly toothed snout jutted out from its wedge-shaped head. A line of spines ran down its back to a tail that twitched with a life of its own, ending in a viciously curved claw that gleamed like a newly sharpened blade.

With another roar, the demon charged, knocking Greyson to the ground again just as he got to his feet.

In a heartbeat, Rane vaulted onto the creature's saw-toothed spine and hooked her metal arms around its neck. She braced one foot and yanked its head back.

The thing's scaly back arched, and it reached behind to grab at Rane. Its claws raked across her metal skin, drawing sparks.

Dru tore apart the pile of crystals, frantic with frustration. Just as she was about to give up, she spotted the cube of galena gleaming happily up at her.

She plucked the shiny lead-colored cube from the dirt and sprinted around the outside of the ceremonial site, taking care to stay well clear of the other trenches and their painted horse skulls.

Before she could reach the creature, its tail snaked up and wrapped around Rane's neck.

With a vicious tug, it broke her grip. As Rane tried to recover, the creature raised one powerful leg and kicked her to the ground.

Then it turned its attention to Dru.

One cold look from those fiercely glowing green eyes made Dru pull up short. A wet, breathy growl boiled up from the thing's throat.

Suddenly, the cube of galena in her hand felt completely inadequate.

A long, forked tongue slipped out between the creature's grinning teeth and flicked the air, as if tasting it.

As it stalked toward her, it moved to step over Rane's body. But it didn't get far.

Rane stood up directly in the creature's path and slammed her metal forehead into its scaly snout, momentarily stunning it. Then she stepped back, widening her stance, and hauled back one titanium fist. With blinding speed, she twisted her body and drove her fist straight into the creature's body. The blow rang out with a sound like metal striking concrete.

The impact flung the demon back into a bookshelf, knocking it down in an explosion of pages and dust.

With one hand, Rane pulled Greyson to his feet. "Time to *go!*"

Dru ran back to her purse and scooped up the crystals, careful to leave the galena sitting on top, then plucked the torch out of the dirt. Its flame sputtered as they ran for the stairs, threatening to blow out and strand them in pitch black.

They made it almost halfway up the steps before the creature emerged from the darkness. Its acid-green eyes burned as it climbed the steps behind them with a clatter of sharp claws. Its toothy jaw opened wide, as if waiting for a tasty morsel to pop into its mouth.

Dru dropped the torch. It guttered against the stone, leaving them in a shrinking circle of dying light. She grabbed the cube of galena tight in one hand, and with the other she fumbled for Greyson's hand, finding it only at the last second.

Touching him unlocked a torrent of magical energy within her. It surged up her arm and shuddered through her fingertips into the galena.

The crystal flared with a cold blue glow, as if spotlights had been trained on it from all directions, reflecting off its pitted, mirrored faces. A high-pitched ringing sound whined in her ears. Loud, sharp, and pure.

At the burst of light, the creature halted its charge. It raised its scaly arms against the surreal glow and cringed behind its gnarled claws. Between its thick fingers, one wide, snakelike eye peeked at the shining crystal.

"Keep climbing," Dru said breathlessly. "Right now."

Greyson backed up a step, then another. She matched his movements. She didn't dare take her eyes off the creature, though the galena's burning light made her eyes water.

As Rane charged up the stairs, Dru kept one hand tight in Greyson's, guiding him up one step at a time. She held the shining crystal high.

The creature climbed after them, pacing them.

Rane's brassy voice echoed down. "Dru! We've got a Mustang!"

Dru risked a puzzled glance back, catching a glimpse of Rane's silhouette at the top of the stairs, dark against the stark, empty whiteness of the doorway to the garage. Then she was gone.

From above, an aggressive rumble surged to life. The sudden noise rolled down the stone steps like a crack of thunder.

As they neared the top, Dru finally identified the sound.

An engine. An old, powerful one, like Hellbringer's. Its heavy exhaust notes thudded through the air like the beating wings of some giant primordial creature, pierced by the sharp squeal of tires.

"Oh," Dru whispered to herself. "*Mustang.*"

24

CARDIO FOR THE
CASUAL SORCERESS

The sound of squealing tires ended in a cruel impact of metal, sending a jolt of cold fear shooting through Dru's body. Without thinking, she let go of Greyson and ran up the last few steps. "Rane!"

Instantly, the galena in her hand dimmed from the glow of a brilliant spotlight to the murky blush of a nightlight. Greyson let out a grunt of surprise.

The creature below them on the stairs shrieked with triumph. Its claws clattered up toward them.

The garage beyond the doorway blazed with blinding sunlight from one of its hangar-style doors, now open to the desert sun. The vast white interior was broken only by the aggressive red outlines of an old Ford Mustang, its tire treads caked with the sand it had tracked in from outside.

Through the windshield, Dru could easily see that no one sat at the wheel. Yet the engine revved with an evil, earsplitting rumble.

The Mustang looked pristine, except for a cavernous dent in its front fender that quickly straightened itself out. The red paint bled where it had cracked, smoothing over to become whole and flawless once again. The chrome trim eased itself back into place.

Across the garage, Rane rose unsteadily to her feet, glaring at the car.

Her whole body had taken on the mottled brown-and-white smoothness of her polished flint ring. As she turned to face the Mustang, she planted her feet with a sound like falling rocks.

The engine revved.

Rane shot a warning glance at Dru where she stood just inside the secret door, then nodded almost imperceptibly toward the open garage door. Telling her to make a break for it.

Dru shook her head no. Rane would not face this alone.

Rane sidestepped away from Dru and beckoned the car with one outstretched finger. "Hey, rust bucket. Bring it."

The Mustang revved in place, hood shaking, rear wheels spinning up stinking clouds of burned rubber. It launched straight at Rane. She dodged out of the way, rolling on one shoulder to come up behind the car.

Greyson charged up the steps, the creature close behind him, and pushed Dru through the doorway into the garage. The green-eyed demon flew up the stairs and boiled out of the darkness, claws outstretched.

"Wait!" Dru turned back and aimed a kick at the halite crystal she'd left in the corner of the doorway, sending it flying into the darkness. With a sizzle of invisible energy, the warding spell on the door slammed shut. A blast of static-filled air blew Dru's hair back.

A split-second later, the creature slammed head-on into the invisible warding spell. It flattened out against the unseen barrier, inches away, its scaly hide pressed up against the ward as if it was a pane of glass. Blinding arcs of energy, no doubt powerful enough to kill a human, streaked out from all edges of the doorway and converged on the demon, driving it back.

"Hah!" Dru backed away and jabbed a finger in the demon's direction. "Gotcha!"

The garage filled with the echoes of the Mustang's engine as it revved higher and higher. But the car didn't move. Rane now stood directly behind it, motionless as an Egyptian monolith, every muscle bulging as she lifted the Mustang by its chrome rear bumper.

Her face darkened into a mask of strain as the car's rear wheels spun uselessly in a blur of black rubber and white letters, suspended a few inches over the concrete floor. Her cheeks bulged. Her lips puckered with the effort, revealing clenched teeth.

Glancing from the demonic Mustang on one side to the fanged creature trapped on the other, Dru racked her brain for a solution. This time, she didn't have any spray paint. But she did have Greyson's potion in the Prius. Could she use that against the Mustang?

Rane's arms shook with the effort. "Can't . . . hold on."

On the other side of the invisible barrier behind them, the demon shook itself off and pressed its scaly hands together. A glyph glowed on its right hand like a hot ember. Not the symbol of scales that had appeared on Greyson's hands, but the symbol of a sword.

An ominous flicker of firelight shone through the demon's claws. With a flare of light, a long blade composed entirely of flames grew from the demon's hands.

Baleful, reptilian eyes locked on Greyson. The demon drew back its sword and swung at the invisible barrier.

Dru pushed Greyson aside just as blinding crackles of electricity from the sword's impact shattered the spell into a fountain of fiery fragments. A piercing sizzle cut through the garage.

"Come on!" Dru ran out through the open garage door, hoping Greyson would follow. "We need the potion!"

The demon's chilling howl followed her out into the brilliant sunlight. She flew down the length of the sandy driveway, toward the diminutive white lump of Nate's car parked in front of the mansion. Her breath burned in her lungs. Her footsteps crunched in the sand.

It took every bit of Dru's resolve not to stop and go back for Rane. But they had to get the potion first, while the Mustang was immobilized. It was their only chance.

In the flat distance, two dust clouds rose on the horizon, drawing closer.

The other two Horsemen, Dru realized. Coming after Greyson, to complete the circle. To gather together the Four Horsemen of the Apocalypse.

Greyson opened the driver's door and started the car.

"Take us back into the garage," she said as she got in next to him. As Greyson whipped the car around toward the garage, she picked up the skull-shaped potion bottle from beneath the passenger seat. "If I pour this into the Mustang's gas tank, it could have the same effect on the car as it has on you. Break the demonic connection."

"One hell of a carburetor cleaner," Greyson muttered.

"*Hell* is right."

Ahead of them, the driverless red Mustang suddenly shot out of the dark mouth of the garage, dragging Rane. Her fingers were locked onto the chrome back bumper, flint feet scraping on the ground, showering sparks behind her.

"Time for plan B," Greyson said. "If the airbags go off, just push them off of you."

"Airbags?" Dru shot a terrified glance at him, but his gaze was locked intensely on the oncoming red Mustang.

Greyson hunched over the wheel, one hand steering, the other reaching for the emergency brake. "Seat belt!" he barked.

Dru yanked her seat belt into place. Just as it clicked home, the Mustang veered straight for them. Its chrome grill flashed, sunlight gleaming from its headlights.

Before the red car could ram them head-on, Greyson swerved the little Prius out to the side, then whipped back in tight, striking the Mustang on its back corner.

The Mustang spun away into the sand, flinging Rane through the air. She hit the ground and rolled, blending into the rocks as she tumbled.

Greyson kept the little car drifting sideways across the sand until it slid to a stop alongside Rane. "Get in!" he shouted through the closed window, making Dru's left ear ring.

Outside, Rane stood up, tottered dizzily, and fell over again.

Wincing, Dru unbuckled her seat belt and burst out of the car. In two quick steps, she was at Rane's side. She tried to lift her, but in stone form, the woman weighed a ton. Maybe literally. "Turn human!" Dru begged her.

"Screw that," Rane said. "Where'd that hunk of junk go?"

The Mustang swung back around onto the driveway, its tires spinning. It straightened out and headed toward them again, engine roaring.

Still in stone form, Rane climbed to her feet. "I can take him."

"No. His friends are coming. Get in!" Dru pointed to the back seat of the Prius, then got into the passenger seat and buckled up. Rane climbed in behind her, making the car sink almost to the ground. With a surreal sense of detachment, Dru noticed that the airbags had never gone off. So much for safety features. Or had Greyson intended that?

"What is that thing doing?" Greyson mused.

Instead of ramming them, the Mustang cruised past to the garage and slowed to a halt, engine thudding. From the darkness of the garage, the reptilian demon streaked out, pounding on all fours toward the Mustang. The red door on the driver's side swung open, waiting for it.

"You've got to be kidding me," Rane said from the back seat. "That's one of the Four Horsemen?"

Greyson swore under his breath and launched the car back onto the driveway, heading away from the garage. No matter how well he drove, Dru knew they didn't have any chance of outrunning the demon car. Especially not with Rane's weight in the back seat.

From the look on Greyson's face as he checked the rearview mirror, he was thinking the same thing. "Even if we make it back to the main road, he'll catch us."

"We still have to get past those guys," Dru said. She pointed into the distance, where the two dust clouds had converged into one huge plume. The mean profiles of a sleek, old silver sports car and a blocky white truck raged toward them, side by side, filling the road.

"Bronco. Ferrari. Late sixties." Greyson glared at the dirt road ahead, the muscles taut in his face. "Each of them has something behind the wheel."

Some*thing*. Not some*one*.

"We have to get off this road." Dru craned her head around, looking for some way out. She spotted the stone archway in the distance, behind the mansion, and remembered the symbols on the diagram.

"*Sekura koridoro*," she whispered. *Safe road. Escape route.*

She pointed. "That way! Turn! Now!"

"Hang on!" Greyson stomped on the brakes. The Prius pitched forward hard, then leaned steeply to the side as he whipped the car into a claustrophobic reverse skid.

The Mustang roared past in a blood-colored blur. It tore off Dru's passenger side mirror with a crack like a baseball bat hitting a line drive.

Greyson drove off the pitted road and into the sand, fishtailing his way up a steep rise. The Prius burst over the top of the rise in a spray of dirt and an explosion of dry grass.

They trundled down the treacherous far side of the rise, toward the archway in the distance. As they went over rocks and bushes, the entire car shook, rattling Dru to the bone.

"You realize," Dru said, her teeth chattering, "this is not an off-road vehicle."

"This was your plan," Greyson shot back.

"I *meant* take the *road* out to the archway."

"Next time, be more specific."

Greyson steered through a maze of rocks, scrub brush, and dry gullies, yanking the wheel left and right. Spiky yucca plants scraped down the sides of the car, the sound like fingernails on a chalkboard. Loose rocks and bushes pelted the windshield.

Dru cringed. Some neurotic part of her brain that she couldn't shut down told her that no amount of car wax or detailing would fix Nate's beloved little earth-friendly car.

The stone archway loomed up ahead. Dru pointed. "Over there!"

"We've got company," Rane said flatly.

Greyson looked back over his shoulder, eyes fierce with alarm. "That thing doesn't give up."

The red Mustang charged down the brush-covered hill after them, bounding over rises like a living creature. Its tires gouged the desert hillside as it closed in.

From behind, Rane's solid rock arms locked around Dru, like a safety bar at a carnival ride. So tight Dru could barely breathe.

"I got you," Rane whispered in her ear. For once, Dru was thankful for Rane's uncomfortable embrace.

"Almost there," Greyson said under his breath, over and over, like a prayer. "Almost there . . ." They darted around one boulder, then another. His eyes flicked up at the rearview mirror again, and his voice kicked up to an urgent shout. "Heads up!"

An impact that could only be the Mustang slammed into them from behind. They slid, hit something with a painful, metallic crunch. Went airborne.

Blue sky filled the windshield. Sparse white clouds rotated clockwise as the Prius lazily rolled over in midair.

Brown sand, sharp rocks, green bushes all zoomed into focus. The car slammed into the ground and rolled.

The whole time, a shrill scream filled the air.

Dru realized it was her.

25

GOING NOWHERE

The crash was over in an instant, so quickly that it felt unreal. As if the thunderous impact hadn't happened in that moment but was just a distant memory. The crushing force and cacophony of shattering surfaces felt like a half-remembered nightmare, too chaotic and short-lived to be real.

The white scorching-hot fabric of the airbag deflated away from her, shriveling in the blinding sunlight shining in through the hollow window frame on her right. The collapsing cloud of the airbag left nothing but dust swirling in the air before her unfocused eyes, a galaxy of infinitely tiny points of light.

She couldn't breathe. Couldn't think.

Maybe it was easier this way. Not feeling anything. Not knowing anything. Suspended in darkness that was nonetheless filled with light.

The palpable silence that cocooned her gradually dissolved into an aching ringing in her ears. A man's voice called her name, over and over. Greyson.

Close to her ear, Rane said, "Dude, I think she's out cold. Get her seat belt off."

Dru forced her heavy eyelids open, even before she realized they were closed. At the top edge of her vision, she was surprised to see her hair standing completely on end. Somehow gravity had reversed itself.

Rane slowly released her stony grip on Dru, and she slid toward the car's rippled ceiling. With heavy arms, Dru propped herself up inside the car, beside the smashed remains of the glass skull-shaped potion bottle.

The heady stench of herbs and potent liquor burned Dru's nostrils raw, jolting her. The broken face of the glass skull grinned up at her.

Greyson's potion lay wasted in a pool before her, slowly soaking into the fabric.

Strong arms wrapped around her and pulled her from the wreckage. The dying sunlight bathed her.

Greyson gently lowered Dru to the rocky ground. He stripped off his motorcycle jacket and folded it, leather creaking, into a pillow for her head. He leaned over her, his glowing red eyes filled with worry. "Dru! Can you hear me?" A trickle of blood ran down the side of his face from a gash just beneath one of his stubby horns. "Are you okay?"

She nodded. "How many fingers am I holding up?"

He frowned. "None."

"Oh, wait." She held up three fingers. "How about now?"

The corners of his eyes crinkled.

Everything came rushing back to Dru. The mansion. The Four Horsemen. "The Mustang!" she realized out loud. "Where'd it go?"

"It can't follow us down here," Greyson said. "Not unless it can fly." He helped Dru to her feet, then handed her glasses to her. She wiped off the dust that coated them.

Fighting a wave of dizziness, she quickly scanned their surroundings. They had crashed at the bottom of a dry, washed-out ravine, surrounded on all sides by uneven ground littered with ruddy boulders and parched scrub brush.

Greyson was right. No car could drive down that incline. "That leaves us with two bad options," Dru said. "Climb out, or stay trapped down here."

Oily curls of smoke drifted around them, from something ruptured in the crashed Prius. When Dru breathed in, a sickly sweet chemical smell coated the back of her throat and scoured it raw.

Above, the relentless sun dipped toward sunset, burning a gold glow into the edge of the crystalline blue sky. An encroaching curtain of dark gray clouds approached from the direction of the archway, cooling the horizon and sapping the color from the landscape.

There was no visible sign of the Mustang, but the echoes of throaty engines thudded all around them. It was impossible to tell where the noise was coming from. The sounds grew louder, then faded, as if the cars were circling around them like vultures.

"They're all up there," Rane spat, hauling herself out through the shattered window. Still in stone form, she crawled through a halo of broken glass that shone like diamonds in the sun. "I want to take those things apart with my bare hands. Pretty sure I can."

"We have to keep moving," Dru said. "If the other demons—the other *Horsemen*—leave their cars behind and find a way down here on foot, we're in real trouble. I don't know what happens when all four get together, but I'm thinking it's not poker night."

Greyson let out a pained grunt, then pressed his hands against his temples.

Still on all fours, Rane shot a worried look at Dru, then back at Greyson. "Hey. He doesn't sound so good."

"I'm fine . . ." Greyson's deepening voice broke into an anguished groan. He leaned against the upside-down wreckage for support. His fingers curled into fists, and the muscles stood out on his arms, beaded with sweat. He shook his head, as if trying to clear it. The red glow in his eyes grew brighter. "Not now," he whispered.

"That magic fire at the ceremonial pits, I think it did a number on you." Dru put a calming hand on his arm. "Greyson. Look at me."

He jerked away. "Stay back!" His skin darkened before her eyes. His fingers bunched the white sheet metal, wrinkling it as if it were nothing more than fabric. He let out a long growl that didn't sound entirely human.

Dru's knees went wobbly. The potion that could stop his transformation was currently nothing more than a puddle soaking into the roof of the Prius.

Rane wearily got up and planted her feet, hands balling into fists. "Dru, get behind me."

Greyson needed the potion. But the bottle was smashed. That meant she had to get it to him some other way. But how? Maybe if she could soak it up into something.

"Wait, wait! I have an idea. Hold him."

"Gladly." Rane stepped around the groaning Greyson and expertly pinned his arms behind his back. He didn't resist.

Dru looked around for something absorbent, but the loose rocks, sandy dirt, and scrubby plants offered nothing.

"Oh, hey, his T-shirt," Dru realized out loud. She reached for Greyson, but he reared back, snarling. A wild look filled his glowing red eyes, and his teeth started to grow into fangs. His darkening chest swelled with muscle. His horns grew longer. His lips curled back and let out a snarl.

Rane struggled to hold him in place. "D, whatever you're thinking? Think faster."

Despite her fear, Dru stepped close and put both hands on the collar of Greyson's T-shirt.

She yanked. The collar stretched out amazingly far, but it didn't rip.

Rane peeked over Greyson's thrashing shoulder. "The hell are you doing?"

"Jeez, it's like spandex or something." Dru kept tugging on his collar, first one way, then the other. "This made more sense in my head." With a final heave, she yanked the collar past its breaking point and was rewarded with the welcome sound of tearing fabric. His shirt tore off in her hands, leaving him bare-chested and glistening in the last rays of the sun.

Rane peeked over Greyson's shoulder again, one eyebrow quirked up. "Seriously?"

"Just hang on." Dru got down on the ground and reached in through the crumpled window frame of the Prius. With some difficulty, she flopped the torn T-shirt down into the puddle of potion and let it soak in.

The whole time, Greyson snarled and fought Rane's stone grip.

"Dru!" Rane said. "We don't have all day!"

When the fabric had soaked up all it could hold, Dru pulled it out, dripping wet. She wadded it up and, after a little ducking and weaving, stuffed it into Greyson's open mouth. "Okay, good! Rane, give him a head lock or something. Don't let him spit it out."

With a kick that was more savage than absolutely necessary, Rane brought the thrashing Greyson to his knees, then snaked a stone arm around his neck. As she held firm against his struggling, Rane lifted her gaze to give Dru a meaningful look, her killer instinct rising to the surface.

"This will work," Dru said. It came out a whisper.

"It better." Rane wrapped her arm tighter around Greyson's neck. "Or else."

26

LAST EXIT FOR THE LOST

Bracing herself for the worst, Dru watched as the damp rag unceremoniously dropped from Greyson's suddenly normal teeth.

"Told you we should've taken my car," he croaked out. His dark reddish skin faded, and his horns began to recede. Not all the way, but at least back to unobtrusive stubs. Rane released him and turned human again.

Dru tilted his head left and right, inspecting him closely. "Feel any pain? Tingling, numbness?"

He shook his head no.

"Well, you're a work in progress. You start feeling anything funny again, tell me."

The red glow in his eyes dimmed until it was nearly imperceptible, but it was still there. His gaze dropped to her lips, and she felt them smile of their own accord. His attention lingered there, then focused back to her eyes. He lifted his chin, a fraction of an inch, to indicate his assent. "Believe me, you'll be the first to know."

"Better be." Feeling shaky, she drew in a long breath and let it out. "Sorry about your shirt."

He picked up his leather jacket and stood. "Sorry about your car."

Dru looked past his bare chest to the demolished wreck. Upside down, half flattened, one wheel folded in at the wrong angle.

"Nate is going to murder me," she said.

"Not if those demons get down here first," Rane said.

Greyson shrugged into his leather jacket, then nodded toward the top of the steep incline. "You two head that way. I'll double back on foot and try to lead them away."

"Good idea," Rane said.

"No, it's a *terrible* idea," Dru said, retrieving her purse from the wreckage. "Look, the schematic of the archway said that it's some kind of hiding place or escape route, and it's unlocked by crystal magic. If that's true—"

"Big *if*," Rane said.

"If it's true, then it's our only chance. We can't outrun them, and we can't outfight them."

Rane folded her arms, disagreement plain on her face.

"We *can't*," Dru insisted. "Not until we know more about these guys. We need to get back to the shop and check the books. Especially that journal with the seven-fingered hand. These Harbingers were serious about bringing on the end of the world. And from the looks of it, they've done a bang-up job so far. So we can't risk going in there all gung ho and making things worse. We need to figure out what kind of escape route is at the archway." She didn't wait for them to agree. She just started climbing up the ravine, hoping they would follow.

Rane caught up quickly, her big feet knocking pebbles loose. "No offense, D. But this archway sounds like a long shot. How's it going to get us back to the shop?"

"Right now we just need a safe place to hide. We're out in the middle of nowhere. We've got three Horsemen of the Apocalypse on our tail, plus their demon cars. Greyson's iffy at best. We don't have a lot of options."

The engine sounds were fading, Dru noticed, but it was too much to hope that the Horsemen had given up.

Rane cast a wary eye back at Greyson as he climbed up behind them. "We need to keep him at a safe distance. Having him around is getting seriously risky."

"We need to risk it," Dru said, thinking it through out loud. "I have to break his curse. Because somehow I'm connected to him, and he's connected to *them*, which means together we might be the key to stopping Doomsday." Dru reached the top of the ravine and stopped.

The desert was ominously silent. There was no sign of the demons or their cars. Ahead, a dry, flat stretch of sandy dirt led past a few boulders and bushes to the tan stone archway.

Up close, the archway's precisely smooth outline stood out starkly against the craggy contours of the desert. The sorcerers must have used obfuscation spells to hide it, she realized, like they'd hidden the mansion.

Rane climbed up next to her and pointed at the sandy ground, where multiple sets of tire tracks dug through the dirt. They circled the archway and headed back the direction they'd come, over a nearby rise. A faint haze of trail dust still hung in the air, tinting it like an old photograph. "They're waiting for us to make a move. Whatever you're going to do, D, make it quick."

Greyson appeared over the edge and joined them.

Dru dug through her purse until she found the dark-mirrored cube of galena. "Ready?"

They both nodded.

She took a deep breath and sprinted for the archway as fast as she could.

Powerful engines growled to life nearby. The red Mustang rocketed over the rise toward them, sunlight glaring off its chrome. A moment later, the white Bronco followed, dirt spewing from its huge, knobby tires. Through the windshield, Dru spied a hulking, spiky white creature with glowing sapphire-blue eyes.

"Incoming!" Rane yelled, transforming into stone as she ran. "I'll hold them off!"

"Keep going!" Greyson grabbed Rane's arm on the way past. "We stay together!"

Dru didn't wait to see if Rane would go along with the plan. She kept running, her breath coming harsh and ragged as she dashed up the smooth stone ramp. Atop that, the archway towered like a sculpture, two stories tall at least.

She stopped before it, breathing hard, looking for some clue that could save them. The ramp beneath her looked like a suspiciously good place to hide something. One block at the top of the ramp seemed slightly different from the rest. The gaps around it were probably just wide enough to pry apart with a crowbar. If there was a secret trapdoor, it would be right here, at her feet.

But she didn't have a crowbar. And there were no discernible levers or controls anywhere on the archway or around it. Just a plain, beveled archway of stone that rose up over her head and arced down the other side.

Crystal magic was supposed to open it. But how, exactly? There were no inscriptions, no circles, no altar. Nothing.

Undeterred, she held the galena crystal high and walked toward the archway. As she got closer, a piercing whine rang through her skull. Like the worst kind of microphone feedback, as if she had speakers clamped on either side of her head.

Her head pounded, making her gasp, sending black shadows pulsing in her vision. She stumbled back from the archway, and the whine faded to nothing.

The galena wouldn't work, she realized. But that was the only crystal she had that related to demons. If the galena wouldn't work, then what would?

A horrible sinking feeling overwhelmed her. Maybe she was wrong.

Maybe she had led them to a dead end, and they would all die here.

Except for Greyson, who would lose his soul and become the fourth Horseman of the Apocalypse. And after that, quite possibly, the world would end.

Worse, it was all her fault.

Rane and Greyson ran up the ramp behind her, breathing hard.

"I could've taken them," Rane snapped at Greyson.

He ignored her. "Dru?"

"I've got nothing," she whispered. She didn't bother to turn around. She couldn't face the doom that was headed their way.

Behind her, tires slid in the dirt and stopped. Engines growled. Creatures snarled.

The Horsemen were here.

"Wait," Dru realized out loud. "If I'm getting feedback, then it isn't *nothing* after all. It's interference."

Two of her crystals had to be interfering with one another. There had to be something else working against the galena. She opened her purse and dug through it. When her fingers brushed against the vivianite crystal from the mansion, it flickered with a pale green light.

Holding up the vivianite, Dru stepped into the archway as car doors slammed and claws clattered on the rocks behind her. Rane grunted, and the sound was immediately followed by the unmistakable strike of her stone fist against flesh. Something roared in pain and anger.

Before Dru could pass through the archway, an invisible force pushed her back, like two magnets repelling each other. She planted her feet and leaned in, the glowing vivianite crystal outstretched in front of her, pushing as hard as she could.

It took all of her strength, but it still wasn't enough. The muscles in her arms and legs strained, but she couldn't budge. It wasn't physical strength she needed. It was magical.

But she had no more to give. After everything that had happened, her energy was spent. She felt it ebbing away. The primal force inside the archway pushed back harder and harder, threatening to knock her off her feet.

In a heartbeat, Greyson was there behind her. Hands on her shoulders, holding her up. Steadying her.

She pried one hand loose from the vivianite and reached back. His grip on her hand was warm and strong. The moment he touched her, she felt his strength flowing into her.

The vivianite glowed brighter. Its unearthly green light transformed the archway into a shimmering window. The snarls of the demons turned into retreating squeals and faded to silence. A serene tranquility spread out in the brilliance of the light.

A tight grin spread across Dru's face. She'd done it.

They'd done it. Together.

The thrill of victory quickly melted into fear as an ice-cold wind blew past, swirling around her. It nipped at her exposed skin like a wild animal, swirled her hair, plucked at her clothes. The air sizzled with an invisible electricity.

A rumble filled her ears, drowning out the rest of the world. She tried to turn and warn Greyson, but her body wouldn't obey. Hot energy danced over her skin, crackled through her clothes like static.

The dry brown landscape on the other side of the archway brightened, the colors bleaching away until they became nothing but a blinding white light. Purer than sunlight. Painfully intense.

Against what felt like impossible weight, Dru raised her hand to shield her eyes. The light shone through her skin, piercing her flesh, silhouetting the long bones in her hand.

The ground lurched beneath her feet, and an irresistible force drew them into the light.

27
UNDER THE MILKY
WAY TONIGHT

The assault of light and noise dwindled into dark silence. The icy wind dropped away to nothing, leaving them surrounded by cool, damp air that felt strangely sticky on Dru's skin. It smelled like the brisk sharpness after a thunderstorm.

After the glare of the desert, Dru's eyes had trouble adjusting to the sudden darkness. Above, a night sky blazed with falling stars and shimmering spiderwebs of ghostly, prismatic light.

The ruins of a stone fortress surrounded them. The unearthly starlight made it impossible to see much more than jutting silhouettes, as if they were trapped inside an enormous fossilized rib cage. Here and there, a few fragments of hideous statues peered back at them from the wet rocks, inhuman faces leering from the shadows.

Overhead, the sky rippled with twisting patterns of color. Pinpoints of light snaked into shimmering curtains. Burning lights, like stars but much bigger and closer, flared into brilliance as they slashed across the heavens, leaving smoky trails in their wake, until they burned out near the horizon, over undulating waves of mist that glowed in the hellish light from above.

A road paved with glistening cobblestones stretched downhill, out of the ruins. On one side of the road, a sheer cliff dropped away into an ocean of clouds. But Dru couldn't see or hear any water. Nothing but a whispering sea of mist that slowly rose and fell in waves according to the wind, like a vast living, breathing creature.

"This is your 'safe road'?" Rane said, throwing anxious glances over both shoulders. "Where the hell are we? What happened to the desert?"

Dru shook her head. "I was kind of expecting another secret door or something."

The three of them stood at the foot of a looming archway that didn't look at all like the smooth, modern arch in the desert. This one seemed squat and primitive by comparison, built of individual weathered stones stacked one on top of another, two curved pillars tilting toward each other until they met at a distinct point at the top.

Dru stared back through this crude archway. Where there should have been desert, there was nothing but haunted darkness. Angry bolts of light flared across the sky, reflecting on the wet rocks of the ruined fortress.

"Why would the Harbingers build a portal to come here?" The night seemed to swallow Dru's voice. "Is this really the netherworld?"

"More important question," Rane said. "Where are the demons? They were right behind me." Fists raised, Rane watched the portal intently, as if expecting the demons to come lunging through at any moment. "We don't know how long we have until they follow us."

She had a good point. "Can we fight them?" Dru said.

Rane hesitated. Which told Dru that they couldn't.

That left them only two choices: run or hide.

The still-glowing vivianite crystal in her hand reflected up into Greyson's face. "Can you take us back to the desert?" he said.

"I don't know," Dru admitted after thinking it through. "But if the demons are waiting there for us? That would be suicide."

"Maybe we can find a good spot to ambush them," Greyson said. "Fight them one at a time."

Rane looked from him to Dru in disbelief. "You're not seriously thinking about sticking around *here*."

Dru got out her cell phone, switched on the light, and played it across the ruins around them. It didn't shine far. The light glistened off high walls and crumbling doorways built of black polygonal rocks. She had no idea what might lurk in the darkness. Each potential hiding spot looked scarier than the last.

Dru took a long look at the primitive archway. Could the demons follow them here? She had no idea. But if they were coming through, they could arrive at any moment.

"We need to get as far away from here as we can," Dru said. "Fast."

Rane brushed past her. "Follow me." She jogged downhill, following the wet cobblestone road out of the ruins and along the edge of the cliff.

They ran in silence, staying close together. The cool, clammy air seemed to absorb the sound of their footsteps on the hexagonal stones, leaving only the disconcerting whistle of wind through the ruins. Above, the alien skies continued their torturous duel of lightning and shooting stars.

The shaky light from Dru's phone illuminated only a meager wedge of glistening cobblestones in front of them. As the road stretched on, her legs began to burn, and her lungs ached. She didn't know how long she could keep up this pace.

Just when she thought she'd have to stop, Greyson halted at a curve in the road and closed a hand over her phone's light, making his fingers glow red. "Turn it off," he said urgently.

Alarmed, she did as he asked, plunging them into darkness broken only by the haunted, ever-changing lights from the sky. Wordlessly, Greyson raised one arm and pointed into the distance.

Up ahead, she could barely make out the black ribbon of the road as it led straight to the edge of the cliff. Past that, an ocean of mist stretched to the horizon, broken only by the long, straight line of some kind of bridge.

A causeway.

"If the legends are true," Dru whispered, "that causeway was built by ancient sorcerers to connect between portals. It might lead us to another way out of here."

"And if it doesn't?" Rane said.

Dru glanced back at the black stone ruins. "Then we'll have to take our chances with the demons."

28

THE LONGEST FALL

The causeway was held together by magic, no doubt about that. Assembled from polygonal black stone blocks, the same kind as the demolished fortress at the top of the hill. The mortar holding the blocks together was sheer enchantment, glowing softly like molten steel poured straight from the forge. But Dru didn't need to know how it was made. She just had to know that every pounding step carried them farther from the demons in the desert.

They ran for another mile, possibly two, before Dru's legs finally gave out. Her breath burned in her lungs. A stabbing pain lanced up her side. She stumbled to a halt, hands braced on her knees, gasping for breath.

Greyson stopped beside her, his face creased with worry. "Dru?"

"Just . . ." She coughed and gasped, face hot with more than exertion. "Just need a sec."

Rane, who had overshot them, came jogging back. "Dude, she's not a runner. And she doesn't have your demon strength. This could be bad." She looked anxiously down the length of the causeway, then back the way they'd come.

Breathing hard, Dru followed her gaze to the ruins of the fortress, which stood in the distance like dark fingers against the sky.

Rane paced. "If those demons drive their cars through the portal and come down the road after us? That's it. We're done."

Greyson turned to Dru. "They can drive down here?"

"I dunno." Dru gulped, feeling nauseous. "Think I'm going to throw up."

There were no guardrails along the edges of the stone causeway, just a sharp drop-off on both sides. Below, eerie billows of mist roiled and reflected the ever-changing lights in the mad sky, only making her feel more seasick. She had to close her eyes to blot it out.

"Come on." Rane grabbed her arm and pulled her along. "Don't stop now, or you'll make it worse. Need to walk it off."

"Walk it off?" Dru complained as Rane's viselike grip led her onward. "Has that ever worked for anybody?" But after a few minutes, the nausea did pass, although the sharp pain in her feet persisted. She tried to run again, but the torture was too much.

She pulled off one shoe and sucked in a breath when she saw her heel, the skin nearly rubbed off. "Definitely not the right footwear for today's activities."

Rane pointed down the causeway. "Cowgirl up. We're sitting ducks. No time to mess around."

Just as Dru started to protest that she needed to bandage her feet somehow, Greyson scooped her up in his arms. She let out a little yelp of surprise, her heart beating faster, and clasped her arms around his shoulders.

"Let's go," he said to Rane.

She gave him a wary look, wordlessly checked with Dru, and set off again at a brisk run. "Try to keep up."

He didn't seem to have much trouble. His glowing red eyes burned in the half-light, and his chest swelled with each breath. He ran without any seeming effort, his strides long and sure.

If there was a bright side to his demon problem, Dru realized, it was the remarkable endurance it gave him.

As she pondered that, Greyson said, "You okay?"

Dru nodded. "You don't have to carry me," she said into his ear.

He gave her a sidelong look. "Just watch my back, in case anything comes up behind us."

She nodded. But there was no sign of movement from the fortress. Dru's gaze gradually strayed to the distant horizon on one side, past the occasional flickering colors in the depths of the mist. In the dark distance, something glittered. She took off her glasses, rubbed them on her shirt, put them back on again, and squinted.

Cleaning her glasses didn't help. And neither did the constant running motion. But she could just barely make out vertical rows or towers that glittered in the shifting lights of the sky. From so many miles away, it almost looked like a city skyline gone dark.

She nudged Greyson. "You see that? Way out there? What is that?"

He blinked softly glowing eyes. "High-rise buildings, maybe."

"Can't be." But she wondered if it was possible. Could there be an entire city out there, beyond the sea of flickering mist?

If so, did anyone—or any*thing*—live there in the netherworld city?

As Greyson carried her along, she kept searching the horizon, straining to pick up any details. "There's so much we don't know. I need to get back to the shop and research the causeways. I never took those old myths seriously before, but if I was wrong about them, I could have been wrong about any number of other things, too."

He ran onward several long strides before he looked down at her again, the angles in his face softening. "You're not so bad yourself."

That wasn't what she meant, but the compliment was still irresistible. She blushed, thankful that the light was probably too dim for it to show.

She tightened her arms around him. He smiled at her, making her feel as if a warm glow surrounded them.

But the moment was broken as Greyson came to a sudden stop. Rane stood stock-still in front of him, blocking the way. "Put her down," Rane ordered. "From here, we walk."

Past Rane, in the distance, the yardstick-straight line of the causeway arrowed into a dark mass that dominated the horizon. An island of black rock rose above the ocean of mist and blotted out part of the eerie lights in the sky.

Greyson gently set Dru down. She winced when her feet touched the ground, drawing a concerned look from him. "I'm okay," she reassured Greyson, although she wasn't.

Greyson started walking, and Dru moved to follow him, but Rane held her back.

"Can I talk to you for a moment?" Rane flashed a carnivorous-looking smile. "Just you and me?"

"We need to keep moving," Dru said.

But Rane didn't seem to hear her. Instead, she said to Greyson, "Go ahead. We'll catch up."

He shot Rane a long, unreadable look, then turned to Dru. She nodded, not altogether willingly.

"Five minutes," Greyson said, tapping his wrist. "Then I'm turning around and coming back." Grudgingly, he walked away down the bridge.

Dru watched him go, fuming. She was fed up with Rane's oxlike blundering. She drew in a breath to say something, but Rane beat her to it.

"What do you think you're doing?" Rane asked in a fierce whisper, throwing off Dru's train of thought.

"What?" Dru whispered back.

"Don't 'what' me. You're going all googly eyes at each other. Five more minutes and you two would've been locking lips."

"No. Absolutely not." Dru yanked her arm free of Rane's grip. She held up her empty hands before her, defensively. "It's not what it looks like."

"Oh no?" Rane moved her head side to side, as if she were sparring in the ring. "You don't think you're playing with fire here?"

"If you're talking about me and Nate breaking up, if you're worried about some sort of rebound—"

"Oh, I freaking *wish* that was it." Rane gave her a hard look. "While you're spending all that time gazing into his dreamy eyes, you notice anything funny? Like, I don't know, the evil red glow of a demon from the fiery *pits of hell?*"

"Well, yes, of course. His symptoms are still present."

Rane paced in a tight circle, fists working the air in front of her. "It's not like he has a cold, Dru. He doesn't need NyQuil. He has a *demon* inside him. Just like the ones back there." She pointed in the direction of the fortress, now too far away to see.

Dru folded her arms. "And I'm going to get the demon out of him. Somehow."

"Maybe you can't see this with total clarity." Rane stopped pacing and faced her head-on. "I've spent my life protecting people. Protecting my friends. From being hurt by monsters, creeps, and freaky-ass demons.

I don't know if you've noticed, but he hasn't been getting any better. He's getting worse."

"Once we make it back to the shop, I can—"

"No. *If* we get back to the shop. At this rate, that could be, like, never. Real soon, that thing inside him is going to take over completely. And when it does, he could kill you. And if you're in his arms, it wouldn't be too hard."

Dru wanted to argue with Rane. But everything she could think of just sounded like an excuse. Deep down, she knew Rane had a point.

Rane moved to put her hands on Dru's shoulders, but Dru stepped back, out of reach. For a split second, Rane looked hurt. "I'm just telling you, D, because you're my best friend. And the last thing I want, when it all hits the fan, is for you to have your head on crooked because you think he's such hot stuff. I want you to be ready."

Seething anger boiled up under Dru's skin. "Ready for what?" she asked, biting off the words.

Rane gave her a long, stern look before she answered. "Look, as the demon takes over, he's going to get destructive, out of control. Dangerous to everyone around him, including you and me. When that happens—not if, *when*—then someone has to stop him. Permanently."

Dru turned away, not believing she was hearing this.

"That's what I do, D. That's my existence. I take down the forces of evil before they kill people. And what sucks is that I know you're falling for this guy. And I don't want to do this." Rane took a deep breath and blew it out. "But if I have to, I will."

Dru shook her head in denial. She could still save Greyson.

She *knew* it.

Couldn't she?

29
THE ONLY EVIL YOU CAN TRUST

They caught up to Greyson a few minutes later. But at his questioning look, Dru just shook her head. No one spoke.

An open cave waited beyond the end of the causeway, its wide mouth a pool of impenetrable darkness. As they approached it, Rane rolled her shoulders and popped her neck, obviously itching for a fight.

Dru glanced over at Greyson, who squinted apprehensively into the cave, his red eyes glowing.

"See anything in there?" Dru asked him, breaking the silence.

He shook his head slowly. "I don't like this."

"Agreed. You're not the only one getting the heebie-jeebies here."

"I don't know about *heebie-jeebies*," he growled. "I just don't like it."

Dru pulled the still-glowing vivianite out of her purse and held it before her like a candle. Warily, she stepped off the causeway onto the uneven black ground. When they reached the cave opening, she leaned one hand against the rough stone. "Well, it doesn't look like anything—"

Before she could finish, a powerful wind swept out of the cave, buffeting her. The vivianite flashed with inner radiance, and an even brighter light flared from the cave.

A sudden sensation of movement tugged at her, threatening to pull her off her feet. Magic shuddered through the blinding light around her, trying to take them somewhere else, deeper into the netherworld. Somewhere vast, ethereal, terrifying.

Her first impulse was to back away, but the magic was too strong. If she couldn't resist it, she realized, then she had to control it somehow.

Take us home, she thought. But without any chance to prepare, she had no idea how to get control of the magic that assaulted them.

"D!" Rane shouted over the wind. "Do something!"

Instinctively, Dru reached out for Greyson. He swept her up with one arm, holding her close as the brilliant light and wind blasted over them.

"I've got you," he said in her ear. The howling wind nearly drowned out his voice, but his touch was enough.

Instead of fighting the vortex of magic trying to pull them into the cave, Dru cleared her mind and focused her thoughts on where she wanted to go. Not deeper into the netherworld, but back to The Crystal Connection. Back to Denver, or even to the Rocky Mountains that overlooked the city. Back to someplace safe.

Take us home.

The rushing energy threatened to blot out her thoughts. It pulled at her hair, plucked at her clothes. A dizzying sense of movement swirled around her. She blinked away tears, able to see nothing beyond the blazing bright energy.

Take us home!

The vivianite grew warmer in her hand. The more she focused on going home, the hotter it became, until it burned brighter than the energy whirling around them. Caught in the currents of magic, she fought for control, and the resistance gradually melted away. A rushing sound filled Dru's ears, painfully loud.

Without warning, the brilliant magic released them, leaving them in darkness. Dru sagged against Greyson, blinking in a futile attempt to get rid of the spots in her vision.

In the thick silence left behind by the dying wind, Rane said, "So you guys still with me?"

"Yes," Dru and Greyson said in unison.

"Good." Rane pushed past them in the dark. Something thumped, hollow. "Huh. Some kind of wall up ahead. Wood, feels like."

"Okay." Dru tried to find her bearings. "Before we break anything, let's find out if—"

The sharp crack of splintering wood interrupted her. A jagged beam of light illuminated Rane and her fists as she smashed her way through into daylight.

"Or, we could just break things," Dru muttered.

Rane tore open a section of wood-plank wall and stepped through into sunlight, exposing a faded metal sign fastened by rusted nails to a wooden barrier that had been weathered silver by the elements. A skull and crossbones leered from the center of the sign, surrounded by block letters:

STAY OUT! STAY ALIVE! ABANDONED MINES ARE DEADLY!

Dru was still trying to puzzle that out as Greyson ducked through the broken lumber and nodded to her.

Past the sign lay a wide tunnel sloping gently uphill, toward the scent of pine trees. The dry dirt underfoot was littered with loose rocks and pine needles.

Greyson helped Dru up the slope, and they emerged into daylight, surrounded by brown rocks and dense trees.

Blinking, Dru turned and looked back the way they'd come. An abandoned mine entrance gaped open behind them, but the dark shaft beyond descended away into the blackness, much farther than they had walked from the cave.

With a grinding sound, Rane turned human again. "Looks like the Rocky Mountains, all right. Did you do this?"

Dru shielded her eyes and took in the mountain landscape around them: endless ranks of pine trees, broken by jumbles of granite boulders and dry ground scattered with wildflowers. "I was trying for Denver, but hey, not bad, right?"

Rane looked around at the pristine mountain wilderness and shrugged. "I *guess*. If you don't mind more walking."

"Ugh." Wincing in pain, Dru pulled one shoe off her tender heel. She sucked in a breath at the blister underneath, practically big enough to have a life of its own. She sat down on a nearby boulder and fished Band-Aids out of her purse, but Greyson took them from her.

"Let me." He knelt and gently lifted one of her ankles, then formed a makeshift bandage out of folded-up Starbucks napkins, using the Band-Aids to stick them in place.

Dru watched him work with a mixture of embarrassment and warm gratitude. "Guess I could've picked better shoes for this trip."

He smiled. She tried to ignore the fact that he still wasn't wearing a shirt beneath his leather jacket, but she was in precisely the wrong position to look away.

He finished bandaging her other ankle, waited for her to get her shoes on, then pulled her to her feet.

"Thanks." A sudden head rush made her feel a little dizzy, and she leaned against him for a moment.

He put a steadying hand on her back. Nothing more than that, but she was intensely aware of his touch.

Slowly, she lifted her gaze until she was looking up into his eyes. This close, their red glow sent a shiver down her spine. In the back of her mind, a little alarm bell went off. It would have been easy to blot it out, and she was strongly tempted to.

But she couldn't.

"Hey, hello?" Rane glared at Greyson's back. "Finished with your emergency pedicure yet?"

Dru backed away from Greyson, avoiding his eyes. "We should go."

Rane shot her a warning glare, which Dru pretended not to see. She pointed downhill, toward a clear-cut strip through the pine trees. "That could be something."

They set off and soon found an old gravel trail that had once been a dirt road, now overgrown with hardy grass and cactuses. It switched back and forth down the steep slope.

Once they broke out of the trees, Dru realized something wasn't quite right about the sunlight. It had an unsettling fiery quality, somewhere between a bloody red sunset and the ominous greenish-yellow sky that preceded a tornado. The wind picked up, carrying a harsh mineral scent, like rotten eggs.

Rane wrinkled her nose. "What the hell *is* that?"

"Hell. Literally." At her baffled look, Dru explained. "Sulfur. You know, fire and brimstone? Hell on earth? The end of days? Guess this is what it smells like."

"Long as it's not me," Rane muttered, checking her armpits.

"We need to get back to the shop." Dru turned to Greyson. "The other Horsemen are loose in the world, so it would make sense that the world is reacting to their presence. And I'm betting this is only going to get worse until we can cure you."

He seemed distracted by something, but he nodded.

The trail finally ended at the weathered blacktop of a two-lane road, divided down the center by a broken yellow line, fringed on both sides by gravel. An old metal sign identified it as a Colorado state highway.

That lone proof of civilization made Dru crack a thankful smile. She almost sank to her knees in relief, and probably would have if Rane hadn't thrown an arm around her shoulders and shook her in triumph.

Greyson just frowned.

"Oh, lighten up," Rane said to him. "Aren't you glad to be back?"

Greyson's eyebrows furrowed. "Something's coming," he said quietly and lifted his gaze to the top of the next rise, where the blacktop road vanished over a crest.

Dru was about to ask him what he meant when she heard it, too. A motor, deep and distant but drawing closer.

It grew in volume, throaty and aggressive. Greyson bent his head down and blinked, as if trying to clear his eyes.

Dru put one hand on his arm, leaning close. "Are you okay?"

He gave her a haunted look, then quickly turned away. But not before she saw that the red glow in his eyes was brighter than ever. "There's a buzzing in my head. Getting louder."

A prickly hot wind swept down the road toward them, whispering through the pine trees, picking up bits of grit that pelted bare skin.

Dru turned to face into the wind. She stepped away from Greyson, gaze focused on the empty road at the top of the hill. She reached into her purse for the familiar cube of galena. When Rane saw her do that, she raised her own fist, ready to transform back into rock.

The engine noise peaked as a black car rose over the crest of the road, hurtling toward them. The thudding of its engine sounded less like a car motor and more like a mob of caged demons trying to pound their way out through the metal.

Rane tightened her fist around her ring, and with a grinding sound her body turned to solid flint. "You two get back. I'll cover you."

Dru put a cautioning hand on Rane's arm, slowly stepping uphill past her. "It doesn't make any sense. How could the Horsemen get here so fast?"

"Hell, *we* got here this fast. Maybe they've got some kind of trick door, too."

The car swooped toward them, a wedge of impenetrable blackness streaking down the asphalt.

"But think about the Horsemen that chased us," Dru said. "There was the red Mustang, a white truck, and a silver car. This isn't one of them."

"No," Greyson said behind them, his voice a husky whisper. "It's Hellbringer."

Dru glanced over her shoulder at him, but he looked as surprised as she was.

Rane scowled. "I thought you zapped that thing into oblivion with the magic circle?"

"Apparently, the circle expired."

The long black wedge shape, with its tall spoiler wing rising up in back, bore down on them. Just when Dru feared it would try to run them down, the car locked up its brakes. The tires howled as the car swung around, scribing black half circles of rubber across the pavement, like smoking claw marks.

Hellbringer came to a full stop across the pavement before them. Its engine barked twice, then settled down into a sinister growl.

No one sat in the driver's seat. It had come on its own.

Like a warhorse of the apocalypse, Dru thought. Smart enough to come to its rider. Mean enough to fight on its own.

For a moment, nobody moved.

Greyson slowly approached the car, his boots noiseless on the asphalt. When he was still several yards away, the driver's door swung open, waiting for him. The engine revved, pounding out exhaust notes that thudded through Dru's rib cage.

Beside her, Rane muttered, "Oh, *hell* no. I'd rather walk."

Dru tried to weigh the apprehension pulsing inside her against their other options, then realized she couldn't come up with any.

That thing was created to be evil, no doubt about it. It was a demon, an instrument of the apocalypse. And it had already tried to kill Rane once.

But now it seemed to be responding to Greyson, and somehow it had come to find them when they needed it most. Could Hellbringer be trusted?

"D? We are *so* not doing this. I don't care if we have to walk back to town. Tell me we are not getting in that car."

"Do you want to save the world?" Dru said.

Rane just grunted.

Greyson looked back over his shoulder at them, his eyes a fierce red. "So. You ladies want a ride?"

Dru and Rane traded glances.

After a tense moment, Rane blew out her breath and groaned. *"Seriously?"*

30

HEART OF THE BEAST

Dru was terrified. Being strapped into the front passenger seat of Hellbringer was like being loaded into a cannon and fired out of the pit of Dante's *Inferno*.

The roar of the engine shook her entire body, reverberating not just in her eardrums but up through her lungs as well. It was a deep, all-encompassing power like nothing she had ever experienced before. She couldn't just blot it out. It swept right through her, undeniable, unstoppable.

The black car assaulted her with its very presence. Its cavernous yet oddly claustrophobic interior made her feel as if it was trying to swallow her whole. Black surfaces boxed her in, and the short windows seemed to let in as little light as possible. The air inside the car smelled of age, not unlike an old library, overlaid with a dense smokiness she remembered from childhood road trips.

The acceleration crushed her back into the seat. Each bend in the road jammed her against the hard door panel on her right or the edge of the console on her left. Since the front seat only sported a lap belt, without any shoulder strap, it didn't do much to hold her in place.

She braced herself the best she could, knuckles white, and raised her voice to be heard over the oppressive motor. "There aren't any airbags in this thing, are there?"

Greyson, grinning, pulled a spare pair of sunglasses from the visor and slipped them on. "If they still built cars as solid as this, we wouldn't need airbags."

Dru decided not to debate the logic in that statement.

After a few miles, Dru relaxed her grip on the armrest and tried to take some deep breaths. Despite the insanely fast speed they were traveling, Hellbringer moved in a sure way that felt practically alive, curling into the turns like a lithe animal.

Soon, she found that she could anticipate the movements and correspondingly tilt her weight one way or another to stay planted in the seat. It was more like being an active rider than a passive passenger. In other circumstances, it could have been exhilarating, but right now it was simply exhausting.

Something about that thought nagged at her. In all her years of research on demons, she had studied reports on hundreds of different varieties. And although none of her books ever made specific references to the Four Horsemen of the Apocalypse, she had read more than one account of supernatural beings riding demonic mounts.

Some mounts were trained to destroy their enemies in battle. Some were chosen for their loyalty to a particular force of darkness. A few, she was sure, were selected simply to terrorize their foes. But one thing Hellbringer clearly excelled at was speed.

Dru glanced over at Greyson, his glowing red eyes hidden behind his sunglasses, then turned around to Rane, who sat in the back seat with arms petulantly folded across her chest.

"I think I know what this thing is," Dru said over the engine noise. Rane leaned forward, one ear cocked, and Dru repeated herself, louder.

"It's going to kill us, is what it is," Rane said. "Come on, you saw *Christine*, right? This thing could just go ahead and flip over, crash into a wall, catch on fire, do whatever. And what does it care? It can heal itself. And dump our dead bodies on the side of the road."

Dru stared at her in horror, struck speechless.

Rane nodded. "Tell me you're not thinking the same thing, right?"

Actually none of those thoughts had occurred to Dru at all. She decided it would be a good time to change topics. "Listen, I have an idea. The Four Horsemen are supposed to ride all around the entire world, bringing the apocalypse. To do that, they'd want to move fast, right? Demonically fast."

"I guess. Why?"

"Well, what if Hellbringer is a speed demon?"

"That's a thing?"

Dru nodded. "Not just a figure of speech."

"Still, going around the entire world?" Rane looked skeptical. "First off, the world is really freaking gi-*normous*, so you'd have to go like NASA speed to circle around it in a day. Second, what about all the oceans? You can't drive across water."

"Maybe this thing can." Dru shrugged, wondering. "But that's not the point. The point is, if it really is a speed demon, I might know how to destroy it."

"Destroy it," Rane echoed, as if savoring the word. She nodded her approval.

The roar of the engine dropped into a guttural warble, then coughed and went silent. The sudden lurch of deceleration threw Dru off-balance. She reached out both hands to steady herself.

"The hell?" Greyson said in the deafening quiet, then played with the gear shift and the ignition key. It didn't seem to do any good.

Dru tried to peer across to see the gauges. "Did we run out of gas?"

"No. Something's wrong."

They coasted down a long slope, a brown rocky cliff rising up on their left, a steep chasm open on their right. Ahead, the road made a sharp left turn, protected by a guardrail. Beyond the guardrail lay nothing but empty air and the distant pine trees of the far slope. If they didn't turn, they would go right through the guardrail and down untold hundreds of feet to the next rocky ledge below, or possibly all the way to the bottom.

Out of the corner of her mouth, Rane said, "Maybe the *speed demon* heard you."

Greyson gave Dru a sharp look. "Heard you what?"

"Nothing." Dru tried to look innocent. "Did you check the gas?"

"We didn't run out of *gas*," Greyson snapped. "What did you say?"

"Just . . ." She tried not to wither under Greyson's glare. "I may have, maybe, alluded to . . . destroying Hellbringer."

They kept rolling downhill without power, the wind noise whistling louder around them. A bad feeling settled in the pit of her stomach. Maybe Hellbringer really *had* heard her.

Greyson stared ahead at the sharp turn and tightened his grip on the wheel. "Hellbringer came to help us. Why would you want to destroy it?"

"Destroy a demon?" Rane said with a mock gasp. "What sort of crazy talk is that? Oh, wait. Here's a wacky idea. Let's just start *trusting* demons. Because how could that possibly go wrong?" She shot a dangerous look at Dru, who tried to ignore it.

"I thought I broke the connection with that spell," Dru said.

"Hellbringer is still connected to me," Greyson said. "I can feel it."

"Apparently," Dru agreed. "But what if this thing is actually driving *you* instead of the other way around? We know it's a demon. Demons generally equal evil."

"Right now's not the best time for a debate," Greyson said.

"But what if destroying this car is a necessary part of your cure?" Dru's pulse picked up as they approached the turn. "Um, you can stop the car anytime."

"Now would be good," Rane added.

"I'm trying," Greyson said through gritted teeth. "We're in gear, but we're just rolling along without power. And right now, I've got the brake pedal to the floor. Nothing works."

Uh-oh. "That's not good, is it?"

The muscles in Greyson's jaw clenched. "I can't stop this car."

They kept picking up speed, rolling straight downhill toward the guardrail, everything quiet but for the wind. A rush of cold fear shot through Dru's veins.

"I know Hellbringer attacked you," Greyson said flatly. "But so did I. The demon inside me did it, and that doesn't excuse it, but that doesn't make me evil, either. Maybe Hellbringer was just protecting me."

"Oh, sure, that's it," Rane said, her voice dripping with sarcasm before it turned serious. "D, say the word, and I'll go stone and jump out. I can take you with me."

Dru noticed that she made no mention of taking Greyson along.

"Dru?" Greyson said, the urgency plain in his voice. They'd almost reached the bottom of the hill, closing in fast on the guardrail. "I'm running low on ideas."

Dru placed one palm flat on the dashboard. "Hellbringer, can you hear me?" She didn't know what she expected. Maybe not a voice, but some kind of response, maybe a creak or a growl from the engine. She got nothing.

Nothing but the rush of wind over the car as it hurtled straight down the mountain highway.

Rane seized her arm and said something about making a jump for it, *right now*, but Dru wasn't listening. She could only stare ahead at the empty air and the endless pine forests far beyond, the trees from this distance nothing more than miniature points tinged blue by the atmosphere.

The thin air. Nothingness. Endlessness.

If someone had threatened to destroy her—and these days, that felt like a daily occurrence—what would she do?

Try to work it out first. Make a peace offering. Offer assistance, especially if that person was in trouble.

And if that didn't work?

I'd try to destroy them before they got me, she thought.

Just like Hellbringer was about to do.

The black metal of the dashboard grew warm under her hand. "Hellbringer," she whispered, "I understand."

Ahead, the guardrail loomed as they rushed straight for it.

"We won't destroy you," Dru whispered. "If you help us, help save us, we'll save you. That's the truth."

But demons didn't believe in truth, only oaths. A sorcio phrase popped into her mind, gleaned from one of her long-forgotten books.

"*Mi juras, Infernotoris*," she intoned solemnly. *I swear to you, Hellbringer.*

Something trembled through the metal beneath her fingers. Nothing she could pinpoint or explain. Just a feeling that something crucial had shifted.

The engine rumbled back to life, and the wheels locked up with a howl of rubber. Greyson, startled into action, spun the wheel. They skidded to a stop mere inches from the guardrail. The noise of the skidding tires etched itself into Dru's brain.

And then all was quiet.

Through the window, all Dru could see was the distant carpet of pine trees on the far slope, and the snowy peaks of blue mountains ranked into the fading distance. For a heart-stopping moment, she thought they'd gone over the edge. It was only when Rane let go of her arm that she fully realized they had stopped.

They sat motionless at the edge of the road, engine thrumming, while Dru tried to get her racing heartbeat back under control.

"We'll talk later," Rane whispered in her ear. She nodded meaningfully, then mouthed the word *Christine*.

Greyson slid his sunglasses off and seemed to contemplate them for a long moment. He blew out a slow breath but said nothing. When he finally looked over at Dru, his eyes glowed a steady red.

"I get it," she said quietly. "And I think Hellbringer understands me. It's worth saving." Dru wanted to add, *And so are you.*

Still, Greyson said nothing.

Dru gave him an awkward smile. "Sorry. Poor choice of words back there." She shrugged and held up both hands.

Rane snorted. "Yeah. Who knew this evil flying monkey death car of yours was so *sensitive?*"

Greyson glanced back at her, his expression wry, then turned to Dru. "So we're done here? I can just drive now?"

Dru smiled nervously. "Can we stop at Starbucks?"

"No." He slipped his sunglasses back on and shifted into gear.

"What if they have a drive-through?" But her words were lost in the sudden roar of the engine.

31

FADE INTO DARKNESS

T he closer they got to the city, the more traffic they saw, but it was all heading out of town. A few hapless accidents were enough to leave the highways jammed to a standstill.

The overcast sky grew darker as they drove, and the strangely rusty quality of the light that filtered down through the clouds made everything feel nightmarish and unreal.

But worst of all was Greyson's state of mind. The longer he drove Hellbringer, the more it seemed to get under his skin. He became irritable. His teeth looked a little bit sharper and his eyes brighter. It was as if the car gave him a constant dose of road rage.

Dru made a mental note to mix up a new potion as soon as they got back.

By the time they pulled up in front of The Crystal Connection, the uncanny sky was already dark enough to make the streetlights come on.

Greyson drove around into the alley behind the shop and backed the car into the narrow parking space. The walls of the adjacent buildings reflected Hellbringer's thudding exhaust notes back at them, nearly deafening even with the windows closed. When he shut the engine off, the silence settled on them as if it had physical weight.

Dru looked Greyson up and down with a critical eye, noticing the horns protruding farther from his forehead and his skin getting ruddier. Definitely time for a new potion.

Greyson eyed the alley with barely contained agitation. "What do we need here, anyway?"

Mentally, she added up a list. "Everything."

When Dru got inside, Opal swept her into a warm, perfume-scented hug. "Oh, my God, Dru. Where have you been? I've been worried sick."

Dru smiled wanly. "It was a long trip."

"You get my messages?"

"My phone died." Dru dug through the pile of books next to the ugly chairs to find the cord of the charger and plugged in her phone. "First, I need to get some midnight jade for Greyson."

Greyson stormed in behind her, glaring at everything around him, including Opal.

"My word." Opal backed up a step, eyes going wide. "You feeling all right, Greyson?"

He bared his teeth. "Fine."

"He will be in a minute," Dru called out from the front of the shop. She dug through her cardboard drawers of jade. It had occurred to her during the drive back that midnight jade, or Lemurian black jade, could be just the crystal he needed right now. She kept digging until she found a polished oblong stone about half the size of her palm.

She came back and pressed the crystal into Greyson's hand. His touch gave her a warm surge of energy, which she directed back into the smooth black rock. Flecks of pyrite glittered and shone within the darkness, like gold stars. "This should help protect you against the other Horsemen."

Without taking her worried eyes off Greyson, Opal put her hands on her hips. "What Horsemen? Dru, you see what's going on with the weather outside? This does not seem natural, by any stretch."

"I'll tell you later." Dru directed Greyson to go sit down in back, then wasted no time heading up front to mix together a new potion. By now, she had it down to a science. Or at least she hoped so.

Opal followed along as if to help but apparently changed her mind and drummed her fingers on the countertop instead. "So I suppose you didn't see the news on TV."

"We've been out of town," Rane said as she came in from the back room. "*Way* out of town."

Opal shrugged. "Anyway. They say it's unusual cloud formations. Spreading out all over the country. People keep asking, 'Has there been some kind of chemical spill or something?' That horrible smell in the air. Whole city smells like a damn frat house on burrito night." Her eyes turned skyward. "I've got to wonder if it's 'cause of the meteors."

Dru paused in the midst of measuring ingredients into a metal bowl. "Um, meteors?"

"Yeah. Sky's falling, for real. Some kind of big meteor shower. It keeps knocking out satellites, so the media is having a field day with it. But you ask me? I don't think anybody's got a clue what's really going on."

Dru carefully stirred the potion. "The signs of the apocalypse."

"Don't I know it." Opal rolled her eyes. "They've been telling everybody to stay indoors. 'Course, you know that means everybody's been getting the heck out of town. Traffic on the highway is a nightmare. That's why I had to open late today, just so you know. And I've got errands to run this afternoon." She paused, one immaculately drawn eyebrow lifted. "Wait a minute. When you say the signs of the apocalypse, you don't really mean—"

Dru nodded somberly.

Opal looked puzzled. "I mean, you don't *really* mean—"

"Hold that thought." Dru decanted the potion into a bottle, covered the mouth with her thumb, shook it, and brought it back to Greyson.

He sat quietly with the midnight jade cupped in his hands, an anguished look on his face.

When she held out the bottle, Greyson looked up. "Do you really think you can get this thing out of me? Or are you just wasting time on me when you could be trying to stop the apocalypse?"

"Stopping the apocalypse starts with you." Fear radiated off him, even though he hid it well. "Now, drink this."

"The whole thing?"

"Don't worry, this one's alcohol-free. I used a petalite elixir this time. Made from the same kind of crystal that I gave you in the beginning. But you might need some Tums later."

Up front, Opal's voice went shrill, the words lost in a frantic tirade. Dru was still debating whether she wanted to investigate when Rane came stomping back. "Dude, she's totally freaking out. I don't have the energy to deal with this. I've been burning calories like a maniac. Got any protein?"

"Fridge is upstairs." Dru nodded toward the stairwell door. "You know where it is."

As Rane headed upstairs to Dru's apartment, Opal hustled into the back room sniffling, holding her phone like a fragile egg. "I can't reach my man." She tottered past Greyson on plum-sequined heels and dropped into the chair next to him. "He's supposed to call me on his lunch break. Why does that man always forget? And now the world's ending."

Dru came over and laid a comforting hand on Opal's arm. "We won't let the apocalypse happen. I promise."

Opal dabbed at the corners of her eyes with a tissue and gave Dru a terrified look. "Tell me you've got a plan."

"Well, um . . ."

Without warning, Opal slapped Greyson on the shoulder. "What did you *do*, Mr. Greyson?"

He finished chugging his potion and set down the empty bottle. Wiping his mouth with the back of his hand, he looked from Opal to Dru and back, obviously uncomfortable. The moment stretched out. Finally, he cleared his throat. "I'm just going to take a walk." He got up and left.

Dru let out a long breath and sat down next to Opal, who sighed.

Then Opal touched Dru's arm and leaned in close. "You did notice that man's not wearing a shirt under his leather jacket?"

"Yeah, kind of my fault." At Opal's sharp look, Dru felt her cheeks reddening. "Well, I sort of ripped his shirt off. But I had a perfectly good, logical reason."

"Mmm-hmm." Opal nodded knowingly. "That's what I always tell myself."

"So I'll just go upstairs and get Greyson a shirt."

"Good thinking."

When Dru came back down with the T-shirt and found Greyson, his eyebrows went up.

"Face?" he said. "I take it that's the front?"

Confused, Dru checked the front of the shirt and laughed. "Oh, yeah. Face Vocal Band. Kind of a rock thing, only no instruments, just voices.

You've got to hear them sing 'How Was the Show Last Night?'" She held out the shirt. "I got this at a concert, and Nate never wanted it, so I figured if maybe you were getting cold . . ."

Opal snorted.

"Thanks." Greyson took the shirt.

As he stripped off his jacket, Opal's gaze lifted from the old book she was slowly paging through and roamed up and down Greyson. Dru shot her a reproachful frown, but Opal feigned innocence.

The T-shirt stretched tight over Greyson's shoulders and chest, distorting the four letters of the Face logo into four oblong shapes. He shrugged his jacket back on, straining the shirt's seams.

As Dru tried to clear the visual of Greyson's bare, muscled chest from her mind, she searched around for the Harbingers' journal. "Opal, we had a book here. A hardbound journal, mid-twentieth century. Had a drawing of a seven-fingered hand on it. Do you know where that got to?"

Opal looked up. "Hmm? Oh, Salem took it."

"What? *Why?*"

"He said you sold it to him," Opal said defensively. "I'm sorry, I thought you were trying to operate a for-profit business here?"

A cold feeling settled over Dru. "I didn't sell it to him. He's lying."

Rane walked in, chewing as she stuffed chicken bones and empty food containers into the already full trash can. "What would Salem want with the Harbingers' book?"

"Hopefully, he wants the same thing we do. It's the only clue we've got about the Harbingers. Opal, could you call Salem, please? Tell him we need that book back. Immediately."

Grumbling under her breath, Opal looked up his phone number and dialed, but a few seconds later she shook her head. "He's not answering. Want me to leave a message?"

Rane crumpled up a paper bag in her fist. "I've got a message for him."

"Tell him it's a matter of life or death," Dru said. "Totally serious."

As Opal left the message, Rane finished disposing of the wreckage of her feeding frenzy.

Dru pointed at the pile of bones. "Was that my rotisserie chicken?"

"I was hungry. Look, we can't just sit around and wait for Salem to get around to calling back. Because take it from me, he doesn't call."

"What else can we do? We can't just break into his house and get it."

Rane snorted. "Why not? I used to break into his place all the time. That's how we met."

Greyson stepped closer, red eyes glowing. "This Salem, he's one of the good guys?"

"Sure. I mean, mostly." Dru wasn't entirely sure about that. "It's not like he's ever done anything bad."

Rane scowled. "Dumping me doesn't count?"

"I mean, not *evil* bad." She wavered, remembering what he'd said in the alley outside. "When I asked him about the Harbingers' symbol the other day, he lied to me. He must know about them, obviously, or else he wouldn't have recognized the seven-fingered hand. And he lied to Opal. I never sold him the Harbingers' journal. He stole it."

Greyson nodded once, decisively. "That settles it. Let's go." With a jingle, he pulled out his car keys.

"Go where?"

"Go find this Salem and get your book back."

32

THE DOOMSDAY WALL

Salem's hideout was squirreled away in an abandoned industrial building overlooking a rusty stretch of railroad tracks. Rather than enter the ground floor, with its smashed windows and blooms of graffiti, Rane led Dru and Greyson up the fire escape.

After debating whether to bring Opal along, Dru had decided she couldn't risk a confrontation between Opal and Salem. Besides, back at the shop, Opal could continue their research. Dru hoped she could turn up something. Right now they needed all the information they could get.

At the top of the fire escape, across a flat stretch of asphalt roof, stood a black metal door, the only entrance to the upper floor. A lone window above the door glowed with candlelight.

"Do you think he's home?" Dru whispered.

Rane shook her head no. "He only closes the door when he's out. It's protected by a pretty badass warding spell. Anyone who touches it will get a gnarly surprise. If they're human, anyway."

"There must be a way for us to open it. Let me have a look." Dru started to dig through her purse for her ulexite crystal.

"Nah. There's an easier way. The trick is to not be human when you touch the door."

At Dru's puzzled look, Rane smirked. "Watch and learn."

Rane crossed the rooftop to the door, then licked her finger and reached up. With her six feet height, she had no trouble reaching the grimy window above the door and polishing the dirt off a tiny circle of glass with her wet fingertip.

Then, tensing, she pressed her fingertip hard against the window.

With an icy ringing sound, her whole body transformed into clear glass. In the starless night, she became nearly invisible.

Carefully, she grasped the doorknob and turned it. The door swung open to the warm glow of candlelight. It glimmered and shone through her glass body.

"And *that*," Rane said from the darkness, "is how you do it."

Dru and Greyson followed her inside. Salem's place occupied the top floor of the abandoned building, a maze of antiques and magical junk packed under a slanted roof. Clusters of candles burned here and there on foundations of built-up melted wax.

An old cigar box sat near the door, its lid flipped open. It was half full of sand, and someone, presumably Salem, had drawn an unfamiliar sorcio sign in it. A grid of four crystals sat at the corners of the box to focus whatever magic power the symbol conjured up. Nearby sat the red zincite crystal Dru had sold him the other day.

Looking around the room, Dru was reminded why she had started dating Nate in the first place. A sorcerer like Salem couldn't have a secure, supportive relationship with anyone. Then again, Salem wasn't typical of most sorcerers. Some of them were even crazier.

"Over here," Greyson called. "You're going to want to see this." He stood before an entire wall turned into a vision board for the end of the world.

Ancient drawings, newspaper clippings, photos, maps, and printouts all hung layered one over another, forming a ragged collage of the apocalypse. It took Dru a minute to soak it in.

Rane let out a long whistle.

"Salem's been at this for a while." Dru pointed out torn sections of city maps that identified three individual houses, colored in with a yellow highlighter. "He told me that he was investigating a string of disappearances."

Hand-drawn lines led from each house to a row of mugshots of three scruffy, unsavory-looking men with sunken eyes and hard stares. Beneath each photo was pinned a printout listing a name, description, address, and a list of criminal offenses: assault, burglary, and worse. Someone had written in bold marker above each, "Red. White. Silver."

In the fourth column, labeled "Black," was nothing but a hand-drawn rectangle containing a question mark.

Rane tapped her finger on the rectangle. "That's where you go, bub."

Greyson shook his head. "Doesn't make sense. These are the other three Horsemen? They're all criminals."

"Weak-willed," Dru said. "Easy prey for demons. But in your case, Hellbringer was drawn to your innate magical power."

"Unless," Rane added, "you've got some kind of sordid, criminal-mastermind past we don't know about?"

Greyson looked directly at her. "It's true. You didn't know?"

Rane rolled her eyes. "Whatever."

His red eyes turned back to Dru, the trace of amusement in them vanishing. He didn't have to say out loud what they were both thinking: he would be the fourth Horseman right now if it weren't for her.

"Hey." Rane tapped her fingers on a cluster of handwritten pages. "Looks like Salem tore these out of your book."

Cursing inwardly, Dru scanned the pages. They were definitely torn from the Harbingers' journal. The scribbled handwriting ranted endlessly about overpopulation, nuclear escalation, the destruction of the environment, even the moon landing. Clearly, whatever nameless sorcerer had written this was disgusted with the state of the world in the late 1960s.

Someone had recently highlighted the phrase she had seen earlier:

The day has come to wipe the slate clean. Do it over, and do it right. Apokalipso voluta is the key. With it, we Harbingers will remake the world the way it was meant to be.

"*Apokalipso voluta.* 'The apocalypse scroll,'" Dru translated aloud. Nearby hung a drawing taken from a faded medieval text, showing a single scroll with seven seals. She skimmed over the lengthy notes pinned around it. "Breaking the seven seals on this scroll supposedly triggers the apocalypse. People have been searching for it for centuries. Some, because they want to save the world. Others, because they want to destroy it."

"Do you think the Harbingers found it?" Greyson said.

"They had to, in order to summon the Four Horsemen. But it couldn't have been easy." Dru pointed to a map of New Mexico. A scanned and blown-up series of hand-drawn symbols laid out the now-familiar sorcio code for *causeway*. "What if there was a reason no one had ever found the scroll before? What if it wasn't anywhere on earth? If the apocalypse scroll was hidden in the netherworld, the Harbingers could've built this portal to gain access to the causeways and go find it."

She spotted a black-and-white photo of the Harbingers. The shot was similar to the one she had already seen, but taken from slightly farther away, revealing that the Harbingers were standing at the base of their archway in the desert.

A detail caught her eye, something she hadn't noticed before: a line of sorcio signs carved into the base of the archway. They were so tiny she had trouble making them out. She took off her glasses and squinted. "I asked Salem if he knew the sign of a seven-fingered hand. He said no. Why would he lie to me?"

"I was trying to protect you," a voice said from across the room. Startled, Dru shoved her glasses back on and straightened up.

Salem stood in the doorway, his top hat casting a shadow over his features. He turned toward Greyson. "Who's your friend here? He seems not so fresh."

Dru pointed angrily at the pages torn from the Harbinger journal. "You stole this book from me. You lied about the Harbingers."

Salem shrugged and strolled inside, kicking the door shut behind him. "I try to keep amateurs out of the line of fire. Misplaced sense of duty, I suppose. Maybe instead I should just let you sacrifice your mortal soul. Your call." He took off his top hat, letting his long hair cascade over his face.

Rane planted a fist on her hip. "You could've just asked us for help and not been a complete jackwad about it."

Inwardly, Dru groaned. She should've known better than to risk putting Rane in the same room with Salem. She certainly hadn't forgiven him yet, and maybe never would, considering she apparently couldn't help but antagonize him.

It seemed to be working. Salem's face stiffened with anger, and he lifted one arm to point his long fingers at Rane. They rippled in a spidery, arcane gesture, and the air around his fingertips rippled with magic.

Instantly, Rane tightened her fist around her ring and transformed her body into shimmering titanium.

"Stop!" Dru shouted, drawing a startled look from Salem. She stepped between him and Rane. "You can keep the book. And we'll just leave. As soon as you tell me how to undo what the Harbingers did."

Slowly, Salem lowered his arm. He shook his hair out of his face and sniffed, smiling sadly. "You can't."

"I don't believe that," Dru said, with more conviction than she felt.

"Ooh. Denial. I like that strategy." He fixed her with a half-crazy stare, made even starker by the black eyeliner around his eyes. "What are the stages again? We've already had anger. Next we're onto, what, bargaining?"

"You think this is some kind of joke?" Dru said.

He gave her a look of mock sorrow. "Darling, it's all one big cosmic joke being played on us. Don't you know that by now?"

With an effort, Dru resisted getting drawn into Salem's unhinged logic. "Look, you've obviously been studying these Harbingers. So just tell me. Did they really break the seals on the apocalypse scroll? Is that what's happening?"

He folded his arms. "Do you actually need me to tell you that?"

With a whisper of metal, Rane turned human again. "Forget it, D. He'll just keep messing with you until you can't think straight."

"No." Dru shook her head. "Salem, you know me. We're in this together. Talk to me."

Salem paced, his twitchy black-outlined eyes studying Greyson, paying considerable attention to the nubs of his horns. Greyson just stood his ground, shoulders back, locking stares with Salem until the sorcerer finally averted his gaze.

"They broke the first seal on the scroll in 1969," Salem said. "The apocalypse has been a long time coming, you know. You can't stop it just like that." He snapped his fingers. "They planned this all out from the beginning. They wanted to remake the world. Wipe the slate clean. Start over fresh and new, and do everything right."

"Sounds like you admire them," Dru said, unable to hide her disgust.

He shrugged. "We all have to die someday."

"But not all on the *same* day. So how do we stop it?"

"You?" He seemed amused by that. "Well, first, find the apocalypse scroll before all seven seals are broken. Good luck with that."

"How do you know they haven't broken all the seals already?"

"Because we're still standing here." With a sigh, Salem slunk across the room and gestured to a section of the wall over Dru's head, where he'd listed the seven seals as bullet points. "The first four seals have already been broken, conjuring up the Four Horsemen. Breaking the fifth seal makes the dead rise from the grave. And considering that the streets aren't crawling with hordes of zombies yet, I'm thinking seal number five is still wrapped for freshness."

"For now," Rane said.

"Who else knows about this?" Dru indicated the whole wall with a sweep of her arm. "We need all the help we can get. Every sorcerer, everywhere."

His crazed eyes turned toward her, suddenly piercing. "You think you're the first one to try to band everyone together into some kind of rah-rah super team to save the world? Please."

A sour feeling filled Dru's stomach. "You've already tried to stop this, haven't you?"

"Darling, half the sorcerers out there think the end is inevitable, and they're just waiting for the clock to run out. Others think the world *needs* to be put out of its misery. The rest suspect it's all some kind of cruel hoax, a trick to get them to show their cards. You know how we sorcerers are." He gave her a gaunt smile. "Trust is an issue."

"Shocking."

Rane put a heavy hand on Dru's shoulder. "Speaking of trust, don't listen to him. You don't know how much of this is gospel and how much is total crap."

Salem didn't seem fazed. "Notice how I've refrained from pointing out that you thieves callously invaded my sanctuary and snooped through my research."

Rane cocked her head. "Notice how I'm not kicking your ass?"

"Okay," Dru said, pushing Rane toward the door. "Okay. Time to go." As much as Dru wanted to count on Salem's help, it was obvious they were on their own.

"Just so we're clear," Greyson said to Salem, "we find the apocalypse scroll before the rest of the seals are broken, and this all ends."

Salem looked him over, one eye twitching. "You're an unusually sharp one, aren't you?"

"Greyson?" Dru called, holding the door open for Rane.

She could practically feel the intensity in the air as Greyson and Salem stared each other down. Finally, Greyson turned and followed Rane out onto the roof.

"Why isn't he like the other Horsemen?" Salem said just before Dru closed the door. His gaze turned icy. "Why is he still human?"

"How should I know?" Dru answered as sweetly as she could. "I'm just an amateur."

33

RADIOACTIVE

Find the scroll. That was all they had to do. But how?

Hellbringer carried them through the crowded night streets back toward The Crystal Connection. Even the growl of its engine seemed subdued by the impossible task ahead of them. The foul, brimstone-tainted air glowed in its headlights.

Dru's mind kept going back to that photo. There was something about that line of symbols beneath the archway that tugged at her, but now there was no way to know what they said. Besides, Salem was more fluent in sorcio signs than anyone she knew. If even he hadn't found anything important in that photo, there was probably nothing to find.

All of which put her back at square one. No clues, no scroll, nothing.

"By the way," Greyson said, breaking into her thoughts, "this is for you." He reached inside his leather jacket, pulled out a crinkled photo, and handed it over to her.

It was the photo of the Harbingers. The one with the line of symbols across the base of the archway.

He glanced up in the rearview mirror for a moment, headlights reflecting on his face, then turned his attention back to the road. "I saw you looking at it when Mr. Personality showed up. Rane was distracting him, so I took a chance and grabbed it for you."

She could have kissed him. Except for the possible magical consequences. "You're the best, you know that?"

Seeing her elated smile, his expression softened. "See? I am a criminal mastermind after all."

*   *   *

Back at the shop, Dru took off her glasses and studied the photograph under a magnifying glass. For once, being nearsighted had its advantages.

The edges of the black-and-white photo were notched and browned with age. A rusty U-shape was pressed into one edge, where it had been paper-clipped to something for many years.

She studied the line of symbols carved into the stone ramp beneath the Harbingers' feet. She hadn't noticed the symbols when she'd been at the archway, possibly because the base was covered up by desert sand, but mostly because they were busy running for their lives. She did have, however, the distinct feeling that the stones were built to accommodate a trapdoor or compartment of some kind.

Lips moving, she puzzled out the meaning of the symbols, occasionally checking them against the books she had opened up beside her. Connecting the dots simply made her more uneasy.

Rane leaned against her back, hair hanging down. "What does it say?"

Dru set down the photo and cleared her throat. "'Herein lies the end and the beginning.'"

Rane wrinkled her nose. "The hell does that mean?"

"We were right there, and we didn't see it. It's in there, buried inside the base of the archway."

Rane shook her head. "What is? I don't get it."

"That's where the Harbingers hid the apocalypse scroll." Dru's finger stabbed down on the photo. "Right there, in plain sight. Well, maybe not exactly *plain* sight, considering all of the obfuscation spells hiding the mansion, but plain enough."

Suddenly, the victorious poses of the seven Harbingers made sense. This wasn't just a portrait. These photos were probably taken right after they had succeeded where centuries of sorcerers had failed. They'd returned from the netherworld in possession of the scroll.

And they set the end of the world into motion.

Dru put her glasses on and reshelved her books. "We're going to need tools to dig that up. More crystals because I'm sure it's protected by spells. But my purse is totally full."

"You don't have one of those traveling jewelry cases?"

"Who am I, Martha Stewart? No. But I have an idea." Dru went up front and poked through the junk crammed under the cash register until she found a hardware kit, the kind that consisted of a plastic tray with assorted screws and nuts parceled into its small compartments. She dumped all of that into the trash, then loaded up the empty plastic case with her favorite crystals, one per compartment. "We'll need to be ready for anything when we get back to the mansion."

"The mansion?" Rane followed her. "Whoa, hang on, cowgirl. You want to go *back* there? Where all the Horsemen are?"

"And where the *scroll* is." Dru paused, crystals in hand. "Besides, I thought you were itching for a fight."

"*Pssh*, yeah, I'll take them on. But we need some kind of leverage. Something big we can hit them with. Some mondo kind of magic."

Rane went on, but Dru wasn't listening. Most of her truly powerful crystals were too big to fit in the plastic tray. She lined the crystals up on the edge of the counter, side by side, careful not to touch any two together that had opposing vibrations. The last thing she needed right now was a crystal accident.

The thought made her freeze to the spot.

Opposing vibrations.

A crystal explosion. She could make it happen. She had exactly the crystal to do it, though she'd kept it locked away in a lead box since she'd yanked it from the clutches of an ancient evil. "You want leverage to fight the Horsemen?" Dru said. "I'll give it to you."

She marched to the corner of the room, where the wall safe installed by a previous tenant was hidden behind a framed photo of Ming the Merciless. Over his enormous, smooth forehead, someone had drawn a word balloon on a yellow sticky note that read, "Pathetic Earthlings! Who can save you now?"

Opal looked up from the book she was reading and followed Dru's gaze to Ming's forehead and back. "Oh, no. Tell me you're not breaking that thing out."

"I have to," Dru said firmly. Ignoring Opal's warning look, she took down Ming's picture and started working the combination dial on the safe.

Opal stood up. "For real? It's not bad enough we had to outsmart a two-thousand-year-old sorcerer's *ghost* to lock that thing away. What was his name again?"

"Decimus the Accursed," Dru muttered.

"Decimus the *Accursed*," Opal repeated. "Now why do you want to go and get that bad mojo out again and risk blowing up the city?"

Rane looked from Opal back to Dru and lifted her chin. "So who's this Decimus dude?"

"Sorcerer in ancient Rome. Not exactly a swell guy." Dru got the safe open and pulled out the thick black rubber Hazmat-certified gloves she kept in there. "He built an impenetrable palace in Pompeii, surrounded by walls of magic warding spells." With a grunt, Dru pulled out a crushingly heavy lead-lined box and set it down on a nearby end table, making it creak. "Decimus drew his evil power from infernal spells that scores of generations of sorcerers had placed on Mount Vesuvius. His enemies were so desperate to stop him that they wiped out the entire city to get him."

"The entire city?" Rane said. "How?"

"With this." Dru undid the latches on the box with a sound like gunshots going off, one by one. She lifted the lid, wrinkling her nose at the musty smell that left a sharp, metallic taste in the back of her throat.

Inside the box, sitting in a square nest of foam rubber, sat a fist-sized angular crystal formed of thousands of stacked hexagonal layers, each one paper-thin, as dark as the darkest tinted glass. Dru carefully reached in with her gloved hand and picked up the crystal. Its black angles glittered with menace. "It's called biotite. It's a little bit radioactive."

"Radioactive?" Rane's eyes opened wide.

Opal gave her a look that said, *I told you so.*

"Only a little teensy bit radioactive. Not even enough to require a federal permit or anything," Dru said, hating the way it made her sound defensive. She had nothing to hide. "Look, there's no safe way to dispose of the biotite. And since this particular crystal has been charged with a huge amount of negative energy, I didn't want it falling into the wrong hands. It's not like I ever expected to actually use it myself. But this is an emergency."

Rane's lips twitched into a frown. "So this is your plan? Nuke the Horsemen?"

"Let's call it plan B. If all else fails, we can use this."

Opal, arms folded, slowly shook her head side to side. "Nothing good is gonna come out of this, I'm here to tell you. You'll be lucky if you don't blow yourselves up."

"True. Not the world's neatest idea." Dru swallowed and explained it to Rane. "Biotite, if it's charged up with enough power, can release destructive vibrations on a colossal scale. It literally reverses the bonds of magic, obliterating everything around it in a blast of total destruction. You want to talk about an uncontrolled chain reaction, this is it. Utter annihilation." She held it out to Opal. "Here."

Opal stood stock-still. "Don't think so, no."

"Fine." Dru put the biotite crystal back in the box and latched it shut. The sudden relief in the room was almost palpable. She stripped off her gloves. "We'll take this with us."

Rane looked like she'd just come face-to-face with a very large and poisonous insect, but she grabbed the box anyway. "Whatever. Where's Greyson?"

Opal pointed toward the back door.

Rane headed that way but paused for a second in the doorway. Over her shoulder, she said, "Hey, when are you going to tell your dude what we did to his car?"

For a split second, Dru thought she was referring to Hellbringer. And then she remembered Nate's car. Smashed to pieces in the middle of the New Mexico desert.

Oops.

"I'll figure something out," Dru said. But right now, there was no time to worry about that. If they were going to fight the Horsemen, she needed to do more research. She pulled down a stack of leather-bound tomes from a narrow space just below the yellowing ceiling tiles.

First *The Grimoire of Diabolical Consorts.* Then *The Cyclopedia of Fallen Angels.*

While she was at it, she grabbed a trio of thick matching folios. A hand-lettered card clipped to the top book's spine read, "Scioptic Whitchcraft and Calamituous Inscriptions Most Noxious."

"Sure," she decided aloud. "Why not."

Staggering under the weight of the books, she headed up front, Opal following along. "Opal, do you remember those doomsday books we got from the Puritan Museum, the tall, smelly ones?"

But instead of answering, Opal stopped by the cash register and stared out the shop's front windows, a mystified look on her face.

As Dru opened her mouth to ask what was wrong, bright lights shone through the night-darkened windows, illuminating Opal's face. Outside, an engine roared, tires squealed, and Dru realized that the lights she was seeing were actually headlights. Aimed straight at them.

The next instant, the entire front of the shop imploded.

34
THE END OF EVERYTHING

The old white truck punched through the front of the shop like a giant metal fist, smashing everything in its path. Headlights blazing, it obliterated the front windows of the shop, then the shelves carefully stocked with glass jars of herbs, rare and delicate crystals, lovingly hand-crafted good luck charms, and everything else Dru had accumulated over the years.

Gone. Every bit of it, in an instant. Crushed, smashed, tossed aside in a tidal wave of destruction before the white Bronco.

Bookshelves toppled and burst apart against its steel front bumper, one after another, falling like dominoes and flinging their contents into the air.

Opal stood frozen at the counter, directly in the onrushing path of destruction.

Dru had no time to plan, only to act. She dropped her books and sprang into motion, arms outstretched. Her legs churned, feeling as if they were stuck in mud. Even though Opal stood only a few strides away, it seemed like an endless stretch of distance. Dru couldn't cover it in time. She couldn't move fast enough.

The growing wave of wreckage, driven by the headlights and chrome grill of the Horseman's Bronco, rushed straight at them. The air filled with flying wreckage.

Dru barely noticed. Her vision narrowed down to a single focus: saving Opal.

She wrapped her arms around Opal, tackling her just as the avalanche of wreckage crashed down around them. The truck drove through the space where Opal had stood a half second before. Some unseen part of the truck caught Dru's foot as it went by, twisting her in midair.

Then the weight of broken shelves and falling debris buried her in darkness.

For a few agonizing moments, Dru didn't know whether she was dead or alive, which way was up or down, or if she was trapped in some kind of horribly vivid nightmare. But the pain of dozens of sharp objects digging into her body was all too real.

She struggled to move, but she was pinned beneath crushing weight, pressed against the soft mass of Opal, whose tightly curled hair tickled her nose with the scent of knock-off Chanel.

"Are you okay?" Dru said, but she couldn't hear herself over the jagged roar of things falling and breaking. Dust choked the air, and the pressure on her back made it nearly impossible to breathe.

"Opal?"

No response.

Dru got one arm free and shook Opal, carefully at first, then with frightened urgency. "*Opal!* Wake up!"

Terrible thoughts swirled around her mind, but at a distance, as if they couldn't make any impression on her. The destruction around her was too vast, too total, to comprehend. It floated on the surface of her consciousness like oil on water, unable to mix.

The Horsemen were here. Her shop was gone. She was trapped. Opal could be dead.

None of it registered.

A scream built up inside some numb part of her, but it felt as if it belonged to someone else. She clamped down on it. She had to fight, even if she had no chance of winning.

She had to fight *right now*.

She twisted beneath the rubble until she worked her legs loose. After a couple of false starts, she pulled them in underneath her and pushed for all she was worth.

The weight on her back resisted at first, then started to budge. A crack of flickering light shone in from beside her, brightening as she forced the gap wider. The light fell across Opal's motionless form, her face turned sharply away, blood running across her cheek.

Seeing Opal lying there, so still, sent a brutal rush of adrenaline coursing through Dru's veins. She heaved with all her strength, lifting up against what she realized was a toppled bookshelf. Her whole body trembled with the effort.

"Dru!" Greyson called to her. "Dru!"

"Here!" she grunted.

A moment later, two strong hands clamped on the edge of the book-shelf and lifted it, freeing her.

She looked up into Greyson's stubbled face, smudged with dust, red eyes wild. He pulled her from the rubble. "Dru!" he shouted. "Are you okay? Are you hurt?"

Her glasses had been knocked loose, and she pushed them back up her nose. "Never mind me. It's Opal."

Greyson's jaw set in a grim line, and he shoved the bookshelf away, letting it topple to the side with a crash.

Dru felt Opal's warm neck for a pulse, but her hands shook so badly she couldn't tell anything.

Greyson knelt beside her and took over. "She's breathing. We've got to get her out of here." As he got his arms beneath Opal and lifted her free of the rubble, Dru turned to look in shock at all that remained of The Crystal Connection.

The lights overhead flickered with a spastic crackle of electricity. The white Bronco had come to a stop in the center of her shop, surrounded on three sides by heaps of wreckage. Behind, its path was swept almost completely clean, from the gaping empty front windows all the way to the cash register, where the truck had finally stopped.

The driver's door creaked open, thumping against a broken wooden cabinet. Out of the driver's seat stepped a hulking white creature, shiny and colorless as newly cleaned teeth. He loomed over the still-rumbling truck, his massive head turning left and right until his glowing sapphire-blue eyes focused on Greyson.

Jagged horns jutted out from every part of the thing's gnarled body, from his tree-trunk legs up to his colossal shoulders. More horns ringed the top of his head, each one curving out and up to a deadly point, the circle of horns forming an infernal crown.

The hellish creature extended a single clawed finger at Greyson. He opened a mouth lined with knife-sharp canines, releasing a string of ropey drool as he spoke two words in a voice like fracturing rock.

"Join. Us."

Dru turned immediately to Greyson, and the unwavering determination in his eyes blew away any doubts she had about him. He wasn't about to complete the set and become the fourth Horseman, bringing about the end of the world.

He had a plan, she could tell. Which was good, because right now, she had nothing.

More car headlights flashed across the wreckage of the store. On the night-darkened street out in front, the red Mustang pulled up with a squeal of tires. The curvy silver Ferrari glided to a stop behind it. The other two Horsemen had arrived.

She recognized the red reptilian Horseman from the mansion, the one that had erupted from the pit. As he stepped in through the gaping hole where the front windows had been, he produced a sword composed entirely of flames. Its flickering light reflected off his shiny scales and the carpet of broken glass. A sinuous purple tongue slipped between his jagged teeth and switched back and forth through the air.

Close behind him came a translucent, skeletal creature with shimmering green eyes. This one scurried on lanky legs. His entire body seemed to be formed of glassy needles, fused together in a malformed mockery of a human skeleton. As he approached, he twitched fingers nearly as long as his forearms. The air between his finger bones wavered, rippling with intense heat or unholy energy.

All three of the Horsemen stared hungrily at Greyson, who slowly lowered Opal's limp form to the floor.

"Wait, wait," Dru said, her throat tight with worry. "What are you doing? Pick her up!"

He shook his head, eyeing the Horsemen closing in on them. In a low voice, he said, "There's no way I can get Opal out of here safely, not with them after me. Our only chance is if I distract them, lead them away."

It took her a second to find her voice again. "That won't work."

"I can get them to chase me." He tensed. "Ready?"

"No. No!" This was a terrible plan, but she had nothing else. They needed to fight their way out, together. They needed Rane.

Dru cupped her hands around her mouth, about to yell Rane's name. But a blur of movement from the back of the shop beat her to it.

The flickering fluorescent lights illuminated a streak of motion. Rane charged out of the darkness, gripping a rust-dotted length of iron pipe in both hands like a super-sized baseball bat. The flashes of light caught her in midstride as her body transformed into rust-mottled metal.

With a flying leap, Rane came straight up behind the white Horseman, her lips drawn back from her teeth with savage fury. She swung the pipe around and down in a deadly arc with enough force to crush any mortal creature.

Without turning his burning sapphire gaze away from Greyson, the white Horseman raised his horn-studded arm and swatted Rane's blow aside.

But Rane had fought demons and monsters all her life. And what the white Horseman hadn't anticipated was that the metal pipe was a feint. A mere distraction.

The real weapon was Rane herself.

In one fluid motion, as the metal pipe spun away, Rane drove all of her mass and velocity fist-first into the base of the white Horseman's skull, plowing him facedown onto the floor.

He toppled with a resounding crash, Rane astride his back.

"I'm on this," Rane said, her voice ringing like empty pipe. "You two grab Opal."

Before Dru could respond, the red Horseman came at Rane with his flaming sword, swinging a fiery crescent at her head. She ducked under the blade, the crimson flames shining off the muscles flexing in her iron body. She stepped beneath the infernal sword and brought her fist up, twisting into the force of the blow.

The impact lifted the red Horseman off his feet, hurling him into his pale skeletal companion. The two of them flew into the far wall, crushing one of the few shelves left intact.

Greyson didn't hesitate. He scooped up Opal again and motioned to Dru with a jerk of his head. She stumbled over the rubble, following him away from the fight, toward the back door.

As Rane closed in on the other two Horsemen, ready to strike, the white Horseman stirred. He got one spiky arm beneath him and pushed himself upright. He stretched out his other arm, his empty fist pointed directly at Rane's unguarded back.

Dru didn't know what that move meant, but it looked dangerous. "Rane! Behind you!"

Rane turned, crouching down just as one of the white Horseman's spiky horns shot out as if fired from a crossbow. It whistled across the open space of the demolished shop, missing Rane's head by inches, and punched a hole through the far wall with a wicked splintering sound.

Immediately, another horn sprouted into place on his arm.

Rane dodged to the side, ducking and leaping as the white Horseman rapidly fired more horn spurs, chopping apart the wreckage around her.

The other Horsemen got to their feet and closed in on either side. Suddenly on the defensive, Rane was quickly surrounded.

"Keep going!" Greyson barked to Dru as he carried Opal toward the back of the shop.

Sparking electrical wires hung down from the ceiling. The lights flickered on and off, illuminating the Horsemen of the Apocalypse fighting through the destroyed remains of her shop. Nothing was left standing, other than a few shelves of crystals along the periphery of the shop.

The Horsemen were all surrounded by crystals, Dru realized. If only she could power them up.

Dru quickly looked around. She needed copper wire, but there was no telling where her spool of wire had gone. Probably crushed under the white Bronco.

She spotted an orange electrical extension cord. The wires in it were copper. There was no time or tools to strip the insulation off them, but it would have to do. She climbed over the massive pile of wreckage to where her biggest amethyst crystal still sat against one wall.

"What are you doing?" Greyson shouted. "Come on!"

As fast as she could, she tied one end of the cord into a loop and fastened it around the huge rock, then jabbed the three copper prongs at the end into the purple crystal.

At the front of the shop, the red Horseman howled in triumph. Rane let out an agonized gasp, retreating from him with a sizzling red-hot gash glowing on her arm.

"Dru!" Greyson waited for her. "Come on!"

"I need your help!" Dru charged across the shop, stumbling over debris. The cord wasn't long enough to reach the knee-high mountain of smoky quartz in the other corner. "Greyson!"

He left Opal somewhere in back, out of sight, and ran to Dru, looking as if he was about to drag her off by force. "We need to *go!*"

"Not without Rane." She put as much fierceness into her voice as she could, and Greyson stopped short. She held out the electrical cord to him. "Take this."

Though obviously puzzled, he took the cord.

"You remember the circle I put under your car? This is a big, ugly version of that. When I say so, grab my hand. But not until I say." She stepped up to the monstrous smoky quartz and put her palm flat against its cold, rough-hewn point. She drew in a deep breath and shouted, "Rane! Bail out!"

Rane's head snapped around, getting a good look at Dru, the crystals, and the wire. Her eyes flashed with understanding. She left the red Horseman behind, dodged around the skeletal pale Horseman, and slid on her knees under the swinging spiky arm of the white Horseman. She vaulted off the side of the white truck and leaped past Dru, landing with a crash.

The moment Rane was clear of the crystals, Dru held her hand out to Greyson. "Now!"

The three Horsemen charged at them.

Dru stretched until her fingers met Greyson's. The moment their skin touched, a spark of magic shot up her arm. His powerful energy flowed into her, completing the circuit, and the quartz beneath her hand lit up from within.

It grew dazzlingly bright in an instant, powered by Dru's fear and rage. With all of the wreckage, she couldn't see the protective grid of crystals that she had evenly placed around the circumference of the store, but she could feel them interact with each other as she closed a dangerous loop.

With Greyson's power amplifying her own, the energy level surrounding the room quickly spiraled out of control. It rang through Dru's bones, whined in her ears, formed a smoky, metallic taste in the back of her throat. Eerie light burned around the periphery of her store, growing brighter by the second as each crystal in turn lit up.

The white Horseman drew up short, as if sensing the danger, and the other two Horsemen hesitated on either side of him. His blazing azure eyes pierced Dru where she stood.

He knew what she was doing. When he bared his teeth and raised both arms to point his deadly spikes at her, she realized she had no way to defend herself.

In a moment, it would be her who died here, not Rane.

A helpless fury rose up inside Dru, focused on the three creatures before her. They had destroyed everything. Everything she had fought her whole life to build.

Tried to kill her and her friends.

Tried to bring about the end of the world.

And she would *not* let them win.

She shut her eyes tight and channeled her anger into the crystals, charging them levels beyond anything she'd done before, letting the awful feedback rip through her body.

Pain scorched through her, out of her, at a terrifying frequency. The magic glow pounded through her tightly shut eyelids. A roaring wind swirled around her.

The Horsemen howled and screeched. Energy sizzled as they hurled their bodies against the magical vortex, trying to get out, trying to escape the pounding destruction Dru brought down on them.

Her ears rang. Her sense of balance abandoned her. She struggled to stay upright, fought to open her eyes, but she was lost in a searing maelstrom. The roar built into a bone-jarring thunder, crashing over and over.

The energy backlash blew out the protective crystals around her one by one, like old light bulbs overloaded by too much current.

When her body could take no more, she collapsed, breaking the connection. Her consciousness faded to a thin, fine line lost in an echoing distance. In the muffled silence, the world toppled and crashed.

She opened her eyes to darkness. Greyson leaned over her, his face inches from hers, calling her name.

She worked lips that felt too dry to speak. "Did we do it?"

He helped her sit up.

Her shop was utterly demolished.

What little had been left intact after the Horseman crashed in through the front windows was now pounded into unrecognizable bits, pocked here and there by guttering pools of fire.

The white truck was crushed into a charred wreck, and beside it, the three Horsemen lay facedown on the floor.

Seeing what remained of her shop filled her eyes with tears. A wrenching despair washed over her, hollowing out the victory until there was nothing left.

Greyson grimly pulled her to her feet. "You didn't have any choice."

She had to lean against him to stay upright. He helped her into the back room, where Opal lay unconscious in the near darkness.

Rane, her body still formed of rusty metal, took Dru out of Greyson's arms. "You're okay, D. Easy does it."

Dru was about to thank her, but a meager scratching sound caught her attention. Slowly, painfully, she turned her stiff neck and looked over her shoulder.

One of the white Horseman's fingers scratched against the floor, and then the rest of his hand quickly joined suit. With nightmarish slowness, he turned his horn-crowned head and opened glowing blue eyes. To either side of him, the other Horsemen stirred. As they did, the crushed hulk of the white truck began to uncrumple and smooth out.

The air seemed to leave Dru's lungs. She couldn't speak a warning, couldn't breathe.

She hadn't accomplished anything. She'd thrown everything she could at the Horsemen, sacrificed everything she had, and still she'd failed.

Greyson saw, but he didn't hesitate. "Rane, get her clear. I'll carry Opal."

"Where?" Rane demanded, her face twisting in rage. "Where else can we go? What the hell else can we do? We can't make a stand against these guys!"

"No," he said in a low voice, "but we can outrun them."

"How?"

In Greyson's eyes, an inner fire burned brighter. "We've got Hellbringer."

35

SPEED DEMONS

As they lowered Opal into Hellbringer's back seat, Dru heard sirens getting closer and louder. "I don't like moving her like this," she said.

"The hospital's not far," Greyson said grimly. "Get in."

Rane swung one long iron leg into the back, then the other, and slid in beneath Opal, cradling her head in her metal lap, using Greyson's leather jacket as a pillow.

Dru could barely tear her gaze away from Opal's motionless body. Even though she seemed to be breathing fine, she was still unconscious, and that could mask any number of injuries.

As Dru got into the front seat, she noticed the biotite lockbox sitting on the carpeted floor mat, next to her plastic hardware case full of crystals. "How did you . . . ?"

"I didn't have a chance to grab everything," Rane said at Dru's questioning look. "But I grabbed the essentials. We had company."

"Way to go."

Hellbringer rumbled to life before Dru even had the door shut. With a lurch, Greyson pulled them out of the parking spot behind The Crystal Connection and sped down the tight alley. The fact that he had already backed in saved them a minute of turning around. It wasn't much, but it could be enough of a head start.

Both sides of the street were lined with parked cars and storefronts, many of them closed up early, probably because of the widespread panic about the foul air and the meteors. The sidewalks were unusually empty. A strange haze choked the air, wrapping a halo around the streetlights, giving a weight to the light.

As they pulled out of the back alley onto the side street, the red Mustang whipped around the corner from the front of the shop, sliding sideways on four howling tires. Its fiery headlights speared through the night, sweeping toward them.

"Damn," Greyson spat and spun the wheel away from the Mustang. Hellbringer's engine revved up with an earsplitting roar, and the acceleration pressed Dru into the seat. They rocketed away down the street, with the Mustang hot behind them.

At the next intersection, traffic screeched to a halt as Greyson forced the long black car through it, swerving through a sea of oncoming headlights and angry honks. When they were clear, he accelerated again, the force of it jolting Dru.

Behind them, the Mustang charged straight across the street without pause.

"Main streets are clogged. We'll take the back way." Greyson spun the wheel, and Hellbringer slid around the next corner, skidding past a slow-moving taxi. Ahead, an oncoming SUV blared its horn.

Hellbringer's engine howled, and they shot around the taxi, swerving out of the SUV's path. Its horn warbled as it streaked past them, its taillights leaving a red glow in the darkness.

As they dodged and weaved through the traffic, Dru craned her head around, looking for the Mustang. It drove up onto the sidewalk, smashed through a blue mailbox, and closed in on their right. "Over there!" She pointed.

"I see him." Greyson's right hand worked the shifter, cranking Hellbringer into a higher gear. "Hold on!"

He spun the wheel left, yanking the car hard across the street, between oncoming cars, and toward a narrow alley framed by trees. The car's long rear end swung around wide, nearly making them overshoot the alley.

As the brick corner of the building loomed over them, Greyson straightened out and steered them back into the turn. They squeezed into the alley. Newspapers and trash swirled in their wake.

The Mustang crossed the street behind them, bumped up onto the curb, and clipped the tree at the corner. Leaves and branches exploded over its hood.

Hellbringer shot down the dark alley. Dumpsters and telephone poles whipped by in a blur. Behind them, the Mustang closed in, and a streak of red-hot fire erupted from the driver's window.

Through the Mustang's windshield, past the glare of streetlights sweeping over the glass, Dru could clearly see the glowing eyes of the reptilian Horseman hunched over the wheel. He held his fiery sword high out the window, trailing flames into the night.

Hellbringer soared out of the far end of the alley and rocketed across lanes thick with cars and trucks. They headed uphill, leaning into a hard turn that brought them into the next lane at easily twice the speed limit.

The Mustang exploded out of the alley behind them, the Horseman's sword billowing with flames. The car plowed between two parked taxi cabs, sending them spinning away in opposite directions.

As Greyson straightened Hellbringer out, Dru got a good look at the pursuing Mustang's smashed front end. It seemed to snarl at them, its headlights glaring from above a jagged, hollow mouth filled with sharp steel teeth.

As she watched, the crumpled grill smoothed itself out with a ripple of chrome. The headlights realigned themselves, staring like a wide-eyed predator closing in on its prey.

They crested the hill, fast enough that the tires left the ground for an instant, and Dru's stomach dropped. They sailed over an empty set of railroad tracks and landed hard with a crunch of metal and a chirp of tires.

Greyson cranked the wheel right and took a fast turn at the next block, cutting off a delivery truck just before it could turn onto the same street.

The truck braked, its tires screaming a shrill warning. The deep, heart-stopping blare of its horn shook Dru to the core. Its huge grill closed in on them, filling the windows on Greyson's side as they flashed past.

A moment later, safely behind them, the truck bumped up onto the sidewalk and stopped, filling the road.

Greyson accelerated down the street. On their right lay a row of broken-down houses with boarded-up windows and junk on their lawns. On their left, a rusty guardrail blocked off the edge of the road, where the dry grass dropped away into the pitch black ribbon of the river below.

Ahead, a frontage road to the highway led to a motionless expanse of headlights and taillights. Traffic was completely locked down.

"Can't go that way," Greyson muttered, his voice nearly drowned out by the thunder of Hellbringer's engine.

Dead ahead, an ominous pair of classic car headlights swung around the corner, coming straight at them. A flush of fear froze Dru's veins as she realized what she was seeing.

It was another Horseman. The silver one.

Behind them, the delivery truck still barricaded the street. The long, flat side of the truck buckled outward and exploded in an eruption of crushed cardboard boxes and flying sheet metal.

The Mustang burst through the side of the truck as if fired out of a cannon. It sailed through the air, the Horseman's sword leaving an arcing banner of fire, and slammed onto the road with a trail of sparks and wreckage.

They were trapped. They had one Horseman closing in from the rear, another straight ahead, charging toward them. The only other route was the highway, and that was dead still.

They had nowhere to run.

In front of them, the silver car swung sideways and skidded to a stop, blocking the road. Its headlights burned twin lines out over the darkness of the inky black river.

Trapped, Hellbringer slowed until nothing moved on the blacktop.

"Greyson?" Dru asked, unable to keep her voice from trembling. "Maybe we can make it on foot?"

The Mustang pulled up behind them. Its door swung open.

The reptilian Horseman slid out, sword flaming in the night. It flourished the blade in a quick figure eight, leaving a dazzling afterimage in Dru's vision. With a snaggle-toothed grin, it lurched toward them, serpentine tongue licking at the air.

In the back seat, Rane snorted. "They think they've got us cornered."

"Don't they?" Dru turned in her seat.

Rane nodded toward the river. "I go running down here all the time. Hello? Bike trail!" She pointed one long metal arm to a gap where the guardrail ended, and a line of dry grass and bushes marked the edge of the road. Beyond, the shoulder dropped down into the dark nothingness where the river lay.

Somewhere in the middle, unseen, the bike trail split the distance between the road and the river.

Greyson's gaze ticked up to the rearview mirror and then over to the darkness at the edge of the road, as if calculating the odds. Then he turned to Dru, his face unreadable.

She nodded once. "Do it."

Greyson's stubbled jaw set in a determined line. He jammed the long shift lever into reverse and dropped the clutch. Tires smoking, Hellbringer flew backward, headlight beams piercing the clouds of burning rubber.

The red Horseman's snakelike eyes widened in surprise just before Hellbringer's wing hit him in the snout. A split second later, the black car's rear end slammed into the creature's body, pinning him against the nose of the parked Mustang.

Greyson shifted again, and Hellbringer lunged forward, releasing the red Horseman. The creature stumbled after them, limping and angrier than ever, and let out a blood-chilling screech.

Greyson whipped Hellbringer around in a tight circle just as the red Horseman's flaming sword flashed down in a deadly arc, too late, carving a red-hot trench in the asphalt road.

Hellbringer headed straight for the gap in the guardrail and the impenetrable darkness beyond.

The black car's long nose dipped, and they sped down the steep slope of dry grass toward the narrow strip of concrete that ran along the edge of the river, nothing more than a sidewalk bisected by a chipped yellow line.

The headlight beams glittered off the swift-moving water as they swept past. Dru could imagine drowning in the cold depths of the river. Her fingers dug into the armrest next to her, fighting the urge to scream.

"Yee-*haw*!" Rane yelled behind her.

Greyson turned the car as they plowed down the steep hill, tilting them sharply to one side. The front tires slid onto the concrete and held on, with the rear tires whipping around right after them. In a heartbeat, they were centered on the narrow concrete track, rocketing along the edge of the river.

From behind, the silver car tried to follow them down the steep slope onto the path. But its demonic driver didn't make the turn in time. It hit the bike trail at an angle, sliding diagonally across the narrow strip of concrete with a squeal of burning rubber, like a terrified animal desperate to hang onto the precarious ledge of land.

For a long moment, the silver car seemed to cling to the bare strip of grass and dirt at the edge of the trail, its headlights shining in the blackness like two eyes glaring out from a wide chrome skull.

Then, unable to resist the forces of gravity, it rolled off the side of the trail, its momentum pitching it over onto its roof before it hit the river with a thunderous splash. Water erupted on all sides as it plowed its way beneath the murky surface, its headlights still burning all the way to the bottom.

Greyson didn't slow Hellbringer down but charged them straight ahead on the tight, uneven trail. They drove beneath the highway, under an echoing expanse of cement and shadows. Graffiti flashed past in the narrow glare of the headlights.

Then they were out, on the other side of the packed highway, where the trail stretched onward into the night, empty and welcome. A minute later, a steep exit ramp led away from the trail. Greyson drove them up, one wheel spinning on bare grass, until they bumped over the sidewalk and back onto a deserted street in front of a used furniture store.

"How far are we from the hospital?" Dru asked, completely disoriented.

"Five minutes, tops."

Back on the road, the engine picked up speed. She peered over her shoulder. "How's Opal doing?"

In response, Opal turned her head and blinked at Dru. "Hey. What on earth just happened? Were we on the bike path?"

Dru could feel the silly grin as it plastered itself across her face. She laughed out loud in relief. Seeing the twinkle in Opal's eyes, she reached back and took her hand. "Are you okay? Don't move."

"I'm all right. Except for lying on the lap of the Iron Maiden here. Not helping my headache any."

"Hey." Rane's metal face scowled. "Could be worse."

Greyson ran a light just as it turned red, swerving around an eighteen-wheeler. They headed back underneath the highway again, as the road ran at an angle through the smog.

Every pair of headlights seemed threatening. Every honking horn made Dru jump. When she saw a flash of red in the right lane, her heart raced. But it was just a red station wagon.

"We're almost to the hospital," Greyson said.

"Dru," Opal said faintly. "You really going back to that mansion in the desert?"

"We have to. The scroll is there." Through the rear window, Dru could see the jam-packed highway above and behind them as they passed beneath it. A river of motionless white headlights.

Except for one pair. A single car streaked along the overpass, hurtling along the shoulder. Its headlights flickered through the fence that ran along the edge of the highway.

With an explosion of twisted metal and concrete, the red Mustang smashed its way through the guardrail and hurtled down toward them.

36

DEATH MACHINES

The Mustang sailed through the air, trailing wreckage, until it bottomed out on the avenue behind them with a brutal crash. Sparks blazed along the asphalt as it clawed its way out of a wild skid and came charging after them.

Despite her choking fear, Dru found her voice. "Greyson!"

"I see him." Hellbringer's engine let out a throaty roar, shoving Dru deep into the seat.

They flew through the next couple of blocks of small car lots and rundown industrial buildings. An empty street opened up on the right, and Greyson aimed for it.

The Mustang came at them from the left, swerving to hit Hellbringer on Greyson's side.

"Hang on!" Greyson yelled.

Dru barely had time to grab onto the armrest as Greyson nailed the brakes, making everything inside the car pitch forward. Hellbringer's tires shrieked.

The Mustang sailed diagonally across in front of them, missing Hellbringer's long black hood by inches. Before the Horseman could recover, Greyson accelerated and struck the Mustang's back corner with a bonejarring impact.

The hit sent the Mustang spinning away on smoking tires. It dropped behind them, shedding velocity as it careened into the side street.

As Hellbringer charged onward past the Mustang, it pulled out of its skid. Quickly, it got onto the road behind and closed in, headlights burning.

Greyson accelerated straight ahead, dodging around a stalled blue pickup into a lane full of oncoming traffic. He charged hard at the honking cars, then whipped Hellbringer back into the right lane just past the stalled truck.

The lane ahead of them was completely clear, and as he sped up, Dru understood Greyson's move.

But the Mustang wouldn't be stopped by a traffic snarl. The red car shoved its way past the blue pickup, stripping off the side mirror.

It kept coming. Unstoppable. Focused. Ferocious.

The Horseman wanted Greyson, and he would kill anyone and everyone in his way. Including her. Dru knew it with frightening certainty. She had to find a way to stop it.

As the Mustang closed in, the car's demolished front end quickly uncrumpled and became whole again.

Greyson swung left around a slow-moving van, and the red Mustang streaked past the van, pulling up alongside Dru on their right.

Through the window, the Horseman's reptilian snout gaped open wide in animal rage, sharp teeth shining in the passing flash of streetlights. For a second, his luminous eyes locked on Dru's.

Then the Horseman yanked the wheel, and the Mustang smashed into Hellbringer's right side, nearly knocking Dru out of her seat.

Greyson fought the wheel for control, trying to get away from the Mustang. But it stayed viciously planted against their passenger side. Ahead, a concrete mixer truck barreled head-on toward them, horn blaring.

Only a few feet away from Dru, on the other side of the window, the reptilian Horseman glared at her, inhuman eyes shimmering with fury. Its long, lizardlike snout stretched open, revealing rows of jagged fangs, and its howl of triumph drowned out the horn of the oncoming truck.

A hellish red flicker of flame erupted inside the red Mustang. With a savage leer, the Horseman brought up its flaming sword, its point aimed at Dru, and drove it home.

Dru tried to get away, but she was trapped in place by the seat belt.

Hellbringer's passenger window shattered in an explosion of glass, a million fragments reflecting the red-hot flames of the Horseman's sword as it pierced inward, aimed at Dru's heart.

A flash of metal came down past her ear in a shining arc. At first, she didn't realize what it was. But when Rane screamed in pain and rage, Dru realized she had parried the Horseman's sword with her bare metal arm.

Rane's fist stopped inches away from Dru. A horrible sizzling sound filled the air, amplified by the foul stench of burning metal.

Truck headlights whited-out the windshield. The unrelenting horn bellowed.

Hellbringer lurched as Greyson pulled a hard left, yanking the car free of the Horseman's blade. The truck passed between the two cars with a roaring blast of wind.

The rushing wind choked off as Hellbringer's window repaired itself, glass growing up from the door like frost on a cold winter day.

From the back seat, Rane choked out an inarticulate cry of pain.

Dru unbuckled her seat belt and turned around. "Rane! Let me see your arm!"

Rane sat hunched in the back corner of the wide rear seat, huddled over her arm, where a red slice of heat burned inside a blackened gash. "*Hhh . . . huhh . . .* hellfire . . ." As the red-hot wound in her arm faded and went dark, a thin curl of smoke drifted up past her pained face.

"Tell me what to do!" Dru begged.

"*Huhhh!*" The muscles stood out in Rane's metal face. She swallowed, her throat working. "Take this . . . bastard out. Before he . . . kills us all."

The tremor in Rane's voice was enough to shake Dru to the core. Rane was never scared.

Until now.

Dru dropped her gaze to Opal's limp form lying across the wide back seat, unconscious again, face half covered in blood. She hadn't made a sound during all of this, and that frightened Dru even more.

She glanced over at Greyson, who appeared more demonic by the minute, as he slammed gears with grim determination, just trying to keep them ahead of the unstoppable creature closing in behind them.

The crystals at her feet. They were her only hope. She bent over, fighting motion sickness, and fumbled with the clear plastic hardware case. She managed to undo the tiny latches and get the lid open, but

Greyson's every yank on the steering wheel threatened to send the crystals flying.

She dug through the case. A sparkling gold lump of iron pyrite. A faceted wand of icy quartz. A spongy metal mass of pink copper. None of them would help.

Then she found the galena, the anti-demon stone. A heavy chunk of it, glittering like cold blue-tinted chrome. As she turned it over in her hand, it left a trail of tiny fragments on her fingers that shone in the streetlights streaking past.

When Greyson had first come into her shop, she had touched a galena crystal against his skin, and it burned him. That burn had taken a while to heal.

If it had the same effect on the other Horsemen—or better yet, on their speed demons—then she had a chance.

But she only had one shot to stop the car dead in its tracks. And there was simply no way to do that, unless . . .

"Bingo." Dru turned around in her seat again, the galena crystal cupped in both hands. She held it out to Rane. "Here. Take this. I need you to crush it."

Between gasps, Rane looked puzzled. "What?"

Dru held out the crystal. "Just do it!"

Hellbringer's engine throttled up to an earsplitting roar. The avenue ahead rose up to become a long, two-lane bridge passing over the railroad tracks below. On either side, short concrete walls choked off the shoulders, topped by chain-link fences that were nothing but a blur at this speed.

"Galena crystals have an octahedral structure," Dru explained. "If you crush them, you break them into lots of little cubes."

Rane grunted in a way that indicated that either she understood completely or didn't care at all. The crystal disappeared inside her big metal hands.

The muscles in her iron arms flexed. Her fingers tightened, and her face contorted with the strain.

At first, nothing happened. A moment later, a sharp pop rang through her long fingers, then another, and then came a rush of crunching noises.

When she opened her hands, she held a little pile of shimmering metallic cubes.

Heart pounding, Dru took the cubes, careful not to drop any inside the car as it hurtled down the road, swerving side to side at breakneck speed.

"I need your hand," she said to Greyson.

"Little busy here." He slammed gears, his right hand on the long lever of the gear shift, his left hand quick on the wheel.

She touched his shoulder. "Greyson. We need to do this together."

His horns were definitely longer than they had been a minute ago. His skin was darker. When he finally met her gaze, his eyes glowed bright red. For the space of a few pounding heartbeats, she was afraid she was losing him to the demon.

But then he lifted his hand off the white knob of the gear shift and held it up. She took it. His grip was strong, warm, reassuring. All the noise, terror, and confusion around her began to melt away. For this one moment, she felt connected to something greater than herself.

Her fingers tingled in Greyson's grip as his energy began to pour into her. It started as a quiet tingle but quickly rose to a sizzling burn.

Magical energy, from Greyson and Hellbringer both, flowed through her body and into the tiny galena crystals in her hand.

They began to glow. Softly at first, then brighter and brighter until she had to turn away from the blinding glare.

"Open the window!" she told Rane.

Rane obliged, cranking a short silver lever that retracted the little window behind the passenger door. Cool air swirled through the car.

Dru stuck her hand out into the wind, trying to reach out as far outboard of Hellbringer as she could. The charged crystals would burn their own speed demon as quickly as they would hurt the Mustang.

The red car weaved side to side, headlights burning.

Dru's arm shook with the effort of reaching out into the wind, and trying to steady herself against Greyson's sharp turns as he dodged left and right. She needed the perfect moment, the perfect angle, because she only had one shot.

"Dru!" Greyson said over the noise of the engine. "Do it now!"

The timing wasn't right. She couldn't get enough leverage to throw the crystals far. But the Mustang closed in, aimed straight at them. She had run out of time.

She had to act. Now.

She took a deep breath, as deep as she could, then twisted her body and threw with all her strength. The burning white lights of the galena crystals flew in a brilliant arc up and over Hellbringer's back wing, through the night, and scattered across the road behind them like a carpet of stars.

A split second later, the Mustang drove right across the shining galena crystals, picking them up in its treads, haloing its wheels with white heat.

Despite the darkness and the blinding speed and the whipping wind, Dru could see the smoke gushing out from all four wheel wells as the galena burned through the rubber.

As one, the Mustang's tires all blew out, sending the red car into a sudden violent swerve, spinning it one way, then the other.

As the Mustang lurched, its tires shredded and flew off one by one, flapping away through the air like giant, malformed bats. Skidding on bare metal wheels, it shot up fountains of white-hot sparks.

Completely out of control, it careened across the width of the road and smashed into the bridge's concrete barrier. It flipped onto its side and tore through the upper chain-link fence as if it were no thicker than a strip of gauze.

The smashed Mustang sailed through emptiness, lazily rotating through the night air. Then it pitched nose-first into the rail yard far below, disappearing between two parked trains.

The space between the trains erupted with an oily fireball of red-and-gold flames choked in peals of black smoke.

Inside Hellbringer, no one said a word as Greyson drove them off the other end of the bridge and turned at the blue H sign. Ahead, the glowing windows of the hospital complex loomed, just blocks away.

Dru turned to look at Rane, expecting to see her own terror mirrored there. But instead, Rane showed her teeth in a savage grin.

"Hells, yeah," Rane said, nursing her arm. "Teach that bastard to tailgate."

37
DEEPER CUTS

Dru sat alone on a puce-colored vinyl hospital seat, phone cupped to her ear, blinking her eyes to keep the tears from overflowing. "Nate, it's me. I . . . I wish I could tell you this in person."

She hated the way her voice sounded stuffy when she was upset. But sitting in the hospital hallway, waiting for word on Opal, she'd had too much time to dwell on Nate and all the things she wanted to say to him. The problem was that he would never understand.

Her entire life, her calling, was too inextricably linked to the world of magic. She knew that now. It wasn't something she could just choose to ignore. Not something she could walk away from or compartmentalize.

As much as she desperately wanted to surround herself with a world of safety and stability, she could never live there. She didn't belong in his normal world.

And he would never accept hers. He didn't believe in magic. It was as simple as that. When things spun out of control, what he thought was a sane, rational response always ended up hurting her.

The heartbreaking truth was that there was no future for them together. There was no way to bridge that divide. She had known that for a long time, she realized, though she had tried so hard to fight it. It wasn't fair to either of them.

She pulled off her glasses and ran an exhausted hand across her eyes. Grit clung to her skin. How could she possibly have this conversation with his voicemail?

"Nate, I just . . . I don't want to leave things in this weird sort of limbo, not anymore. I think we both know . . ." A hard lump rose in her throat, and she had to squeeze her eyes shut to keep going. "We both know this isn't working. And I'm so sorry about that. About your car. About everything."

Now that she was actually saying the words, they seemed so small, so inadequate. None of them conveyed the pain of losing him, the relief of letting him go, the torture of all the things she still wanted to say. But this was no place to say them. And in truth, she was better off leaving them unsaid.

"Good-bye, Nate."

She hung up, overcome by the finality of it.

That was it. No more Nate.

She stared off into space, trying to blot out the emotions crashing down around her, feeling oddly detached from it all and at the same time raw with hurt.

At the end of the hall, on TV, a newscaster spoke earnestly into the camera. The closed-captioning read, "Unexplained meteors nationwide." It switched to footage of burning lights streaking across the night sky, then went to a map showing half the northern hemisphere blanketed by storms, punctuated by meteor strikes.

The sky was falling. Literally. The end of the world was at hand, and here she was breaking up with Nate. There was something so surreal about that.

A heavy hand landed on her shoulder, making her jump. Rane looked down at her with intensity. "Hey." That one monotone word was loaded with meaning: a question, a comment, a vote of confidence.

Dru held up her phone. "Had to tell his voicemail."

Rane's face filled with compassion. "Oh, dude. That sucks."

Dru nodded in agreement.

"Hey. Check this out. Serious bragging rights." Rane held up her forearm, swaddled from thumb to elbow in a thick bandage. "Good news is both cuts were on the same arm. So I'm still packing a mean left hook."

Dru winced. "Does it hurt?"

"The hell do you think? Damn right it hurts. But I'm looking for positives here."

"Did they give you some pain meds?"

Rane snorted. "Tried to. But, dude, my body is a temple."

Dru tried to give her a reassuring smile, but it faltered. "Are you still good to go to New Mexico?"

"Quit worrying about me. You sound like Todd."

"Todd?"

"The doctor. I'm not even sure he's old enough to be a real doctor. But I'm a sucker for freckles."

"Did he ask how it happened, your arm?"

"I told him there was a tragic welding accident."

Dru nodded, somehow unsurprised. "And he believed you?"

"Not the first time I've fed him that line. Besides, I acted all cute and gave him my number." She smiled in a way that might've looked coy on most people, but on Rane it was slightly unsettling. "Actually, it's your number, so if you get any weird calls, don't answer. You ready to go?"

"What about Opal? They haven't told me anything yet."

"Todd said they're going to keep her for observation. A wallop of a concussion and a head laceration. Other than that, no big."

A wave of relief washed over Dru. "Could've been so much worse." She stood up.

"Hey, do me a favor." With a sly smile, Rane held out a magic marker and presented her bandaged arm. "Draw a big old heart on this bad boy and put 'Dru plus Rane 4-eva.'"

Dru had no intention of writing anything on Rane's bandage, but she took the marker anyway because she knew Rane would hammer on that same ridiculous note all night. Together, they headed down the hallway. "Where's Greyson?"

"Sitting in his evil car, watching the road, being all martyr-y. Let's go say hi to Opal, then get out of here."

"Did you try Salem again? I know it's a long shot, but if you tell him the scroll is buried at the archway, maybe he'd finally come over to our side? We need all the help we can get here."

"He knows. He just doesn't care. Kind of detached from the whole human race. We're on our own, D."

"Lovely," Dru muttered.

"I know, right? It's the end of the world. You'd think *somebody* would step up."

"At least we have Greyson," Dru said. "And Hellbringer."

"Road tripping with two demons." Rane shook her head. "That's so messed up."

38

UNSPOKEN

Nothing moved in the lone blackness of the desert highway.

If any witnesses had stood at the side of the road, where the asphalt ended in the silence of sand and cactus, they would have heard the soul-chilling wail of the speed demon's engine long before it appeared in the night. Even then, all that arose on the horizon were twin pale halos that preceded headlights in the distance.

The two pinpoints of light were all that broke the endless desolation of the desert. Smothered under a starless sky, the night tried to swallow the shining headlight beams as they approached.

The dead stretch of asphalt lay motionless except for the play of light across cracked pavement still warm from the vanished sun.

The thrumming sound of exhaust rose to a frenetic roar, like an army of mad devils pounding on the drums of war. In a blink, the black car roared past, piercing the night.

It left nothing behind but a rush of wind that stirred the dead sand, and a pounding thunder that echoed out into the emptiness behind the dwindling red glare of its taillights.

Inside Hellbringer, no one spoke.

Dru took the last few crystals out of her purse, and one by one, she slid them into the individual pockets of the plastic tool case with a soft click. Fitting each crystal into its own slot somehow felt like loading a bullet into a gun.

The green vivianite was too big to fit, so she left it in her purse, belatedly remembering that vivianite crystals slowly degrade with exposure to air. She wondered what had happened to the old oilcloth she had found it wrapped in. But it probably didn't matter anymore.

She tried not to dwell on what could go wrong when they reached the archway. Everything could fall apart in so many ways. But the more she tried to think positive, like Rane suggested, the darker her thoughts became.

What if they couldn't pry open the base of the archway?

What if there was no way to reseal the scroll?

What if the scroll wasn't there at all?

With every new thought, her anxiety level rose, forming a bitter taste on her tongue. And yet, despite the nervous energy, she was exhausted. Every part of her body felt as heavy as solid rock. She couldn't remember the last time she'd eaten or slept.

She probably looked like hell, she realized, and Greyson wasn't far behind her. His eyes glowed a steady red. The nubs of horns stubbornly poked up from his forehead. He could be on the verge of a transformation any minute.

But she didn't have any potion left to give him. If Greyson's horns suddenly sprouted and his fangs grew and his skin turned dark, there was nothing she could do to stop it. She just had to hope that they got to the mansion in time. Because as long as he was still part human, there was hope.

They rode together in deathly quiet until she couldn't take the pressure of her own thoughts anymore.

"At least there's no traffic," she said finally.

Greyson looked at her for a moment as if she were completely insane, and then the corner of his mouth quirked up in a wry smile, a welcome glimpse of the old Greyson. "No. No traffic."

"How much farther?"

"Almost there." Greyson glanced over his right shoulder at the back seat.

Dru followed his gaze. Rane slouched deep in the seat, looking sound asleep, as she had for the last hour or so. But she had to be awake. Dru knew from unfortunate experience that when Rane was truly asleep, she snored like a rhinoceros.

Greyson, on the other hand, seemed convinced. He leaned a little closer to Dru. "You can do this. With the crystals. I know you can."

She looked away. "Is it that obvious?"

"That you're doubting yourself? Yeah." They drove on for a while until Greyson added, "I've gotten to know you pretty well, Dru."

That wasn't exactly a ringing endorsement. "Sorry about that."

His red eyes glinted with amusement. "You don't give yourself enough credit. From what I've seen, you know what you're doing. You're the only one who can pull this off. Not Salem. Not even Rane. You."

His vote of confidence brought a flush of heat to her cheeks. "I can't do it alone." She stared ahead at the endless blur of sand-dusted pavement racing toward them and disappearing beneath their headlights, as if Hellbringer was devouring the desert.

"They're still out there, you know," he said. "I can feel them. They're not far."

She wanted to ask who. But she knew who he meant. The Horsemen. "Any idea where they are?"

Greyson hesitated. "I can't tell. I just know they're coming."

Dru nodded, thinking of how quickly the red Mustang had straightened itself out after every crash. How long would it take for it to put itself back together after its fiery plummet over the bridge?

"It could be days," Greyson said, as if reading her thoughts. "Or they might already be back at full strength. I just don't know."

Dru glanced through the back window, but of course she could see nothing behind them. Outside, the night was as black as if the impending apocalypse had dropped a shroud over the world.

Greyson gave her a long look, studying her, but his expression was impossible to read.

Their eyes met, and she was reminded of the moment he had walked into her shop. Back then, her biggest worry had been ringing up enough sales in the cash register to pay the rent at the end of the month.

So much had happened since then. So much craziness. They'd been through hell together.

Maybe not *literally* hell. Not yet, anyway.

She felt that, in so many ways, he had helped her discover who she truly was. And no one had ever done that before.

"Dru," he said softly. Then he hesitated.

She waited, wondering at the sudden intensity in the air between them.

He cleared his throat. "The truth is we don't know how this is all going to go down." He swallowed. "There's something I need to tell you."

She found herself hanging on his every word, breathless and somehow terrified. She tried to shake off the feeling. But she couldn't.

"I don't know when this happened. But things have changed. *I've* changed. Because of you." He closed his eyes for a moment, blotting out their red glow. In the pale dashboard light, he looked entirely human again. Vulnerable, determined, real.

She wanted to reach out to him, but she thought better of it. Instead, she kept her hands firmly folded in her lap.

When he opened his eyes again, the way he looked at her made her heart beat faster. Despite the fiery glow in his gaze, she could see the anguish and longing there. She could easily let herself get lost in it.

His voice came out husky. "Dru, I want you to know that I—"

Her phone rang. She jumped.

"Sorry. Hang on." She bent and dug through her purse until she found her phone.

It was Nate.

From the back seat, Rane's heavy hand fell on Dru's shoulder. So much for pretending to be asleep.

"Don't answer that," Rane whispered in her ear, the words urgent.

Dru had the inexplicable sense that she had tiptoed up to the edge of something, right here, right now. A little voice inside her told her to put the phone away without answering it. But it kept ringing.

The phone was only getting one bar of reception. She might never get another chance to talk to Nate again, to say the final things that had to be said.

She had to answer.

Before she could talk herself out of it, she took the call. "Hey."

"Are you okay?" Nate said. "I'm worried sick about you."

Rane let go of her shoulder. In her peripheral vision, Dru saw Greyson and Rane exchange meaningful looks. But hearing Nate's voice again completely overwhelmed her.

"I'm at the hospital," he went on, the words tumbling out. "I came as soon as I got your message. Where are you? What happened to your shop? Opal said someone stole my Prius. Are you all right?"

Good old Opal. Trying to spin a cover story, even now. More than anything, Dru wanted to be back there with her, safe.

But instead, she was hurtling across the desert in a demon car, on a mission to stop Doomsday. "Listen, Nate, about everything that's happened. You deserve to know the truth."

Nate's voice faded into robotic white noise and went silent.

"Nate? You're breaking up." She pressed one finger into her other ear. As if that would help.

"Call . . . matter. Let's . . . tomorrow."

There might not even be *a tomorrow*, Dru thought. She had to say goodbye, and she had to do it now. She drew in a breath to speak.

"Dinner together," he said, his voice suddenly back at full strength. "I booked a private table for us at Chez Monet. The back table, with all of the miniature red peonies, the ones you like." Before Dru could process that and respond, he pressed on. "Look, I was wrong. I know that now. With everything going on around us, the meteor showers, the clouds, it puts everything in perspective. Life is too short, Dru. You deserve . . . I shouldn't . . . you." Whatever he said next dissolved into electronic noise.

Was he actually apologizing? Admitting he was wrong? Asking her to consider getting back together? She never would have expected that from him, and she had no idea how she felt about it, much less what she should say.

The phone warbled, chopping Nate's voice into incomprehensible bits.

She was losing him as Hellbringer carried her farther out into the desert, toward the endless blackness beyond their headlights. She was speeding away from her home and Nate and everything in her life.

Before they had left, she was sure she was done with Nate. But now that she might never come back, suddenly she was overwhelmed by the fear of losing him.

She squeezed her eyes shut, blocking out the rest of the world, because this might be the last time she heard his voice.

". . . work things out," he said fuzzily. "Will you give me another chance?"

No, she thought. *Yes . . . I don't know.*

A wave of emotions crashed over her. Hot tears burned at the corners of her eyes.

He said something else, and she strained to hear him, finger jammed tightly in her other ear.

"Nate?"

Nothing came back but static. She had no idea if he could still hear her at all. This was her last chance.

Part of her insisted that they were done, that she was better off without him.

But at the same time, he was such a fixture in her life, such a reassuring constant, that she couldn't imagine going on without him. Without his steady presence keeping her down to earth, would she eventually end up as crazy as Salem? Or worse?

Could she salvage things with Nate? *Should* she? Or should she just let him go? The decision tortured her.

She thought of his boyish smile, his soft voice, his warm arms around her. And then the anger from him when he had so bluntly broken things off. Which one was the real Nate? Who would he be in her future?

Would there even *be* a future?

"Nate?"

A fragment of his voice broke through the static, saying her name.

She swallowed. "Nate, maybe we can try." The words left her like a desperate message in a bottle, flung into stormy seas, where it was instantly swamped by the waves and sunk.

A long hiss of unbroken white noise unspooled in her ear, and then her phone beeped three times. She'd lost the signal for good.

As she stared at the useless phone, helpless and adrift, she realized she hadn't promised anything, hadn't decided one way or another. It left her feeling like she'd made the wrong choice, even though she hadn't actually chosen anything at all.

Only then did she realize the stony silence that filled Hellbringer. Greyson stared straight ahead at the road, gripping the wheel. Despite the steady thrumming of the engine, he must have heard every word of that conversation.

"Greyson, I'm sorry, I couldn't—"

"Forget it. You don't have to explain anything to me." His eyes burned a brilliant red, brighter than before.

An ache stabbed through her, the pain that came from trying to block out how she truly felt about Greyson, because admitting it now would tear her apart. "Greyson, listen to me. Everything has been so fast. Like you said, we don't know what's going to happen. To any of us. To the *world*."

"Then let's find out." He yanked the shift lever into a lower gear, making Hellbringer growl in protest. "We're here."

He turned the wheel, and they left the highway, tires crunching on the dirt track that led to the end of the world.

39
THE DUST OF TIME

Hellbringer rolled to a stop at the end of the dirt trail, its head-lights illuminating the graceful curve of the Harbingers' archway. Greyson turned the ignition off. In the abrupt silence that followed, Dru could still hear the ghostly echoes of the speed demon's engine.

They got out, and the squeak and thump of the shutting car doors echoed out across the cool desert night. Apprehensive, Dru looked around in a complete circle, but the starless night revealed nothing. Not even the white curves of the mansion that she knew lay just up the hill, like a giant, sun-bleached skull watching them from the darkness.

Only the archway stood out against the inky night.

Their shoes crunched on loose rocks as Dru led them through the pool of light to the base of the archway. Bending down low, she brushed and blew away the layer of accumulated sand until she found the carved symbols she'd seen in the photo.

Herein lies the end and the beginning.

"I didn't see these symbols when we were here before. But I did notice this." She pointed out a rectangular stone laid at the top of the ramp. Hellbringer's headlight beams elongated the shadow of her pointing finger until it looked like a slashing sword. "This one block in partic-ular looks different. See the gaps around it? They're wider than the rest. There's something under this."

Rane folded her arms. "So you think the Harbingers just happened to leave the most dangerous artifact in the universe sitting out here in the desert?"

"They didn't leave it unprotected. You can be sure of that. The wards on it are probably astronomical. That's why I brought these." Dru opened her new plastic case of crystals and pulled out her round-cornered rectangle of ulexite.

Taking a deep breath, she pressed the crystal to her forehead.

But to her surprise, hardly anything registered. Multicolored magical residue drifted up from beneath the stone, visible around the edges of the stone block. But it was barely there. Nothing was left but a mere whisper of the power that must have once protected the apocalypse scroll. As if the Harbingers' warding spells had just gone up in smoke. Vanished.

But how?

"Something's wrong. This thing should be locked up like Fort Knox." A bad feeling gripped Dru as she wedged her fingertips into the gap between stone blocks. "We need to pry this out. Quickly."

Greyson headed back to Hellbringer and returned with a tire iron.

Rane took it from him, tightened her fist around it, and transformed herself into shining black steel. Then she handed it back. "Ready?"

Together, they pried up the stone block. With a scrape of rock, Rane pushed it aside, revealing a hidden compartment beneath.

Inside, nestled on a drift of fine sand, lay a sinister black cylinder, open at one end, the other end enclosed by a crownlike cap with twelve wicked spikes.

Under the glare of Hellbringer's headlights, the cylinder sparkled. Fine etchings covered its length, depicting massive armies clashing with hordes of terrifying creatures, mountains toppling into boiling oceans, falling stars shooting past a blazing sun whose rays set fire to the lands. And throughout it all, panicked crowds raised their entreating arms to the heavens as they died.

A gust of wind rustled past Dru. It picked up the dust from the scroll's resting place and blew it out in a cloud that twisted in the air like grasping claws.

Heart beating faster, Dru reached into the small compartment.

Despite the fine etchings that covered the container's surface, it felt smooth and curiously light to the touch, as if the passage of ages had worn away its very existence to almost nothing. As she lifted it out, the wind whistled a mournful note over the open end.

Dru peered inside, turning the mouth of the cylinder into the head-light beams.

It was empty.

She stared into it, uncomprehending.

Wordlessly, she looked at Rane and Greyson, and she could see her own shock mirrored in their faces.

"Son of a *bitch*," Rane spat. "Someone else got here first."

Dru shook the empty container, as if she could somehow dislodge the missing scroll. "I don't understand. If someone has the scroll, then why is Doomsday still happening? Why haven't they stopped it?"

"Maybe they don't know how." Greyson frowned. "Or maybe they *want* it to happen. These evil sorcerers, these Harbingers, do you know for a fact that they're all dead?"

Slowly, Dru shook her head no. "You don't think, after all these years . . . ?"

His red eyes scanned the darkness, burning like hot coals. "Wait. Did you hear that?"

Only then did Dru hear footsteps pounding through the darkness. The bright beams of Hellbringer's headlights were broken by the unmis-takable reptilian silhouette of the red Horseman. It charged toward them, and a blade of hungry red-orange flames erupted from its claws.

As Greyson pushed Dru behind him, Rane charged directly at the Horseman with a furious yell, fists raised.

The Horseman screeched, jaws open wide, and swung his flaming sword.

It passed harmlessly over Rane's head as she dropped and slid through the sand, feetfirst, and knocked the Horseman's scaly legs out from beneath him.

Dru fumbled with her plastic case of crystals, trying to find some galena. But she'd used it all up fighting the Mustang.

She didn't see the pale Horseman until he was almost upon her. He scuttled up over the top of the archway, his glasslike, skeletal body nearly invisible against the dark sky. He leaped down headfirst, long, sharp fingers outstretched to impale her.

Greyson was faster. He pulled Dru out of the way, his strong arms holding her tight, his wide shoulders absorbing the impact as they hit the ground together and rolled. Where she had just been, the pale Horseman's claws cracked into the stone, splitting it.

As Dru got to her feet, Greyson pushed her behind him again. "When I say so, run for Hellbringer! Got it?"

A single set of heavy footsteps circled around the other side of the archway. A looming white figure strode into the beam of the headlights, his body covered in long spikes, his skull ringed with a crown of horns.

The white Horseman.

Greyson glanced his way, red eyes widening slightly, and the pale Horseman used the distraction as his moment to strike. With a single crunching blow, he sent Greyson tumbling across the sand, then went after Dru.

She scrambled back away from the pale Horseman. He swung at her, his sharp, skeletal arms slicing through the air around her.

She ducked and turned to run. Her foot caught the edge of the open scroll compartment, and she landed hard on her back.

The Horseman threw a lightning-fast blow at her. The long blades of his fingers pierced the stone on either side of her neck, pinning her in place.

He grinned a mouthful of glass needles.

Unable to move, Dru looked around desperately for help. Rane lay on the ground, the red Horseman's flaming sword a mere inch from her throat.

Greyson lay at the feet of the white Horseman. With a muffled cough, he got to his hands and knees. Blood dripped into the sand beneath him.

The white Horseman's glowing sapphire eyes glimmered with evident satisfaction. He raised his spiky arms to point one at Rane and the other at Dru, aiming.

Dru's breath caught in her throat. She had seen how those shooting spikes had punched through the walls of her shop, and she had no illusions about what they would do to her. Rane's iron body might blunt the worst of the blow, but Dru had no way to protect herself.

This was the end.

"Let them go." Greyson's words came out rough and raw.

All eyes turned to him.

Greyson bared his teeth. They shone in the flickering light of the flaming sword, sharper than any human teeth should have been. His eyes blazed with fiery intensity, and his short horns gleamed.

"Let them *go!*" Greyson ordered again.

The white Horseman ground out a single word: "*Why?*"

Greyson's red eyes flicked to Dru's, and for a moment, she could almost see the tortured decision being forged behind them. Then he looked up at the white Horseman again.

"Let them go. And in exchange . . . you get me."

40
EVERYTHING IS WRONG

"*G*reyson!*" His name tore from Dru's lips before she could stop it. "No!"

His gaze left the white Horseman for a moment and cut across the darkness to meet hers. "If I don't, they'll kill you. Both of you."

Dru fought to get more words out past the hard lump in her throat. "You'll fulfill the prophecy. You can't—"

"You have to stop me."

At first, she didn't understand what he meant. *Stop him? How?*

"You have to find a way. Whatever it takes." His voice grew husky and harsh. "When the time comes, you can't hesitate."

Hot tears burned Dru's eyes and spilled down her cheeks.

"Dru, you can do this. You're strong enough. I know you."

"No," she whispered, slowly shaking her head side to side. Whatever faith he had in her, she didn't share it. She couldn't be that strong.

"You and Rane can pull this off. You can find a way to stop Doomsday."

With the flaming sword at her throat, Rane didn't speak a word. She just stared at Greyson, her expression transfixed with growing horror.

All this time, the only thing Dru had wanted was to save Greyson. But now, she'd lost the last shred of hope.

Everything was wrong.

Everything.

A terrible emptiness opened up inside her as she realized they were beaten. She tried not to accept it, tried to fight against it, but it was no use. They had run out of options. If she wanted to live, she would have to let him become the final Horseman.

And then she would have to destroy him. But she knew she couldn't do it.

"This is the only way," he said.

"No. Let me die." She couldn't keep the tremor out of her voice. "Because if you become the last Horseman, the world will end. Do you understand? The world will *end*."

"Not if you stop it." He fixed her with his glowing red gaze, and it seemed to carry an impenetrable sadness. "Dru, if you die, *my* world ends."

Too late, she saw how deeply he loved her. She reached toward him, though he was much too far away. She just wanted to touch him again, feel the heat from his body, cling to the strength within him. She had to tell him all of the things that she had pent up inside her, all of the things that she knew she'd never get a chance to say.

For a fleeting moment, she wanted to believe there was some way to save him. Some way that she could outthink the Horsemen and stop this from happening.

The white Horseman held his hand over Greyson's head, as if giving some sort of benediction.

But it was no blessing.

A heart-wrenching shout of sheer agony escaped from Greyson's lips. Every muscle in his body stood taut, and he seemed to grow within his own skin, becoming physically bigger, less human, more menacing.

His skin changed, darkening like a burned-out coal. The arcane symbols of stylized scales glowed white-hot across his hands.

His head snapped back in pain, giving Dru a terrifyingly clear view of his teeth growing into fangs, his horns sprouting and curving away from his skull.

In a few agonizing moments, the searing transformation was complete.

He had become the black Horseman of the apocalypse.

The prophecy was complete.

Lightning flashed, and a crack of thunder boomed out across the desert, followed quickly by another, and immediately another. All around the archway, twisting bolts of lightning blasted down from the heavens, blistering the desert floor. The ceaseless crashing surrounded Dru, but she barely noticed.

The pale Horseman released her, having lost all interest in her, and marched toward the others. At the same time, the red Horseman abandoned Rane to join his brethren.

Immediately, Rane scrambled over to Dru and grabbed her with iron hands, pulling her to her feet.

The clouds above them lit with streaks of blood-red light. Blazing stars descended and punched holes in the cloud cover before finishing their journey in fiery streaks of light. All around them, craters blasted sand and rocks high into the air.

A hot wind blew across the land, carrying the stench of death.

"This is it!" Rane shouted over the noise. "It's starting!"

But Dru didn't answer. For her, everything had already ended.

41
SET THE WORLD ON FIRE

Dru stared in speechless horror at the vile creature that had once been Greyson. With looming horns, vicious fangs, and a rippling leathery skin as black as Hellbringer's paint, he bore no resemblance to the man she had known and trusted.

He got to his feet and pulled off the tatters of his shirt, now split at the seams. His onyx-black chest shone in Hellbringer's headlights.

The other Horsemen crowded in around him. The crystalline skeleton of the pale Horseman, with his long, insectlike arms. The snarling, snaggle-toothed red Horseman, with his swishing reptilian tail. And the jagged, snow-colored expanse of the white Horseman, his crown of horns towering over all of them.

They stood back-to-back, four pairs of glowing eyes staring out at the horizon in all four directions. Surveying the world they were about to destroy.

The desert beneath their feet trembled as falling stars pounded the horizon, throwing up clouds of black dust lit from within by the angry red fires of impact. Lightning flashed all around the archway, illuminating the night with an incessant flicker of blinding light from every direction.

From the direction of the mansion, three pairs of headlights streaked toward them through the night, growing closer. In a minute, the Four Horsemen of the Apocalypse would climb aboard their speed demons to spread destruction across the world. And Dru had no way to stop them.

Her gaze went to Hellbringer.

Hellbringer. If Greyson didn't have it, he couldn't ride. If she got Hellbringer safely away, would that be enough to stop the prophecy?

Or would Greyson—now the black Horseman—call it to do his bidding? There was only one way to find out.

"Get into the car!" Dru sprinted around the Four Horsemen and yanked the driver's door open. As she got behind the wheel, Rane climbed in the other side.

Greyson hadn't left the keys in the ignition. But it didn't seem to matter. As if sensing her presence, Hellbringer rumbled to life of its own accord.

"Gah, I haven't driven a stick shift since high school," Dru realized out loud. "You?"

Rane's dark iron face revealed nothing. "Dude, I don't own a car."

Dru gripped the wheel with both hands, willing the demon car to feel the intensity of her desperation. "Hellbringer, if you can hear me, we need to go. *Now!*"

But Hellbringer didn't budge.

In the headlight beams, the ground ahead of them trembled. Small rocks danced on the sand, shaken by the shattering impact of the falling stars. The black Horseman turned his burning red gaze toward Dru.

"Hellbringer, you have to help us." She put one palm flat on the warm dashboard. How could she convince the speed demon to listen to her instead of the Horsemen?

"Go!" Rane said, grabbing her arm. "We're sitting ducks here!"

Dru awkwardly shifted into gear and pressed down the gas pedal, but Hellbringer wouldn't move. It still waited for its master.

She remembered its desire to run free, its fear of imprisonment. She had to use that to her advantage. "Do you want to stay here, where you were locked up for decades? Do you want to remain a prisoner of those who enslaved you? Or do you want to *go?*" She leaned closer to the steering wheel. "*Mi juras, Infernotoris.* I swear to you, I can set you free. But you have to take us far away from here. As far as you can. *Now.*"

Before she could say more, Hellbringer's engine revved, and they launched forward with neck-snapping acceleration. It was all Dru could do to hang onto the steering wheel and turn them around in a wide circle until they headed back down the dirt road toward the highway.

And directly toward the three oncoming speed demons.

"What do we do?" Rane said. "We can't outrun them."

"Even in this car?"

Rane gave her a worried look. "D, I love you, but you can't drive like he could."

It stung, the fact that Rane already referred to Greyson in the past tense. But Dru pushed the pain aside. It wouldn't take long for the other speed demons to catch them.

"Hey, we've still got this Mount Vesuvius thing," Rane said, picking up the metal box of biotite from the floor. "Let's blow them up like Pompeii." She shook the box.

"Don't do that!"

"Can you make it go boom?"

"Yes," Dru realized out loud. In that moment, she knew what they had to do. She spun the wheel again, swinging Hellbringer around and heading back toward the archway.

Rane stared at her, mouth gaping open in shock. "The hell are you doing, D? You can't take us back there!"

In answer, Dru pointed to her purse on the floor at Rane's feet. "There's a big green crystal in there. It's vivianite. Grab it for me."

Obligingly, Rane dug through Dru's purse. "Jeez, you've got like *everything* in here." She held up a mashed granola bar, now flattened and bent in half. "Is this even food?"

"Here. Just give me—" Dru reached for her purse.

Rane yanked it away, her eyes going wide. "Wait. You're going to open up the *causeway*? Can you even do that on your own?"

"I think so. Now that I know how. At least, I have to try. I can't let Greyson get behind the wheel of this car. If he does, it's over. Everything's over. And he will chase us . . ." Dru choked down a sudden sob and swiped brimming tears from her eyes with the back of her hand. "He's a Horseman now, and that means he won't stop pursuing us. Ever."

"Yeah, but maybe—"

"He *will* catch us, sooner or later. There is nowhere in this world that we can go to escape him. So we have to *leave* this world." Dru fought to keep Hellbringer pointed in the right direction. She had no idea how Greyson had done it so effortlessly. "This is a one-way trip. Once we go through the archway, and I charge up that biotite, bad things are going to happen. *Really* bad."

Rane's eyes shone in the reflected glare of the headlights behind them. "You're going to blow up the Horsemen?"

"Not them, exactly. Biotite reverses the bonds of magic, destroying any enchantment. I don't know what it would do to the Horsemen, if it would work or not. But I know what it'll do to the causeway," Dru said with finality. "Total destruction. If we lure them out onto the causeway and destroy it, we can send the Four Horsemen straight back to hell."

As they hurtled toward the portal, the wild look in Rane's eyes transformed into steely resolution.

"We're going to make it," Rane said as she pulled the vivianite crystal out of Dru's purse. "You and me, D. Together to the end."

As they raced toward the archway, Dru swallowed down the hard lump in her throat and held out her hand. Unlike Rane, she didn't have any hope left. But she had to try.

Rane placed the green crystal in her palm, its heavy weight cold against her skin. It started to glow.

42
NEVER COMING BACK

T he archway flared with blinding white light.

Hellbringer streaked through the portal like a black arrow fired into the writhing chaos of the netherworld skies. Engine roaring, tires spinning, it soared in a long arc over the black stone ruins and landed hard on the cobblestone road, kicking up sparks.

Rubber shrieked across the wet stones as the long car skewed at an angle, leaning into the skid. Then it straightened out and hurtled down the road toward the glowing line of the causeway.

Immediately behind them, the other three speed demons jumped out of the fading light, one after another: red Mustang, white Bronco, and silver Ferrari. They shot over the shattered foundation of the black fortress and landed on the wet path, skidding. Their headlights pierced the night like the flashing eyes of a pack of hunting animals. Engines growling, they chased after Hellbringer.

Dru gripped the steering wheel so tightly that her fingers prickled. The road had taken so long to travel on foot, and now it flashed past them in the blink of an eye.

Ahead, the causeway led away over the roiling cloud sea. Beneath the fiery madness of the sky, the road stretched razor-straight out to the far horizon, its black stones lit by the ruddy glow of the ancient enchantment that bound them together.

Dru planned to annihilate that enchantment with the biotite crystal. Destroy the magic, obliterate the causeway, and send the Horsemen plunging into the abyss. That was the plan.

If she could power up the biotite crystal on her own without Greyson.

A big *if*.

She'd managed to open the archway on her own, but this was different. Powering up the biotite would require infusing it with her own magical energy, and she didn't know how much she had left.

Over the roar of the engine, Rane said, "Dude, if you nuke the causeway, what happens to us? Won't we go down too?"

"Not if we're fast enough." Hellbringer hit the lip of the causeway with a metallic bang that jolted up through Dru's feet. "We need to get off the other end before they do. Off the causeway, onto that black rock island with the cave."

Dru struggled to keep the steering wheel centered on the bumpy road. The causeway had no guardrails. Nothing but the sheer edge separated them from the cloud-filled abyss on either side.

Behind them, headlights burned brighter as the other speed demons closed in. The red Mustang and the white Bronco came up side by side, only inches between them, entirely filling the width of the causeway.

Dru pushed the gas pedal to the floor. Without any landmarks to gauge distance, it felt as if they were standing still but for the roar of the engine and the drilling whine of the bridge beneath their tires.

She risked a glance down at the speedometer, shocked to see it steadily climbing past one hundred miles per hour.

Then 120.

Then 130. The white needle kept rising.

But even as Hellbringer's engine howled up in pitch, the headlights behind them grew steadily closer, burning in the rearview mirror.

Squinting into the glare, Dru saw a dark figure climb out of the Mustang's passenger window.

It was the black Horseman, horns standing out in sharp profile against the glowing sky. He scrambled onto the Mustang's roof, clinging to the metal in the hurricane-force wind.

"Please, no," Dru breathed.

He grinned a mouthful of fangs that glowed red in Hellbringer's taillights, then bent into a crouch and leaped off the Mustang's hood, arms outstretched. He sailed toward Hellbringer, claws reaching out to grab.

Dru stomped on the gas pedal, but it was already on the floor. She hoped for a miracle, a surge of speed that would widen the gap between the cars, wide enough to make him miss and leave him tumbling down the road face-first.

But although Hellbringer had already buried the speedometer needle at 150 miles an hour, they still weren't going fast enough. The black Horseman caught the edge of Hellbringer's tall back wing. In one smooth motion, he swung beneath it, feetfirst, and landed atop the trunk.

The twin impacts of his cloven hooves reverberated through the car, making Hellbringer sway. For a panicked moment, Dru feared they would swerve over the edge.

"Take the wheel!" Dru said, hunching in the seat.

"*What?*" For once, Rane sounded shocked. "Dude, I can't drive this thing!"

"Just keep us from going over the edge!" Dru bent closer to the steering wheel. "Hellbringer, keep us on the road."

"Oh, *seriously*." Hyperventilating, Rane took over the wheel, sliding her iron body into the driver's seat. Her monotone voice took on an uncharacteristic edge of panic. "Hurry!"

Climbing over into the back seat, Dru grabbed the metal box of biotite. Fingers shaking, she pulled the lid open and yanked out the angular dark crystal from its nest of foam rubber. She cradled the biotite in her hands, willing it to charge up.

But there was only the merest flicker of light in its murky brown depths. Without Greyson's aid, her energy wasn't nearly as powerful. She didn't know for sure how much energy the biotite needed, but she clearly didn't have enough.

The black Horseman's bunched fist smashed through the rear window, sending broken glass flying everywhere. A tornado of breath-stealing wind blasted through the shattered window, forced in by the turbulence of their extreme speed. The wind tugged at Dru's hair, grasped at her clothes.

Rane ducked low in the seat. "Take the wheel back! Take it! Let me at him!"

Dru almost did, but that would mean giving up on the biotite. And the crystal was the only chance they had left.

Hellbringer's window tried to reform itself, glass growing inward from the edges of the frame like spreading ice crystals, sealing the black Horseman in place. With a sinister roar, he forced his way through, smashing the glass away faster than it could form.

Dru's every instinct told her to scramble back away from the Horseman, jump over the seat, and squeeze into the front corner by the dashboard. But she stayed put. If there was any trace of Greyson left in him, she needed his power. Now, desperately.

As he fought his way into the back seat, claws digging deep into the upholstery, she realized he was at a disadvantage. The cramped quarters limited the strength he could bring to bear. And she had a fleeting chance to use that against him.

Instead of backing away, she came straight at him. The Horseman thrust out one clawed hand to grab her, and she caught his fingers in hers.

Instantly, she connected with him, as she had with Greyson. Even though the demon had taken over Greyson's body, his soul was still linked to hers.

He was still an *arcana rasa*, and she was still a sorceress.

Without hesitation, she reached out with her feelings and unlocked the vast reservoir of magic within him, letting it flow into her. She deliberately dropped her defenses, drawing in the Horseman's power. It burned, dark and foul, and every fiber of her being wanted to reject it.

But she needed that energy, as much as she despised it. She needed it desperately for the crystal. She soaked it up, every bit she could, and channeled it into the biotite.

Caught by their connection, the Horseman's strength wavered. Beneath his long horns, his furrowed face twisted in rage, then confusion. He slumped, as if tranquilized, and slid down into the back seat.

Dru shifted aside and let him settle into Hellbringer's wide black seat, his clawed fingers still intertwined with hers.

Dru focused all her attention on extracting the seemingly limitless flow of dark magic from him. Its intensity scorched through her, burning like acid as she poured it into the biotite crystal in her other hand.

At first, nothing happened.

But as she held the connection, pinning the Horseman against the seat with her knees, she willed more and more of the infernal energy into the crystal. It began to glow from within. A coarse, primal light, like lava under a bloody sunset sky.

His howl of rage became a strangled gasp. He sagged and collapsed into Hellbringer's back seat, and still she held on.

"Dru!" Rane shouted over the still-roaring engine. "We're running out of bridge!"

Through the windshield, Dru could see the cliff growing closer, like a black wall of stone rushing at them.

Behind, the white Bronco closed in fast, its grill flashing in the chaotic light. The red Mustang swung around to the side, and the reptilian Horseman leaned out the window, raising his flaming sword high.

But the biotite crystal wasn't yet charged. Dru kept pulling the dark energy from the Horseman, letting it sear its way through her soul and sizzle into the ever-brightening biotite. At this point, it didn't matter what scars the energy left within her. She had nothing left to lose.

The intensity of the crystal's glow went from hot coals to bare light bulb, then quickly became too bright to look at. Like holding a fragment of the sun in her hand.

A smoky smell filled the air, the foul stench of burning rock. Teeth gritted, she ignored the scorching pain in her hand.

She charged it further than she had ever charged any crystal. Further than she expected this crystal could take. Any moment, she expected to overload it to the point of fracture.

If that happened, it could release all of its energy in an uncontrolled firestorm, killing everyone inside Hellbringer but leaving the causeway untouched.

They had only one shot. She had to make it count.

The red Horseman's fiery sword came down, carving a red-hot path through Hellbringer's roof. Molten metal dripped from the edge of the blade, burning into the seat next to her, setting fire to the upholstery.

The next instant, the white Horseman rammed them from behind. The impact sent Hellbringer skidding. The sudden movement wrenched the flaming sword free, and it spun away to disappear over the edge of the causeway, lighting the mist as it fell.

It left behind a gaping hole in the roof, revealing a wedge of chaotic sky filled with rippling light.

Rane let out a wordless yell of fear, trying to steer the car back into control. For a terrifying moment, Dru thought they would go over the edge and plunge into the endless abyss below.

Then Hellbringer straightened out on its own, sending them hurtling directly toward the black rock island ahead.

Pinned beneath Dru's knees, the black Horseman let out a final gasp and slumped in the seat, spent. The energy flow stopped. There was nothing left to charge the crystal.

Dru held the biotite for a moment in her hands, so bright it drew streams of tears from her eyes.

This was it. This was all she had. There was nothing more.

She had to make sure it hit the causeway behind them. If it missed, they were doomed.

With a ragged breath, she cocked back her arm and hurled the crystal up through the already-closing gash in the roof. The moment it left her fingers, she felt the energy ripped away from her, as if there was nothing left within her.

The crystal sailed up into the sky, blinding bright, until it came down behind them in a lazy arc, like a new sun setting on the horizon.

"Dru?" Greyson's gravelly voice was unmistakable.

He stared up at her. Though every inch of him still had the demonic appearance of the Horseman, the white-hot glow of his eyes had faded to nearly human. Slowly, his fangs began to recede, his horns shrank, and his face started to look like his own again.

Her heart leaped in her chest. She could see the recognition in his eyes. It really was Greyson. He was back.

By drawing the dark energy out of him, she realized, she had drawn out the black Horseman as well. Pulled him right out of Greyson and trapped the evil essence within the glowing inferno of the biotite crystal.

At last, in this darkest hour, she'd managed to achieve what she had wanted all along. She had saved Greyson. Despite the tears that stung her eyes, she smiled.

"What happened?" he asked. "Are you okay?"

She cradled his face in her hands, trying to ease his confusion. "Shh."

"Don't cry," he said, raising one hand toward her cheek. But before he could touch her, a flash of light erupted behind them, so bright and hot she could feel it on her skin as much as see it.

It was too late.

She couldn't help but look back through Hellbringer's rear window, squinting into the glare as the causeway whited out in a blaze of light.

The black polygonal stones some nameless sorcerer of ancient times had used to build the causeway flew apart as the biotite reversed the enchantment holding the stones together. Epic bolts of unbound magic flared in all directions, like lightning, in colors Dru had never seen before.

For a moment, the eerie beauty of the energy blossoming behind them almost made her forget its deadliness. But as the white-hot wall of the shock wave raced toward them, obliterating the causeway as it came, she held on tight to Greyson's hand.

He knew something was coming. She could see it in his eyes.

"Dru," he whispered, "I—"

She opened her lips to say, *Don't let go.*

But she didn't get the chance.

That instant, the blast overtook them, flinging stones and cars like dry leaves swept before a storm wind.

The last thing she saw in the searing light was the twisted wreck of the red Mustang flipping end over end. Below it, the other two cars trailed fire as they burned through the mist and tumbled into the endless abyss below, vanishing forever.

43

FOREVER REMAINS

Nothing remained of the causeway. Its destruction had ripped a hole in the edge of the cliff, leaving nothing but a smoking depression in the black rock. Dark stone blocks, the size of coffins, lay scattered across the rocky ground of the island. The long troughs and craters from their impact bore mute witness to the all-devouring power that had flung them there.

The aftermath of the explosion had reached high into the heavens and swept away the shimmering spiderwebs of fiery color from the netherworld sky, leaving only cold, naked stars staring down from above, punctuated by the bright slashes of meteors streaking toward the horizon.

Under the chill of the starlight, a lone figure moved across the barren landscape, staggering away from the wrecked black car.

Rane trudged a short distance and laid Dru's limp form down across a flat rock, then gripped her wrist to check her pulse. Leaning close, she bent until her ear nearly brushed Dru's lips, listening to the soft rhythm of her breathing.

Satisfied, she patted Dru lightly on the cheek. "Hey. D. Wake up."

By the time Dru came around, Rane was peeling up her eyelids and staring into them with wide-eyed intensity. "Helloooo? Anybody in there?"

Dru jerked away, blinking dry eyes. "Ugh." She swatted ineffectually at Rane's large hands. "Leave me 'lone."

"Love to, but I can't. Got your bell rung pretty good. Could be worse, though. I got you out of the car in one piece. Come on, easy does it." Rane helped her sit up and handed over her glasses.

"Where's Greyson?" Dru slipped the glasses on and looked around at the scattered black stones. They stood out starkly beneath the cold star-light, like the crooked teeth of some long-vanished giant.

Rane's face was smeared with soot. Her blonde hair had come undone from its ponytail, sticking out in random directions. Her red-rimmed eyes looked back at Dru, wide and wild. "Dude. We survived. That's what counts."

"What?" Dru nodded slightly. "Yeah, I guess so."

"You *guess* so? Don't you get it?" Rane insisted, her voice high and tight. "We stopped the Four Horsemen of the Apocalypse. We saved the *world*. We are officially the most badass sorceresses. *Ever.*" She let out a trickle of a laugh, but there was a high-pitched brittleness to it, as if it could crack and shatter. She held up her hand for a high-five.

Dru hurt too much to respond. She placed her palms flat on the cold, gritty ground and pushed herself up. A splitting pain shot across the back of her skull and down her neck. Wincing, she reached up to probe her tender scalp.

Rane caught her hand. "Don't touch. You should get that looked at. We'll go out through the old mine shaft, get back to town, get you checked out. Sound like a plan?"

With a pained grunt, Dru sat down again and blinked up at the sky full of unfamiliar stars, bisected across the middle by a shimmering ribbon of hazy light, then another. Gradually, the netherworld sky began to come alive again. "Is that the Milky Way up there?"

"Nuh-uh." Rane shook her head no. "I don't know where this neth-erworld is, exactly, in the grand scheme of things. All I know is it freaks me out."

Out past the edge of the cliff, nothing was left of the causeway or the sea of clouds. Just an infinite blackness that stretched out as far as she could see.

A rustle of chilly wind blew out of the empty darkness and across her skin, raising goose bumps. The air smelled sooty and electric, like the aftermath of a thunderstorm mixed with smoldering ashes.

The only other sound was a pinging of cooling metal. Nearby, Hell-bringer lay on its side, the car's long body warped and crumpled. Every part of it was smashed, as if it had tumbled end over end before finally coming to rest. Its windshield and windows gaped, empty. Broken glass lay scattered across the ground, sparkling like gems in the starlight.

Dru stared at the wreckage, aware that there was something inherently wrong about it but still too fuzzy to think about it clearly.

"Good thing I was still in iron form," Rane said. "Held onto you tight the whole time. We came cartwheeling off that bridge, hit the island, and rolled maybe three, four more times. Never been in a crash like that. Never want to do that again, either. Damn."

"It's not fixing itself," Dru realized out loud.

"What's not what?"

"Hellbringer. Look. Why is it still smashed? We've always seen it pull itself back together." Dru painfully pushed herself upright and limped toward the car, a hard lump rising in her throat. She felt responsible for Hellbringer's well-being, as if the car were a stray animal she'd adopted.

Rane followed close behind. "Forget it. There's nothing left in there. I checked. Did find your purse, though. Amazed it didn't go down into the clouds."

But she didn't care about her purse. With every step, the pain in Dru's ankle jabbed up her leg and met with the pain that shot down her neck, slowing her down. Deep inside, she felt a desperate need to get back to the car. To check on it. Make sure it was okay.

But she was too late.

As Dru reached the lifeless wreckage, tears welled up in her eyes. After a moment of hesitation, she reached out and touched the crumpled metal. Where the paint was broken, it crumbled and fell away, revealing naked steel beneath. The bare metal shone in the starlight.

But the steel itself felt cold and dead to the touch.

She leaned close until she rested her cheek against the metal. She had sworn to the speed demon that she would save it, if it helped them. She'd sworn to set it free.

Hellbringer had carried them through to the end. And now it was gone.

"I'm sorry," she whispered to the wreckage. "I'm so sorry."

"Come on," Rane said gently. "Let's go."

Dru swallowed. "Where's Greyson?"

Rane's eyes turned haunted. "I tried, D. I tried to grab him in the crash. But . . ."

"What?"

"I grabbed you, but then we were rolling. It happened so fast."

Dru shook her head, not understanding. "What do you mean? Where's Greyson?"

"I'm so sorry." Rane reached for her, long arms starting to circle around her.

Dru pulled away and limped to the edge of the cliff, cupping her hands around her mouth. "Greyson!" she shouted. Ignoring the stabbing pain in her back, she clambered over the scattered black stone blocks, searching. "Where is he?"

In the darkness of every shadow, she searched for him. Wide-eyed, she scanned every inch of the tortured ledge. But he wasn't there. "Greyson!"

"I looked everywhere already. He was thrown out in the crash. I don't know where he ended up." Rane followed her, looking as if she wanted to grab her. "D! Come down. You don't need to do this right now."

She stood at the shattered footings of the causeway, peering down at the bottomless cliff of black rock. He wasn't there.

"*Greyson!*" Dru screamed his name, over and over, into the black depths of the abyss. Screamed until her voice became cracked and hoarse. Screamed out the pain and the loss of knowing that he was gone forever.

She sank to her knees at the lip of the cliff, sobbing tears into the endless darkness below. She swayed on the edge of the abyss, bereft of words or thought, feeling the incredible lightness inside her that came from having nothing left.

The crushing grief threatened to destroy her. Steal her away into the endless nothing. Forever. Like Greyson.

Before she could fall, Rane's strong arms wrapped around her. With uncharacteristic gentleness, those arms pulled her back from the edge. They held her, unwavering, steady, the only safety and stability left in this world.

"I'm sorry," Rane whispered, rocking her slowly side to side as Dru cried. "It's okay."

Dru wanted to answer, wanted to deny that it would ever be okay. Because it wouldn't. But she didn't have the strength left to speak.

They sat together on the cold, rocky cliff, under the light of the netherworld's dying stars, silent except for Dru's ragged sobs.

44
THE SILENCE WHEN YOU'RE GONE

Dru sat alone on the floor in the boarded-up wreckage of her shop, trying to blot out the rest of the world. With most of the overhead light fixtures destroyed in the fight with the Horsemen, the only light came from the single bulb of a battered table lamp with a dented shade.

Her phone rang. Nate again. He'd been calling ever since she'd made it back.

She tossed the phone aside without answering it. Not trying to hurt Nate or shut him out. She just couldn't deal with thinking about him now.

As the cracks of pale daylight around the plywood-boarded windows faded into darkness and became slivers of cold light from the street lamps, Dru occasionally thought about getting up off the floor. Maybe eating one of the crispy cinnamon Duffeyrolls that Opal had brought her.

But she didn't. Hunger had become just another kind of pain to try to ignore.

She felt as if she was drowning in an endless emptiness of waiting. But she didn't know what she was waiting for.

Because Greyson was gone.

The outside world should have gone back to normal, but it hadn't. While the mysterious meteors had stopped, the foul brimstone air and overcast of tainted clouds were spreading around the world. Some tiny part of Dru wondered if it would gradually fade away or only grow worse.

She would look it up, do some research, if she had any books left under the rubble. But she didn't have the strength to dig.

Once, footsteps scraped outside her door. They came right up onto the step and paused just long enough to read the hand-lettered "Closed for Remodeling" sign Opal had taped up. Then they faded away.

Later, the foul smell of spray paint reached Dru, and she went outside with a flashlight to find that someone, presumably Salem, had added a U-turn arrow to the sorcio symbols painted on her back door, reversing their meaning.

Now, instead of saying, *Crystal sorceress will help you in need*, it said, *Crystal sorceress needs your help.*

She blinked away tears and went back inside. Of course, she still wanted to help others. But what could she do? She had nothing left to offer them. Her store was empty of anything useful. Everything was broken. And so was she.

A palpable emptiness hollowed her out inside. She sat alone in an island of lamp light, waiting for the darkness outside to lift.

But it didn't matter. Greyson was gone. And he wasn't ever coming back.

It was a plain fact, clear and cold. Somehow, though, she refused to accept it. As if it didn't make sense. As if every part of her being utterly rejected the truth.

With her head leaned back against the hard wall, she listened to the quiet murmurs of the city, trying to find some calm center inside her. But every time she closed her eyes, she could see Greyson looking back at her.

Against her will, she kept slipping away into the weightless descent of sleep, only to jerk awake in horror, heart pounding. Even awake, she still felt as if she were endlessly falling and Hellbringer was tumbling end over end around her, carrying her through the fire.

Feverish snatches of dreams haunted her. She reached out for Greyson, but her hands closed on empty mist. He whispered her name, but every time she turned to look, he was gone.

The pale half-light before dawn brought heavy footsteps tromping up outside. Someone rattled the locked doorknob. Dru didn't have the strength to yell at whoever it was to go away.

With a splintering of wood, the door flew open, letting in the glare of the streetlight and the flickering red-and-blue neon lights of the all-night liquor store next door.

Dru didn't even look up. Whatever dark fate was heading her way, she felt she deserved it.

Heavy footsteps crossed the room. A woman's hand, with long, thick fingers ending in chipped pink fingernail polish, set down a ring on the concrete floor next to her, directly in Dru's line of vision.

The ring was pitted and blackened from magical feedback, but she would have recognized it anywhere. It was Greyson's titanium ring.

Dru looked up into Rane's worried face.

"I thought you might want it," Rane said, her voice rough and deep. "To keep."

Tears stung Dru's eyes. She bit her lip as she picked up the pitted ring and held it in the palm of her hand, cradling it as if it were a wounded bird.

Rane shoved some wreckage aside and sat next to her, bringing the mingled scents of pine trees, city streets, and sweat from her predawn run. She seemed so alive, so vibrant, so opposite of the way Dru felt.

Rane nodded her chin at the box of stale cinnamon Duffeyrolls sitting nearby. "So. Opal's been here. How's she doing?"

"Better." Dru nodded. "I told her to stay home and rest, but she came by anyway, at least for a while. We hung out. Watched the handyman board up the windows. Mostly, I was useless." Dru pointed to the cinnamon-stained box. "Want some?"

Rane shook her head. "Carbs city." Then she seemed to think better about it. "Splitsies?"

By that, Dru took it to mean that Rane only wanted to eat half of a cinnamon roll. But when Rane opened the lid of the box, her eyes lit up. She picked up one of the miniature cinnamon rolls and sniffed it carefully, like a curious animal. "What's with the green sprinkles?"

"That one's Irish Cream, I think."

"*Nice.*" Rane crammed the entire roll in her mouth and chewed. She pointed at another. "Mmm. That one?"

"Pecan something."

"Mmm." Rane bit that one in half, then reluctantly offered the other half to Dru, who waved her off.

After a minute of grunting and chewing, Rane nodded, satisfied. "I needed that." She looked directly at Dru, suddenly serious. "How about you?"

With a sniff of a laugh, Dru stared off into the distance, seeing all of the wreckage around her and yet not seeing it. Everything was a blur of destruction. "I have absolutely no idea what I need."

"Sure you do," Rane said. "Dig deep down inside. Tell me what you need."

"I need to be safe again." The answer came bubbling up from somewhere deep inside Dru. She didn't even think of it consciously. It just popped into her mind. But it felt like the right answer. She said it again, savoring the taste of the words in her mouth. "I need to be safe. Secure. Out of harm's way. That's what I want."

Rane snorted and grabbed another roll. "Whatever. Have one of these little guys. They're like *crack*."

"I'm not kidding." Dru fixed her with an earnest look. "I'm done. I can't do this anymore."

Rane chewed. "Do what?"

"This." Dru waved her hand to indicate the utter destruction surrounding them. "Everything is gone. Everything that ever mattered."

"Hey, *I* matter. And I'm still here. What are you complaining about?" Rane grinned, but the light behind her smile quickly faded as she studied Dru. "Come on, dude. We can buy you new stuff."

Dru shook her head. "I don't have that kind of money. I can't afford to start over."

"I know some guys who can have your shop tip-top in a week flat. Besides, that's why you have insurance," Rane said, then looked worried. "You *do* have insurance, right?"

"I'm pretty sure my policy doesn't cover Doomsday."

"Are you kidding? Do you have any idea how many times the average sorceress has to cover up magical destruction? Just call it a gas leak." Rane shrugged. "Works every time, trust me."

Dru slumped against the wall and sighed. "I'm not cut out to be a sorceress."

"You so totally are. And you're getting better. You opened that portal on your own this last time."

"Wait." Dru held up a hand. "Just let me finish. Before all this happened, I used to think that I was somehow stuck. That I was just going through the daily motions of life. Helping customers, answering the phone, trying to scrape up rent money."

Rane tilted her head to the side and faked a snore. "Oh, *waah*. You're breaking my heart."

"But maybe that's where I'm *supposed* to be. Maybe I'm not really meant for all this weirdness, this epic battle against demons and curses and everything else. Other people can handle it. Other people *want* to handle it. Like you. I mean, look at you. You were practically put on this planet to kick ass. You've got the attitude for it. The power for it. The body for it."

"Dude, it's not easy staying this buff." Rane arched one eyebrow. "But you need to do your magic."

"Not me. Not anymore." Dru shook her head resolutely. "I mean, before all this, I could do a teensy bit of crystal magic, and that was enough. But with him, there was just so much more. Everything turned out more powerful than I ever imagined. And now he's gone." She squeezed her hand shut, feeling Greyson's ring dig into her palm. "Maybe I can do it on my own, but I don't *want* to. Not anymore."

"So, what, you're looking for some sort of cosmic fairness? A quota? You get your ticket punched once, and you're set for life?" Rane looked unimpressed. "It never gets any easier, D. You just have to get better."

Dru looked at her. "No. This is not my thing."

"This *is* your thing. You have these powers for a reason." Rane's voice turned urgent. "Only like one in a million people have any kind of magical ability. And there might be no one else on the *planet* who can do exactly what you can do. If you don't get it together, if you don't learn how to take this crystal thing to the next level on your own, you're not going to make it. *That's* how it works."

"I can't. Don't you see that?"

Rane stared at her in disbelief. "Did those words really just come out of your mouth? Did you miss the part where you stopped the forces of darkness in their tracks? Seriously, D, we just saved the world!"

"But what's the price of that?" Hot tears flooded Dru's eyes, and her voice grew thick. "Greyson is dead because of me. I killed him."

Rane surveyed the debris on the floor around them. "I miss him, too. You might not believe that, but I do. He was a good guy."

"I should've found another way, besides the biotite crystal." Dru sniffed. "I screwed up."

"No." Rane jabbed a finger at her. "You don't get to do that. You don't get to look back and blame yourself for saving the world. What happened, happened. You can't change it. You had a tough call to make, and you made the right one."

Dru slipped Greyson's ring onto her thumb. She closed her fist around it, feeling the metal warm quickly against her skin.

"I loved him," Dru whispered. "And I never told him."

Rane caught her hand and held it. At first, it looked as if she intended to say something sarcastic, but her expression softened, and she nodded. "He knew."

Tears streamed down Dru's face. She hunted around her for a box of tissues but found nothing and ended up wiping her eyes on her sleeve.

"Listen, you're just freaked out." Rane patted her leg. "Don't worry. Best thing to do is get back in the saddle. Start some serious training. You know, when I first started transforming, I used a stopwatch. Ten seconds. Twenty seconds. But I kept at it, and now I can go all day if I need to. You can do it, too. We'll find you a mentor. Someone who can teach you to build up your powers on your own."

"Easy for you to say." Dru let a sharp edge of anger into her voice. "You've been fighting all your life. But not me. I'm not going to risk getting anyone I love killed. Never again."

"So what are you going to do? Close up shop, marry Nate, move to some beige subdivision, and start popping out kids?"

Dru sniffed again. She couldn't meet Rane's gaze.

"Oh, you have *got* to be kidding me." Rane folded her arms. "Seriously? You? No way."

"Well, not with Nate," Dru admitted finally. "Never with him. That's done. But safety, security, what's wrong with that? Why put ourselves in harm's way anymore? Maybe it's time to go find someplace safe."

Rane shook her head. "There's no safe place anywhere, D. Have you looked outside? The entire world is freaking out. The brimstone clouds haven't gone away. Maybe the lightning and meteor showers are over, but it's not like everything is all rainbows and puppy dogs. Something's up. It's like the world is waiting for the other shoe to drop." Rane's eyes narrowed to dangerous slits. "Somebody out there took the apocalypse scroll. Are you going to let them have it? Or are you going to take it back?"

Rane's words stirred something inside Dru. The desire to discover. Study. Analyze. Decipher. Put together the rest of the puzzle. Still, she shook her head. "I don't know. But we did destroy the Four Horsemen of the Apocalypse."

"Last I heard, the Four Horsemen came from breaking the first four seals. Right? How many seals does that scroll have?"

"Seven seals," Dru replied hollowly.

"Yeah. So get it together, D. We've got work to do. Before the rest of the seals get busted open and things really go to hell." Rane stood up and crossed over to the door. When she opened it, the first bloody rays of dawn spilled in.

Dru looked up, startled. "You think . . . you think this is all going to happen again?"

"*Again* isn't the right word." Rane paused in the doorway, silhouetted in the tainted amber light that suffused the morning air, beneath dark clouds that promised a rainstorm later. "Maybe we slowed down the apocalypse. But we sure as hell didn't stop it."

Dru climbed stiffly to her feet. The two of them locked gazes, and Dru swallowed. "I'll need a hand with these bookshelves."

Rane smiled, teeth flashing in the fiery dawn light.

45

THE END OF THE WORLD, AS WE KNOW IT

By the end of the day, Dru had given up trying to sort out the debris and just focused on finding anything salvageable in the wreckage. As the rain pounded down outside, she dug like a woman possessed, carefully collecting every useful scrap she could find and setting it aside in a growing pile. Eventually, even Rane couldn't keep up.

Most of her inventory was destroyed or too far damaged to serve much use. But beneath one pile of broken bookshelves, scattered crystals, and shattered jars, she found a treasure trove.

Books.

The leather spine of *The Grimoire of Diabolical Consorts* was sheared off, and half its pages were ripped apart, but there was enough left to be worth saving. Beneath that, she found the only known copy of *The Cyclopedia of Fallen Angels*. She gathered up its pages, clutching them like the lifeline they were.

"You know what we need to do?" she said to Rane breathlessly.

"Take a nap." Rane wiped sweat off her forehead.

"No, no. We need to make a wall. Like Salem did. These books are torn up anyway. We can take all of the pages and pin them up. Maybe we can figure out what we missed."

"We missed lunch, for one thing." Rane headed for the door up to Dru's apartment over the shop. "I'm going to raid your fridge, see if anything's left. You want anything before it's all gone?"

"But I just went to the store the other day."

"You mean like a week ago? Trust me, you want anything, better claim it now."

Before Dru could reply, the phone rang. It was Opal.

"What kind of bags you want again?" Opal said, sounding flustered. "Compactor bags?"

"*Contractor* bags," Dru said. "The thickest you can find."

"Can't find a single thing in this place. Doesn't help that the entire town is going bat-crazy. And it's raining," Opal grumbled. "You should've sent Rane on guy-store detail."

"Rane doesn't have access to my credit cards," Dru reminded her, silently thankful for that fact.

Up front, the familiar rattle and snap of the mail slot caught Dru's attention.

That's weird, she thought. It was far too late in the day for the mail to come.

That meant someone else had slipped something through the mail slot. And she knew from experience that such an occurrence was not usually a welcome surprise. "Opal, gotta go. Stay safe out there."

"Uh-huh. Have fun without me." Opal hung up.

Quickly, Dru picked her way across the cluttered floor to the mail slot.

On the floor lay a single black rock, a polished oblong stone half the size of her palm. As she picked it up, its surface glittered with flecks of iron pyrite.

Midnight Lemurian jade. Just like the one she had given Greyson.

As she turned it over in her hand, she realized it *was* the one she had given Greyson.

But that was impossible.

Like a shot, she yanked the door open and stepped outside into the steady rain. The wet sidewalk was empty. A few cars swished past, windshield wipers sweeping back and forth. No one waited at the bus stop. For once, there wasn't a soul around.

She looked down at the stone, watching the rain spatter it as shiny black as Hellbringer's paint. She tried to calm down the sudden storm of emotions inside her by telling herself that she wasn't losing her mind. There had to be a rational explanation. There always was.

Except when there wasn't.

Thunder rolled across the city. And it kept rumbling, steadily.

She realized it wasn't thunder at all. It was an engine: deep, thudding, and all too familiar.

Hellbringer.

Tires chirped in the alley behind her shop. Before Dru even thought it through, she charged down the narrow gap between her building and the next. Her feet slipped on rain-slick leaves, splashed through muddy puddles.

She reached the back of the building just in time to see the tall wing on Hellbringer's rear end pull out of her parking space and slip away down the alley.

She charged into the alley and pounded along the wet concrete, ignoring the throbbing pain in her still-sore leg.

Hellbringer's wide red taillights glowed at her like the slitted eyes of a sinister demon, retreating into the rain, mocking her.

She waved her arms overhead, slinging raindrops from her soaked sleeves. "Greyson!" she shouted at the top of her lungs. "Greyson!"

It was impossible. She and Rane had searched every inch of that cliff face, and there was no trace of Greyson. How did he survive? How did he return?

It didn't matter.

All that mattered was that he was here now. And he was slipping away forever.

She wouldn't lose him again. She couldn't.

She chased him down the length of the alley, shouting his name. Squinting through the raindrops on her glasses.

She ran for all she was worth.

At the end of the alley, Hellbringer's taillights flashed brighter as the car slowed to a stop.

As she ran toward the black car, she couldn't see Greyson through the dark rain-spattered windows, but she could imagine him looking up at her in the rearview mirror, the set in his stubbled jaw resolving into a lopsided smile. She could practically hear the creak of his leather jacket as he turned around to look at her.

She wanted to ask him where he'd been. Find out how he'd come back. Tell him all the things she wished she'd said. But more than anything, she wanted to throw her arms around him and lose herself in his embrace.

Dru pounded toward the end of the alley, breathing hard, smiling so wide it made her cheeks ache. Greyson was back. Nothing else mattered.

Then everything inside her shattered as Hellbringer's tires spun, shrieking on the wet pavement. The black car turned onto the street and rocketed out of sight around the corner, its engine roaring away.

Had he seen her? Why would he leave?

She ran to the end of the alley, but Hellbringer was already gone, as if it had never existed. Nothing was left but the sound of its engine throttling up into the distance.

Was that really Greyson?

Was he alive?

Was he human again . . . or something else?

Dru sagged against the wet brick wall, oblivious to the cold rain pounding on her head, plastering down her hair, raising goose bumps on her skin.

She puffed clouds of fog into the chilly air, trying to catch her breath, and stared down the length of the empty street, where nothing moved but raindrops hitting the puddles.

She would find him again, she swore to herself. She would never stop looking.

Not until the end of the world.

ACKNOWLEDGMENTS

This book would not exist without the steadfast determination and encouragement of Kristin Nelson, a true gem among literary agents.

I'd also like to thank the whole team at Nelson Literary Agency for their sterling work over the years: Lori Bennett, Angie Hodapp, James Persichetti, and even Chutney the Wonder Dog.

Extra special thanks to Rene Sears, for her consistent insight and editorial vision.

Thanks also to the fine folks at Pyr for making this book possible.

Heartfelt thanks to all of my fellow writers and critique group members, here in Colorado and around the world, for their insightful feedback and for their friendship.

Finally, words cannot express my gratitude to my lovely wife, Cyndi, for her unflagging support, tireless wisdom, and boundless faith.

ABOUT THE AUTHOR

L aurence MacNaughton grew up in a creaky old colonial house in Connecticut that he's pretty sure was haunted. He's been a bookseller, printer, copywriter, and (somewhat randomly) a prototype vehicle test driver. When he's not writing, he bikes and hikes the Rocky Mountains, explores ghost towns, and wrenches on old cars. His books include *It Happened One Doomsday*, *The Spider Thief*, and *Conspiracy of Angels*. Visit him online at www.Laurence MacNaughton.com.

Author photo © Kelly Weaver Photography